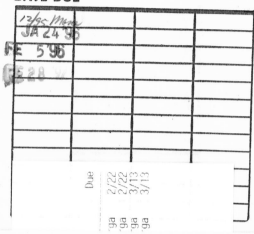

MURDER ON THE POTOMAC

Margaret Truman

MURDER ON THE POTOMAC

Published by Random House Large Print
in association with Random House, Inc.
New York   1994

Library of Congress Cataloging-in-Publication Data
Truman, Margaret [date]
Murder on the Potomac / Margaret Truman.
— 1st large print ed.
p. (large print) cm.
ISBN 0-679-75387-7
1. Smith, Annabel (Fictitious character)—Fiction.
2. Women art dealers—Washington (D.C.)—Fiction.
3. Smith, Mac (Fictitious character)—Fiction.
4. Law teachers—Washington (D.C.)—Fiction.
5. Large Type Books.   I. Title.
[PS3770.R82M88   1994b]
813'.54—dc20   94-1757   CIP

Manufactured in the United States of America
FIRST LARGE PRINT EDITION

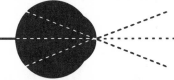

This Large Print Book carries the
Seal of Approval of N.A.V.H.

MURDER ON THE POTOMAC

1

When Mackensie Smith closed his criminal-law practice to teach law at George Washington University, he vowed to find time to smell the proverbial roses. Which didn't necessarily mean he planned to turn to gardening. In truth, he did not enjoy gardening, although his appreciation of a delicate scent, especially from Annabel's throat or shoulders, was as strong as anyone's.

For Smith, indulging in quiet leisure time could mean many things, for he was a man of many interests. But two purely personal pursuits were most important to him: spending more time with Annabel, his wife, and enjoying reflective hours on or along the banks of the Potomac River, a Washington symbol as surely as most of the city's monuments. Like most rivers, it was one of the principal reasons the city had sprung up there in the first place.

Somehow, for Smith, the Potomac and Annabel were kindred spirits. Not in any strained philosophical or poetic sense; Smith was too much the pragmatist for that sort of thinking. Maybe it was that both woman and river provided him with the sort of peace he craved. Annabel was an oasis of calm, as was the river. Both moved smoothly and with a touch of the stately, but no pretenses of grandeur. And there certainly was a parallel beauty. Annabel Reed-Smith was the loveliest female creature on earth as far as Mac was concerned. That she'd chosen him as her life's mate was a reality for which he thanked Someone on a fairly irregular basis.

This day in late August, after having done so again, and taught a class and lunched with a friend from the State Department, he'd thought to stop by the river for an hour. Ordinarily, he would have found a secluded spot near the city and strolled the river's bank, watching crews from the universities practice their smooth but arduous sport, appreciating lovers walking hand in hand or lounging on the grass, or just taken time to drink in the river's tranquillity as it quietly slid past the city to empty into Chesapeake Bay. He occasionally fished the river for bass, smallmouth upstream, bigmouth down, usually in the company of a friend, Wendell Tierney, who fished to catch fish. Not Smith. Sure, it was fun hooking one on his barbless hooks, carefully guiding it to Tierney's bass boat and gently releasing it to be caught another day. But catching fish wasn't as important as being there. Yes, that was it. Just being there was worth it. Maybe that's what rivers were for.

But he decided to do something different this particular afternoon. He drove north on the Virginia side of the river until reaching Great Falls, whose foaming rage creates Washington's most stunning act of nature. (Its tumultuous waters, Smith thought, were rivaled only by the turmoil of politics-as-usual downriver.) He walked to the edge of the Potomac River Gorge and looked out over this scenic, moving masterpiece. Far below, water that had poured over the falls swirled in fast-flowing circular patterns. Like all intense beauty, awe-inspiring, producing fear as well as admiration.

The sunny warmth of the day had lured hundreds of tourists. Schoolchildren squealed with noisy delight as they romped through groves of oak and hickory trees. Photographers propped their cameras on tripods and waited for the perfect slant of sunlight. Bird-watchers trained binoculars on the sheer granite slopes that formed the gorge, fractured in many places after the molten lava of millions of years ago had cooled, the resulting fissures now filled with rich deposits of white quartz.

Lovely, thought Smith. Like her.

In time, with the visceral pleasure of warm sun on his face and the bracing clean air off the falls, he decided to head home. He might get dinner started. Or at least set up the ice in glasses. He turned and walked a few steps in the direction of his car, thinking that this might be one of life's big moments, not big at all but a quiet time when you want nothing more than you have, and then the scream sliced the air like the fissures in the rocks. He turned and saw people running to the gorge's edge. He quickly went to the rail and looked down. The small body below was caught in the swirling currents, tiny arms flapping in vain search of a grip. There was no sound, although the child must have been screaming; there was only the roar of a hundred thousand gallons of water a second cascading over the falls, majestic in its power, unforgiving in its violence.

2 Somewhere in Washington, D.C., on the Sunday following the tragedy at Great Falls, a funeral was conducted for the girl who'd drowned. The newspapers made even more of it than usual because the tragedy had happened where it did: another fatality claimed by the falls. Of all the parks across America managed by the National Park Service, Great Falls produced the highest number of victims—seven, eight, sometimes ten drownings a year. Few were the result of falls into the gorge. Most stemmed from reckless swimmers or boaters failing to respect the water's power. In this case, the child, part of a class that had made a visit to Great Falls to celebrate the end of a hot summer-school session, had slipped away and had gone around the low railings that defined safety. What glorious freedom after two months in a sweltering classroom. You could almost think you could spread your tiny wings and fly.

The grieving family had already announced a lawsuit against the Park Service, as well as against the administration of the school attended by the deceased girl.

But aside from those people emotionally involved in the child's death, for most D.C. residents nothing had changed. It was too pretty an afternoon to dwell upon unpleasant events. People were out on the streets. The heat of the summer, like the death of the child, would soon be another pale memory. Autumn beckoned, Washington's finest, most palatable season.

" 'Morning, Sam," a tall, slender young man with a neatly trimmed black mustache said to another young man he'd intercepted. He wore a soft tan leather vest over an American University T-shirt, tight jeans, and sneakers.

As the two men exchanged banal words, a few men and women sauntered past them. Then a third young man approached wearing a SAVE THE EARTH T-shirt beneath an outlandishly oversized gray double-breasted suit jacket, a small revolver in his right hand. Sam backed away, although the weapon was pointed at the other fellow.

"You bastard!" The newcomer's voice matched the threat in his hand. And then the revolver's report violated the scene's tranquillity. Others who watched recoiled with horror, then braced like mannequins, mouths and eyes opened wide.

The young man slowly backed away, hands raised as though shields against another bullet.

"Don't murder me," he said. "*Please* don't murder me."

Another shot, this time the weapon pointed at the victim's groin. His expression was more bewilderment than pain. "I'm . . ." He gasped, wrapping his arms around a tree in an attempt to stay erect. But his thigh and groin melted into a wet red stain, and his body seemed to melt, too, into the ground.

His attacker stood over him and now held the revolver inches from the man's head and squeezed the trigger. A misfire, a dull, metallic *thunk*. The assailant recocked the weapon, pressed it to the chest, and fired again. The fallen man's shirt became a crimson Rorschach. Again, the revolver was held to his head. Another misfire.

He placed the weapon in his pocket, smiled at the stunned onlookers, and asked of no one in particular, "Is he dead yet? Is the bastard dead?"

He walked off, slowly, casually; one expected to hear him begin whistling a happy Disney tune.

Another dramatic scene in the larger production that is the nation's capital.

3 The Next Night

This was Annabel's first meeting; she'd been elected to the board two weeks ago. She was introduced by the chairman as "Annabel Reed-Smith, wife of former criminal attorney and now distinguished George Washington University law professor Mackensie Smith—and herself a former attorney who gave up the law to become proud owner of a thriving Georgetown art gallery." She took her seat at a large oak conference table on the second floor of the National Building Museum on F Street NW, between Fourth and Fifth, across from Judiciary Square and adjacent to Washington, D.C.'s "Chinatown," such as it is.

The chairman, Wendell Tierney, was in his customary position at the head of the table and called the meeting to order. Tierney hadn't learned yet not to introduce women by giving the occupation of their husbands and their status as wives first. Before addressing the formalities, reading minutes from the previous meeting and other routine things done by boards of directors rather than giving direction, he had a few more words of welcome for Annabel. "Mrs. Smith's distinguished career as an attorney, and more recently as a valued member of the arts community, is well known to all of us. Her husband's fund-raising efforts on behalf of this institution are also well known—and sincerely appreciated." He smiled. "We're honored to have you join our board, Annabel. You will surely be of aid to us. I might also add that you provide a welcome and attractive visual aid."

Annabel politely thanked the chairman for his "kind words," glancing at two other women in the room. Did they resent the sexism, too? And the implied insult? One, Pauline Juris, had been Tierney's administrative aide and personal assistant for years. She was a tall, slender, pretty woman whose plainness of makeup and dress was by design, suitable, perhaps, to Tierney Development Corporation, Inc., the conservative company headed by her boss, but that did little for her. Annabel had observed that Pauline's legs had a ballet dancer's muscularity, like the pronounced calf muscles on some San Francisco women, developed from trudging up and down that city's hills. The other observation made by Annabel upon first meeting Pauline—once at Annabel's gallery, a few other times at the inevitable Washington fund-raisers—was that her lips were more fleshy than one would have assigned to her otherwise small facial features. Sexy lips, Annabel thought.

Physicality aside, Annabel found Pauline Juris to be pleasant but businesslike. *All* business. She had little doubt Pauline kept Tierney's ship running on an even keel.

The other woman, Hazel Best-Mason, an accountant who specialized in nonprofit institutions, Annabel had seen a few times, too. Hazel was the museum's controller. She was short and borderline chubby, a chocolate sundae away from spilling over the edge into outright obesity. Unlike Pauline, Hazel enjoyed makeup and was adroit in its use. Black hair flecked with gray was worn short and neatly styled. Her orange oval glasses made a fashion statement, as did her clothing—suits with vivid splashes of color provided by a blouse, sweater, or scarf. Nicely manicured hands were a fleshy display case for a multitude of rings; hand-hammered gold earrings dangled to her shoulders.

Neither woman appeared to have been hurt by Tierney's acknowledgment of Annabel's indisputable raven-haired, creamy-complexioned beauty. Of course, they might have been but simply repressed it. Unstated truths. It would have been professionally indiscreet to show annoyance. Another unstated truth, Annabel knew, was that all things considered, Tierney would have preferred that her husband be seated in the chair she occupied. He'd asked Mac on several occasions to join the board but had been politely turned down. Annabel represented second choice.

But so be it. She was pleased to have been invited to help guide the fortunes of the National Building Museum, whose mission it was to recognize and celebrate America's historic achievements in building and to encourage excellence in the building arts. With her art gallery humming smoothly and demanding less of her time, she'd found freedom to pursue academic pursuits for purely personal enjoyment, and the architecture of Washington had become a favorite subject. She'd joined groups that studied and fostered public interest in the diverse, often startling, sometimes inspiring, occasionally distressing architecture of the nation's capital. It all tended to heighten her interest in how things were built, old and new. Her seat on the Building Museum's board was a natural extension of that interest.

As the new kid on the block, Annabel contented herself with listening for two hours as Tierney ran through the agenda. She was impressed with the way he maintained control. No heavy-handedness. No surprise. Tierney Development had made him one of the richest men in Washington, and he conducted himself with the natural assuredness of a man secure in his success. Handsome, elegant, with patrician features, Tierney bore all the vestiges of someone who takes care of himself—and who takes himself seriously. A personal trainer came to his home gym early each morning to help his client stay fit. His tan bloomed perpetually, thanks to a tanning machine also located in his home. Grooming was impeccable—hands painstakingly manicured, a full head of gray hair bordering on white, always in place, even on windy days. A rich and successful CEO and chairman of the board from the files of Central Casting.

Across the table from Annabel sat another man, not as rich as Wendell Tierney but not missing any meals, either: Samuel Tankloff, the New York investment banker who, ten years ago, aware that his primary source of business was Tierney Development, opened a Washington office, bought a second home in Virginia, and now found himself spending most of his time in D.C., leaving the running of the New York operation to trusted lieutenants. Tankloff lacked Tierney's smooth demeanor or smooth features. He was short and squat; his nickname in school had been "Tank," which fit his name as well as his build. He was, indeed, tanklike.

Swarthy skin did not need artificial sun to give it a burnished sheen, nor was a trainer necessary to pump up his muscles. Frizzy tufts of black hair fought a losing battle to cover the broad expanse of his bald pate. His eyes were almost black, his ears large. Annabel had never seen so much hair sprouting from anyone's ears before.

Tankloff bought his suits from the same tailor as Tierney, and expensively, but they didn't look as good on the shorter, stouter man. What file in Central Casting would Tankloff occupy? Annabel wondered. Mafioso underboss? Arab deal-maker? Turkish dictator?

He was none of those things, of course. He was Sam Tankloff, investment banker and Wendell Tierney's best friend. And likable, Annabel had decided. Behind his scowling, often menacing facade was a surprising warmth. Tankloff gave you the feeling that he was deeply interested in everything you thought and said; nothing else mattered while you expressed yourself. Mac and Annabel knew both Tankloff and Tierney socially. Although Annabel respected Tierney, she preferred Tankloff's company, and that of his wife, Marie, a woman bemused at everything her husband did and said.

As the meeting neared conclusion, the final business was a reassignment of committee memberships. Annabel had replaced a departed member of the board who'd served on the finance committee and its compensation subcommittee. She was assigned to both. Laughing, she said,

"Me on the finance committee so soon? Wouldn't happen that way in the Senate. Mac isn't happy with the way I balance my own checkbook."

Hazel Best-Mason, finance-committee chair, offered pleasantly, "Balancing a personal checkbook is hard. Being on the finance committee is easy. Welcome aboard."

"Thanks," Annabel said. "But I'd still better brush up on what is an appalling lack of knowledge about money."

"And I can't think of anyone better to teach you than Hazel," Tierney said.

Pauline Juris chuckled softly and said, "Better that Hazel teach you than Wendell, Annabel. He's a brilliant businessman, but his own checkbook will never qualify as a model."

Tierney laughed loudly. "She should know," he said. "Pauline's been balancing my checkbook for years." He surveyed the faces at the table. "Well, shall we adjourn?"

While the board members stood and chatted, Annabel went to where she'd draped her raincoat on a chair in the corner. She paused before picking it up as a hushed conversation between Tierney and Pauline Juris reached her ears: "I'm pretty goddamn fed up with Seymour's temperamental outbursts and disregard for budget," Tierney said. "Straighten him out when you see him tonight." Annabel slipped into her coat and headed for the door. Suddenly, Tierney was at her side. "I'll walk you to your car," he said. "A hell of a building, but not the best neighborhood."

They descended to the first floor over a wide, redbrick staircase grooved by a century of shoes and stepped into the Great Hall, the scene of inaugural balls dating back to 1885 and Grover Cleveland. Harrison, McKinley, Teddy Roosevelt, and Taft had also feted their elections there. Woodrow Wilson chose not to have a ball in 1913, and it wasn't until after World War II that such gala events again lit up Washington's social calendar. One of Richard Nixon's three 1968 balls was held in the National Building Museum. Presidents Carter, Reagan, Bush, and Clinton had also used it as a setting to celebrate their elevation by voters to the White House.

The building's architect and chief engineer, Montgomery C. Meigs, quartermaster of the army, had been mandated in 1881 to find a suitable site and to design a fireproof building for a centralized Pension Bureau. Originally created in 1792 to serve disabled veterans and dependents of the Revolutionary War, the Pension Bureau had facilities scattered all over Washington and had become overwhelmed as the War of 1812 and the Mexican and Civil wars created new generations of needy veterans. Meigs's budget was not to exceed $300,000.

After researching Renaissance architecture around the world, including the Church of Santa Maria degli Angeli of Rome and the Temple of Jupiter at Baalbeck (Meigs was determined that *his* columns would be larger than those at Baalbeck) and Palazzo Farnese of Rome, whose basic design would be his inspiration, he submitted his plans. Ground was broken in 1882, construction completed in 1887. The central section of the Great Hall was the largest of three courts separated by two screens of four huge Corinthian columns, each constructed of seventy thousand bricks and rising seventy-five feet into the air, their bases eight feet in diameter. It was the largest brick building in the world—more than fifteen million of them at a cost to the taxpayers of $886,-614.04, testimony to the fact that government cost overruns are not a contemporary phenomenon.

The huge hall now was in virtual darkness as they walked together, talking. Small perimeter lights dimmed to conserve electricity provided only faint, ethereal illumination. Annabel leaned against the hall's central fountain and looked up to the gabled roof, 160 feet above. One of the many swallows that were the bane of the building's management flew over her head, soared upward, and disappeared into the center bay's cornice.

"This has to be the most unusual building in Washington," she said.

"No argument from me," said Tierney.

"I'm just beginning to learn about it," Annabel said. "I suppose being on the board will hasten the process."

"Heard all the ghost stories? Heard about the canaries?"

Annabel laughed. "Ghost stories? Yes. Canaries? No."

"When Cleveland held his inaugural ball here, the roof wasn't completed, so they draped the hall with a tarp. Then they released a cage full of canaries during the festivities. Up they went, straight to the tarp, where they immediately died from the cold and fell at the feet of the gathered."

"How terrible," Annabel said.

"It was—for the birds."

"Oh, my."

"Sorry. But true story."

When they reached her car, Tierney said, "Be sure to say hello to Mac for me."

"Of course."

"Shame what happened to the child up at the falls. You say Mac saw it happen?"

"Horrible. Mac had driven up to get away for a few hours and was about to leave when it happened. He can't shake it, keeps seeing the child in the water."

"I suppose we don't easily shake such images," Tierney said. "My foundation is setting up a scholarship fund in the girl's name."

"That's good," Annabel said.

"You do what you can do. See you and Mac on the cruise?"

"We'll be there. Thanks, Wendell, for putting me on the board. I think it's going to be extremely interesting and fulfilling."

"A proper mix of both, I hope. Safe home."

4 That Same Night

"No! No! No! No! No!"

Seymour Fletcher, director of the Potomac Players, flung his script across the room and stomped onto the stage. His baggy blue pants, unlaced white high-top basketball sneakers, khaki workshirt, and multicolored bandanna, tied around the neck to give the appearance of a bow tie, combined with long strands of colorless hair flowing down and around wire-rimmed glasses tethered to his neck by a pink-and-white string, gave him the appearance of a man coming loose.

"You are making a mockery of this script," he shouted at actors and actresses on the stage.

Stuart, the young actor playing the role of Congressman Dan Sickles, swore under his breath. "You said we could take liberties with the dialogue, Sy," he barked.

"That's right," said Carl, who played Key. "You did say that." Key had been U.S. district attorney for the District of Columbia and son of Francis Scott Key, author of "The Star-Spangled Banner."

"Liberties? Yes. Butcher it? No! No! No! Sickles and Key did not call each other 'bastards.' The dialogue is very clear and important. Key has been cuckolding Sickles for a long time. He's been climbing under the sheets with his wife, and half of Washington knows it. That's why when Sickles approaches Key with the revolver near Lafayette Square, he says, 'Key, you scoundrel, you've dishonored my house.' He didn't say 'you bastard.' "

A female voice offstage said, "Maybe this is a good time to discuss that line again, Seymour." The voice was that of Madelon St. Cere, who had written the script. She stepped into the light. " 'House' falls so flat," she said. "Key hadn't dishonored Sickles's *house.* He'd been sleeping with Teresa Sickles for a year, waving his handkerchief to let her know he was on his way to that house they rented. He dishonored Sickles's *bed,* not his whole house. Besides, 'house' is a weak word. Bed has strength. It says something. This was lust, not housebreaking."

Fletcher fumed. "I thought we resolved this two weeks ago. I will not discuss it again."

St. Cere went to the stage apron and looked out into the house. Scattered throughout the small auditorium was an assortment of onlookers, including "Chip" Tierney, son of developer and National Building Museum chairman Wendell Tierney; Chip's fiancée of most recent vintage,

Terri Pete; Sun Ben Cheong; and Monty Jamison, a professor of American history at George Washington University. Jamison was unofficial historical adviser to the theatrical troupe rehearsing in the basement of a small, run-down church on O Street.

The Potomac Players had been performing in the D.C. area for ten years. As with most small, semiprofessional theater groups, its existence was perpetually precarious—an occasional handout from a Washington arts organization, ticket sales that rose, when they did, for Neil Simon, and were modest for Beckett, dinner-theater performances in which badly scripted murder mysteries competed with bad food for audience attention—until Wendell Tierney caught one of their whodunit dinner performances at a Maryland Holiday Inn and recruited them to reenact Washington crimes from the past for his Scarlet Sin Society, "the scarlet sin" being Shakespeare's label for murder.

The society, commonly known as Tri-S, represented a special *agacerie* for Tierney. An inveterate crime buff with special interest in historical misdeeds, he often explained, "With all the crimes committed in D.C. these days, most of them connected with drugs or government or both, it's nice to focus on what the man called a kinder, gentler time when crimes of passion and jealousy prevailed."

Eventually, Tri-S developed into one of Washington's premier fund-raising groups. The newspapers and TV programs enjoyed the recall of crimes less current than the Six O'Clock News. But Tri-S's staged reenactments, despite patches of bad acting, were historically accurate and drew large audiences and generated considerable sums of charitable money. When not playacting, members of the society enjoyed lounging around Tierney's mansion in the Potomac Palisades discussing and dissecting crimes, old and new.

Despite Tierney's infusion of steady money into Potomac Players, Seymour Fletcher, Madelon St. Cere, and other guiding lights were unhappy on his payroll. The Tri-S productions did not constitute theater as they defined it, preferring Mamet, Albee, Shepherd.

But money talked, and art walked. Tierney's subsidy was generous and didn't demand full-time commitment. Once the historic murders had been performed for their adoring public, the players were free to perform other, less distasteful productions.

"Monty, please," Fletcher yelled from the stage.

Professor Jamison, a heavyset man whose front bowed out like the Hitchcock caricature, pushed himself up from his cramped seat and waddled down the aisle. He wore what was his "uniform"—heavy tan twill pants, blue button-down shirt, Paisley vest, brown Harris-tweed jacket, and one of hundreds of bow ties from a proud collection. His white beard and fringe of white hair were trimmed short. Tortoiseshell glasses were thick.

Jamison cleared his throat before speaking, as he always did. It was as though a tiny pump needed to be primed before each sentence. "I've done some additional reading on the Sickles-Key case, and I must admit, Seymour, that the body of evidence grows heavier in favor of 'house.' In his 1976 book, Kelly has Sickles saying, 'Key, you scoundrel, you have dishonored my bed—you must die.' But in Nat Brandt's excellent re-creation of the sordid affair, he has Sickles saying, 'Key, you scoundrel, you have dishonored my house—you must die.' Other trustworthy sources favor the use of 'house,' rather than 'bed.' I can cite these other sources if you'd like."

"*Please,* no," Fletcher said.

"What the hell does it matter?" St. Cere said haughtily. "The dishonoring took place in Teresa's hot bed. 'Bed' and 'sex' are synonymous. 'House' can be the little house on the prairie, for Christsake."

Fletcher gritted his teeth and clenched his

hands at his sides as he glared at Stuart. "I can't get this excuse for an actor to say house *or* bed. All he wants to do is call everybody bastards."

"I've had enough," said Stuart. He slammed his script to the floor and walked away.

Fletcher now directed his wrath to Carl, who played Philip Barton Key. "And when Sickles shoots you," Fletcher said, "look as though you're in *pain* instead of dumb and confused." Then, salt for the wound: "And be bloody careful when grabbing the tree for support. It's as shaky as your performance."

Carl, too, disappeared into the wings.

"Please, please," Jamison said after a false start. "We had already decided that 'house' would suffice."

"What would suffice," said Fletcher, "is for this cast to say anything that even approximates Madelon's script."

"Maybe we should take a break to calm down," the assistant director suggested.

"We already have," Fletcher said disgustedly. He vaulted the stage and fled into the auditorium.

Everyone scattered, leaving Monty Jamison with Suzanne Tierney, the actress playing the adulteress Teresa Sickles.

"Much ado about nothing," she said lightly.

They were joined by Chip Tierney, Terri Pete, and Sun Ben Cheong. "Chip knows everybody's lines," Suzanne said. "He's been here for every rehearsal."

Which was true. What Chip hadn't told his sister was that their father asked him to be there. His eyes and ears on how things were progressing.

"How can you put up with these prima donnas?" Chip asked Suzanne.

"They're not prima donnas," Suzanne said. "They're actors."

"And directors, I might say," Jamison said. "Volatile chap, isn't he?"

"Insufferable is more like it," Chip Tierney said. He turned to Sun Ben and said, "As opposed to inscrutable."

Cheong shook his head. "It's good none of you handle large sums of money," he said.

"Why?" Suzanne asked.

"Because money and emotions don't mix."

Cheong had been brought to America through the efforts of the Chinese-American Connection, a nonprofit, altruistic group to which Wendell Tierney lent his name and money. Its predecessor had been the Chinese Educational Mission, an organization funded by an indemnity reluctantly paid by the Chinese government after the United States had helped quell the Boxer Rebellion.

President Teddy Roosevelt decreed that the money be used to educate promising Chinese students, and the mission began bringing them to

America. Although it ended in bloody scandal in the early 1920s, the Chinese-American Connection picked up on its spirit. Sun Ben Cheong was one of many recipients of its generosity.

He'd been scheduled to return to China following his education in America. But after receiving a Ph.D. in economics from Harvard, Tierney placed him in a job with his close friend investment banker Sam Tankloff. It took Cheong less than a year to establish himself as Tankloff's financial wizard. "I don't make a money move without him," Tankloff often said. "He knows ways to make money that haven't been invented yet."

Not only did Tierney arrange for Cheong to stay in America, he legally adopted him. Cheong had told his rich benefactor that he had little reason to return to China. His only living relative there, he claimed, was an older brother, John, whose business was precious gems. They hadn't seen each other in years.

Jamison observed the two brothers and their sister. Chip and Suzanne shared few features to visually link them to the same family. Chip had his father's fine features, the aquiline nose, resolute mouth, and lean, supple six-foot body. Although Suzanne was tall, only a few inches shy of Chip's height, her body was angular in a masculine sense. Her features tended to the coarse—

mouth too small for her broad face, heavy, dark eyebrows, and large, watery green eyes. Not wholly unattractive, simply lacking the refinement of Tierney genes.

Cheong, of course, had not been born to Wendell and Marilyn Tierney. But, Jamison decided, he looked more comfortable as a Tierney than did Suzanne. He was Chip's height but more solidly built. He wore his clothing well; the deft hand of a Tierney tailor helped. His ebony hair was combed straight back on top and at the sides. Pitted remnants of teenage acne on his full cheeks were visible in the right light.

As Jamison watched them, he wondered at the relationship between Sun Ben and Suzanne. They sometimes looked at each other in a way that led him to speculate whether there might be more between them than simply sister and adopted brother. Nothing tangible to fuel his speculation. But Monty Jamison considered himself astute in picking up on subtleties. He'd never expressed such thoughts to anyone, even to close friends. But these and other observations would be dutifully recorded each night in one of many diaries he hoped to publish one day in the tradition of his literary idol, Edmund Wilson.

"Can we go?" Terri said to Chip. She was a pretty little thing with breasts and hips better fitted to a larger woman. Jamison had noted in his diary that she represented this generation's brooder, pondering anything and everything but, in reality, lacking spark. *She appeals to those young men who savor sour sucking candies rather than sweet chocolate,* he'd written, pleased with his metaphor.

"In a minute," Chip replied. Terri pouted and sighed, something at which she was thoroughly rehearsed.

Director Seymour Fletcher returned to the stage, clapped his hands, and resumed the dramatization of the murder of Philip Barton Key by Congressman Daniel Sickles on February 3, 1859.

"Before we begin," Clarence, the actor depicting Sam Butterworth, said, "could we discuss my motivation in this scene?"

"What about it?" Fletcher asked.

"Well, I'm not quite certain what my motivation is. I mean, there I was with Sickles when he looked out the window and saw Key waving his handkerchief as a signal to Teresa. Was I dispatched by Sickles to detain Key long enough for Sickles to get his revolver and confront him? Or was it purely chance?"

"What difference does it make?" Fletcher asked.

"It makes a great deal of difference to me," Clarence said. "You told me to act apprehensive, nervous when speaking with Key. *Why* would I act that way unless I knew Sickles was about to kill him? If I know that, it certainly will color the way I speak, hold my body, everything about my performance."

"We'll discuss it later," Fletcher said. "Places, everyone. Let's go over the murder scene again." He pointed to Carl, who played Key. "Please don't act as though Sickles has gunned you down with a machine gun. He grazes your shoulder, then shoots you in the ribs. Grimace all you wish, but stop flailing your arms like an insect in its death throes." He turned to Stuart. "Remember, you say when you approach him, 'Key, you scoundrel, you have dishonored my bed—you must die.' "

"House!" the assistant director yelled, her face buried in the script.

"House. Yes, house. Can we p-l-e-a-s-e get on with it?"

They rehearsed the murder scene twice more. Then Fletcher decided to go over the trial scene in which Teresa, forced to testify, was ripped apart by eight prominent defense attorneys retained by Sickles. In order to keep the cast numbers down, only one attorney was represented in the production. He was an older man, Brent Norris, an accomplished Shakespearean actor who'd had a modicum of success on Broadway and returned to Washington to bask in that glory. The rest of the cast watched as Norris attacked the young Teresa, played by Suzanne Tierney, with assurance and professional bearing. But Suzanne constantly flubbed her lines and seemed capable of only two emotions—tearful hand-ringing and comic indignation.

"God, she's awful," a cast member whispered.

"Yeah, but look at the way Fletcher coddles her, then gets on Brent's case. Sy sure as hell knows where his bread is buttered."

The final scene was one in which Sickles met briefly with President James "Old Buck" Buchanan. Their close friendship was an open secret in Washington. Buchanan promised Sickles to do what he could to squash the case, offered him traveling money to get out of town, and gave him a razor as a gift.

"Great. Terrific," Fletcher proclaimed when it was over. He took aside the actor playing Buchanan, who was also the church's pastor, and said, "Maybe you could tone down your voice a little, Reverend. You and your friend Sickles are alone in a room. There's no congregation."

"I just want to be heard," said the reverend.

"Oh, you will. Believe me, you will." He announced to the rest of the cast, "That's a wrap."

"Ride home?" Chip Tierney asked his sister.

"No, thanks. I'm having a drink with Seymour.

He has a friend in New York who might have a part for me off-Broadway."

Sy's casting couch? Chip wondered. Oh, well, there wasn't anything he could do about it, any more than his father had been able to dissuade Suzanne from pursuing a theatrical career. But it saddened him. Suzanne's open defiance of her father had caused unbearable tension in the household.

"See you then," Chip said. "Sun and I are out of here."

"Ginny and Mitch are at Bullfeathers," Terri said. "I promised to meet them there."

"Not tonight, sweetie," Chip said, pulling her close and kissing her ear. "Another time."

Pout.

Chip and Sun Ben each maintained an apartment in the three-acre Tierney complex high on the Potomac Palisades. Chip's quarters were in a wing at the rear of the house. Cheong lived in rooms over a six-car garage that had been renovated especially for him.

Suzanne lived by choice in a shabby apartment on Fourth Street, in the shadow of I-395's overpass. She worked during the day as an assistant to a Washington theatrical booking agent who specialized in providing magic acts, singing telegrams, and strippers for private parties.

"Ready?" Suzanne asked Fletcher after the others had left.

His back was to her. "Have to cancel," he said. "The Dragon Lady is coming to discuss the budget."

"When did you find that out?" she asked.

"This morning."

"But you said we were going out after the rehearsal."

"Yeah, I know." He turned. "Go on home."

"What about that part in New York you wanted to talk to me about?"

"Tomorrow. We'll discuss it tomorrow. I can't brush off Juris. You know that."

"Oh, of course not. The Dragon Lady happens to be Daddy's bag lady. You couldn't possibly offend Pauline Juris, could you, Seymour?"

"Knock it off, Suzanne. You know I hate her as much as you do."

"But I don't try to hide it. Ms. Juris knows exactly what I feel about her. Does she know how *you* feel?"

"It doesn't matter. Look, sorry about breaking our date. We'll do it tomorrow after rehearsal. Okay?" He kissed her on the cheek.

She spun on a heel and marched from the theater, leaving the director, a failed thespian, standing alone in the harsh, naked light of a single bulb that scrawled his shadow across the scarred floor.

5 Later That Same Night

"Well, how did it go?" Mac asked Annabel when she returned. "They make you chairperson by proclamation?"

Smith had devoted the evening to reading briefs written by his students while Annabel attended her first meeting of the National Building Museum's board. Their Great Blue Dane, Rufus, had wedged himself beneath Smith's desk for most of the time, forcing his master to prop stockinged feet on the beast's torso. At the sound of Annabel inserting her key, the dog got up quickly, nearly tipping Smith out of his chair.

"Interesting," Annabel responded, kicking off her shoes and vigorously rubbing Rufus's sizable ears. "Fill you in soon as I change."

She emerged from the bedroom wearing Smith's favorite frayed blue terry-cloth robe over a shortie nightgown. "Make me a drink?" she said, settling on the couch and tucking her bare feet beneath her.

Smith poured a cognac, picked up his almost empty snifter from the desk, and joined her. They touched crystal rims. "To the new member of the board," he said, kissing her.

"Thank you." She sipped and smacked her lips.

"Was that in appreciation of the kiss or the cognac?" Mac said.

"Both were vintage—very smooth and very warm. Wendell Tierney runs a smooth ship."

"I wouldn't expect less. What was the chief topic of conversation?"

She put her head back and thought. "Money. Raising money, which I suspect always heads the agenda. They're going after additional federal funding and—"

"*They?* You'd better start thinking *we.*"

"Yes, I suppose I should. *We* spent most of the evening talking about raising money. Sam Tankloff had some good ideas. At least I thought so. Joe Chester presented a proposal for a new exhibition on New Orleans architecture. I brought my copy home. You might want to read it." Chester was the museum's paid director.

"I will."

Annabel laughed. "He's a tightly wound little fellow," she said. "There must have been a shortage of personality genes when he was born. The animosity between Wendell and Chester is thick enough to cut with an ax."

"Doesn't sound like an especially productive

atmosphere," Smith said. "Why does Tierney put up with someone he dislikes?"

"From what I gather, Chester does a terrific job. And Wendell is a shrewd enough business-man to go with a proven executive no matter what his personal feelings."

Smith finished his drink. "You aren't going to leave me with the impression that the entire eve-ning passed without Tierney mentioning the Scar-let Sin Society."

Annabel regarded him quizzically. "Mac, this was a museum board meeting. Why would Wen-dell bring up Tri-S?"

"Because it's his obsession. Same with Monty Jamison. Monty and I had breakfast this morn-ing. He went into his usual pitch, why you and I should join Tri-S. I told him I dealt with enough real crime in my life as an attorney to last me for the rest of it, but you can't dissuade him. He's all excited about their next theatrical re-creation, Barton Key's murder. Monty claims it's going to be their biggest production yet. Something like six hundred tickets already sold for the dinner. I hope they have good weather. Doing the production outdoors seems dumb to me."

Annabel shifted position so that she directly faced him. "Why are you so critical of Wendell and Monty and the Scarlet Sin Society?" she asked.

"Because it's sophomoric, that's why."

"Based upon your definition of sophomoric."

"My definition isn't a bad one, Annabel. For grown men and women to—"

She finished his thought. "For grown men and women to raise considerable money for worthwhile charitable causes. What's wrong with that?"

"There are other ways to raise money." He realized his voice had taken on an edge.

"I think you're jealous," Annabel said.

He got up and splashed more cognac into his glass. "Jealous?" he said. "What could I possibly be jealous of?"

"Maybe I used the wrong word. Frankly, I think it would be fun to get involved with Wendell's group. After all, it's only history. You love history."

"Yes, I do. The discovery of continents and the resulting oppression of the natives. Big wars. What Churchill said to Stalin, what Stalin said to his wife. That kind of history. Run-of-the-mill murders from the past have little appeal for me."

"I think they're fun, if they're far enough back. Apart from the human tragedies. Do you know there was a murder committed in the National Building Museum not many years ago?"

"Uh-huh. A jealous lover pushed a young woman over a railing. Am I right?"

"Of course. But doesn't it pique your interest?"

"Because it happened in the National Building Museum? Afraid not. Besides, that's hardly history. Only a few years ago. Almost yesterday."

"Pity," she said lightly, getting up and walking from the room. Smith started to follow but held back. Should he continue the debate with her over Tri-S? A silly argument at best. They almost never argued, and certainly never fought. Negotiated, perhaps, but then they were attorneys by training and experience. Their day-to-day relationship was, as far as he was concerned, perfection. Calm. Reasoned. Seeing both sides and bending.

He followed her into the bedroom. "Why is it a pity? Why this sudden infatuation with the Scarlet Sin Society?"

She sat at the dressing table and brushed her long hair. "Interest, that's all," she said. "Interest in something other than the mundane business of Washington and politics and street crime and the like." She stopped her motion with the brush, turned slightly, and added, "If you want to talk about something sophomoric, try politics the way it's played in this city."

No, he thought. No political debates at this hour. Like drinking caffeine before bed.

"I suppose you're right," he said. "Tri-S does support good causes."

She resumed the vigorous stroking. "Wendell reminded me of the cruise next Saturday."

"I forgot about that," Smith said. "Didn't write it on my calendar."

"Better do it," she said. "Should be a nice day."

"Yes, I'm sure it will be."

The cruise would be on Tierney's luxury cruiser, *Marilyn,* named after his wife. It was a beautifully appointed boat, fully crewed, and it would be replete with entertainment, inexhaustible food and drinks, and a guest roster of Washington's movers and shakers. Mac and Annabel had been on previous Potomac cruises with Tierney. Smith had found some of Tierney's shipmates to be too precious for his blood, but in the main these had been relaxing events.

"Ready for bed?" he asked.

"Not at all sleepy," she replied. "I think I'll read Chester's proposal on New Orleans architecture. I also never got to the *Post* today. You packing it in?"

"I think I will. An evening of student briefs can be fatiguing, to say nothing of frustrating. Where do they get that polyester that passes for brains? I'll walk Rufus. Back in a minute."

He'd intended for the walk to last only long enough for Rufus to take care of business in preparation for the night. But the minute he stepped out of their narrow two-story taupe brick house on Twenty-fifth Street, with its Federal-blue trim, shutters, and front door, he decided he was in need of a brisk walk for himself—to relieve a set of unsettling, undefined feelings.

Man and dog crossed Eye Street and slowed in front of the River Inn, home of one of Smith's favorite restaurants, the Foggy Bottom Cafe. It was closed for the evening, but he saw through the windows the staff unwinding at the small bar after a busy night. Had he knocked, they would have invited him in for a nightcap, even with the dog. He wasn't in the mood.

He continued north until reaching K, turned left, and went to Twenty-seventh, then left again to the Watergate complex. He'd lived there in a two-bedroom apartment following the Beltway slaughter of his wife and son by a drunk driver. That tragic event had been the turning point in his decision to abandon his lucrative law practice and to accept the teaching position at GWU. As part of his "clean sweep," he'd bought the small house on Twenty-fifth and settled into the quiet bachelor life of a professor of law.

But then he met Annabel, and the light that had been extinguished on the Beltway was lit again, different but still a lovely light.

They'd met at a party at the British embassy. Annabel was a lawyer, specializing in matrimonial cases. But like Smith, she'd harbored a desire to pursue something else, in her case a love of pre-Colombian art and a dream of owning a gallery. When she broached this to Smith after they'd been seeing each other for more than a year, he was enthusiastic and encouraged her to follow her dream. She cleaned up pending cases, closed her office, and leased space on Wisconsin Avenue in the heart of Georgetown. She'd never been happier. She was doing what she loved, was *in* love, and knew that her love was returned by the handsome and urbane Mackensie Smith.

Smith and Rufus continued walking south until reaching the gleaming white Kennedy Center for the Performing Arts. It, too, spurred memories. A staff assistant to his friend, former senator Paul Ewald, then running for president on the Democratic ticket, had been slain outside this living memorial to the slain JFK. Smith and Rufus had discovered the body during just such a walk, and Smith found himself sucked into the vortex of the case, much to Annabel's chagrin.

And that was *before* they were married.

Their marriage took place in a simple service in the Bethlehem Chapel of the National Cathedral. It was performed by another friend, Reverend Paul Singletary. Only days after the wedding, Singletary was found murdered in that same chapel, his skull crushed. Once again, Mackensie Smith, former criminal attorney, now docile and contented law professor, was brought into it by yet another friend, the cathedral's bishop, George St.

James. Again, Annabel was displeased with Mac's decision to allow murder to intrude upon their quiet, loving life. But she seemed less adamant in her objections; perhaps she was getting used to that cell in him that sounded a bell on occasion and compelled him to become involved. He enjoyed teaching law, but he simultaneously missed, now and then, the practice of it.

But knowing how much Annabel preferred that he stick to teaching, Smith promised himself, and her, following the resolution of the cathedral murder, that he would assiduously avoid further involvement.

That resolve lasted a year. A former law student, Margit Falk, air-force major, helicopter pilot, and on the secretary of defense's general-counsel staff at the Pentagon, was assigned to defend the accused murderer of a leading military scientist. She sought out her former mentor for help, and he responded, but only after considerable soul-searching. And with Annabel's reluctant, but nonetheless supportive, blessing.

Since his Pentagon involvement, no one close to Mac and Annabel Smith had been mugged, much less murdered. Things were quiet and calm, for which both were grateful. He believed his wife was content with things as they stood. But he also sometimes sensed a vague restlessness in her that was uncharacteristic. Not that she wasn't a proven go-getter. She'd built her art gallery into one of substance and had recently expanded it into an adjoining storefront. Simultaneously, she'd taken courses in a variety of subjects to, as she put it, "keep this brain oiled."

Now she was on the board of directors of the Building Museum and expressing interest in the Scarlet Sin group, that childish obsession of Wendell Tierney's that had captured the imagination of half of Washington, including his friend and distinguished professor of history Monty Jamison. What was she looking for? What are women ever looking for?

Each time he'd ventured out of his safe and secure academic cocoon, it had been Annabel who'd urged him back. Well, he was back, but it was as though she were attempting to escape the silky threads of her own cocoon. It was getting complicated. That had been the point of the dramatic shifts in their lives in the first instance, hadn't it? To cut down on complications, to become more self-contained and enjoy their considerable love in a peaceful atmosphere.

He continued his stroll, taking a route that took him through the George Washington University campus. He started to feel better, less apprehensive. These were familiar surroundings; rubbing shoulders with the spirited young people who sat on the front steps of their housing units—laughing, joking, enjoying the lack of complication in *their* lives—was a welcome tonic. By the time he reached Twenty-fifth Street and came through the front door, anxiety had drained from him. He was ready to join his wife for a good night's sleep.

"I was worried about you," she said sleepily from the couch in the study.

"Sorry. I felt like a longer walk. Rufus can use the exercise."

She smiled. "Rufus? Come on, Smith, let's hit the sack."

As he clicked off the light next to the bed, she turned and touched his arm. "Want to hear something silly? I mean, *really* silly?"

"Silly? You? Sure."

"I have this fantasy—and that's all it is, a fantasy—a silly one, too, because I know it could never be a reality, not with you—I have this silly fantasy that when you take Rufus for a *long* walk, you're meeting some mystery woman with whom you're having a torrid affair."

He sat up and turned on the light. "An affair? On a street corner with Rufus standing guard? Tough to be torrid with ol' Rufe looking on. More likely he'd be having an affair."

She giggled. "I told you it was silly."

"It isn't silly. It's—it's the dumbest thing I've ever heard."

"It isn't dumb. It's *silly*. You used to be silly

sometimes. At least you enjoyed it when *I* was silly."

"I still do."

"Then laugh at my fantasy."

Instead, his face turned even more serious. "Sure it's just a fantasy? I mean, it doesn't represent a deep, dark suspicion about my fidelity, does it?"

"No, it does not. Sorry I brought it up. Good night."

"Good."

"Huh?"

"Good. I'm glad it's just a fantasy. Come to think of it, a pretty funny one, too." He chuckled as the room went to black.

6 Very Early the Next Morning

National Park Service ranger Lloyd Mayes sat at the base of the seventeen-foot bronze Paul Manship statue of T.R. He wasn't due to conduct his first nature walk until ten, wasn't even supposed to report for work until eight. But here it was five-thirty, the sun poised beyond the brightening horizon.

It wasn't a heightened sense of duty that had brought Mayes this early to Theodore Roosevelt Island. It was Grace. They'd been fighting a lot lately. When she'd married him six years ago, she was impressed with his uniform. Maybe he didn't have medals to wear like soldiers had, but Mayes carried his unadorned uniform and wide-brimmed hat with soldierly pride. A cowboy-without-chewing-tobacco, hat tilted forward over leathery face and narrowed eyes, chin strap secure, stomach sucked in, pants tight over his rump.

Now, six years later, Grace Mayes no longer looked at her husband with the same adoration. Gone were the compliments on how he looked, or that when tourists tentatively approached him, especially kids with wonder and respect in their eyes, it sent shivers up her spine. Sure, he'd grown a little thick around the middle, and his stories about the people he met each day had become predictable, probably even boring. But she'd married him for better or for worse and knew from the day she'd met him how much he loved his job and intended to make it his career.

She simply didn't understand.

Since he was a boy, Mayes had wanted a job that would keep him outdoors and close to nature. Being hired as a ranger for the Interior Department was the fulfillment of that boyhood dream, a dream Grace no longer shared. "Get another job," she said to him most nights. "We can't live on what you make."

"Like a goddamn broken record," Lloyd usually replied, sometimes to her, more often to himself. He said it now as he looked up into the bronze face of Teddy Roosevelt, the country's conservation president. Four twenty-one-foot-high granite tablets flanked the statue. Written on them were things Roosevelt had said about the environment, some of which Mayes had committed to memory. His favorite: *"There is delight in the hardy life of the open. There are no words that can tell the hidden spirit of the wilderness, that can reveal its mystery, and its charm."*

His second-favorite line from ol' Rough Rider

was, "A man's usefulness depends upon his living up to his ideals in so far as he can." As many times as he quoted that to Grace in the hope it would help her understand him, she only hardened. And last night she delivered her ultimatum. The job or her. Good there were no kids, he thought, as he slowly walked from the oval terrace that comprised the Roosevelt memorial, crossed one of four small footbridges spanning a water-filled moat, and started down a foot trail, one of two-and-a-half miles of trails that crisscrossed the eighty-eight-acre preserve. The first flight out of nearby National Airport whined above; Mayes looked up and watched the jet become a black dragonfly against the reddening eastern sky. He stopped a number of times on his way to the river where a 170-foot pedestrian causeway linked the island to a parking lot just off the northbound lane of the George Washington Memorial Parkway. A startled red fox fixed him with wide eyes, then disappeared into a grove of tulip trees. A chipmunk crossed his path. Mayes smiled as the tiny, curious creature darted out of his way, perched on the fallen trunk of a maple, and sat up. " 'Morning," Mayes said.

He enjoyed the early-morning peace at this place. There was no peace at home these days.

As he neared the river, the ground became spongy. The island, he would point out to his first batch of tourists, consisted of three biological communities—swamp, marsh, and upland forest.

Minutes later, he stood at the island end of the causeway and looked out over the Potomac. A small bass boat moved south, its two occupants heading for a day of fishing. Mayes envied them. Maybe he'd drag out his fishing gear that weekend.

Every morning since being assigned to duty on the island, it was Mayes's responsibility to cross to the opposite end of the causeway and unlock a padlock that secured a metal gate through which visitors would pass. There was no need this morning. When he'd arrived in the darkness, he'd noticed that the lock was undone, the gate partway open. The ranger who'd finished up yesterday must have forgotten; Mayes made a mental note to mention it to his colleague when he came on duty.

He leaned on the railing and peered down at the shoreline below the causeway. He shook his head. Although the Potomac had been cleaned up over the past few years—it no longer was a vile, brown, polluted waterway and now supported an ample fish population—people still dumped garbage into it. "Slobs!" he said at the sight of plastic bags, tin cans, and other vestiges of human consumption that had drifted in to shore and were trapped by small broken branches and rocks. He turned and started back up to the memorial, hesitated after only a few feet, and returned to where he'd stood. He leaned over the railing as far as he dared and squinted.

Then he said, "Oh, my God."

7 That Afternoon

Mac Smith looked out over his one o'clock class and frowned. He was tired; he'd been lecturing for two hours on the subject of plea bargaining and its place in the criminal-justice system. The more pragmatic of his students accepted his thesis that plea bargaining was a necessary evil in a system choked with cases. Others, their idealism worn on their earrings, saw no rightful place for the distasteful practice of cutting deals with criminals. One, a pale young lady who'd been arrested more than once at White House demonstrations for causes unknown, was the most vocal. He enjoyed debates with most people, on most subjects, but she bothered him. There was an expression on her thin face that spoke of scorn for him and his anachronistic ideas. Disagree with me, but keep your scorn to yourself, he thought.

That day, she'd droned on about the government's penchant for granting immunity, or reduced sentences, to violent, vicious members of organized crime in order to put away the top guy.

"Like the Gotti case," Smith said, checking his watch.

"Exactly," the student responded. "That guy, Sammy the Bull, was an acknowledged murderer. But because the feds had a thing for Gotti and his in-your-face style, they let slime like Sammy the Bull walk free."

Smith said that it was an imperfect world and that he was glad it was, because a perfect world would be boring. He patiently pointed out again that plea bargaining was necessary because of the overcrowded court system. "More than that," he said, "by putting away the boss of a major crime family, you disrupt it. Chances are good that it will fall into disarray. And, Ms. Clausen, I suggest you read the papers more carefully. Mr. Sammy the Bull Gravano did not take a walk. He'll do twenty years' hard time."

"But what about the attorney for Gotti?" she persisted as Smith gathered up his papers and books and prepared to leave. "He can't see it your way. His client is away for life."

"True," Smith said over his shoulder. "But Sammy the Bull's attorney is as happy as a pig in mud. Have a good evening, ladies and gentlemen. I intend to."

As he walked from the classroom to his office, he couldn't help but second-guess himself on his exchange with Clausen. In all honesty, he agreed that going to bed with a devil like Gravano in order to make a prosecutor's case against a mob boss was distasteful. Perhaps even wrong. But he was no longer interested in crusading to change the legal system in which he'd functioned—flourished—for so many years as a criminal attorney. His current responsibility was to prepare his students for the real world of justice. The imperfect world. And hopefully, along the way, to slip in a dose of ethics, moral truth, fidelity to principle and, in Ms. Clausen's case, an understanding of how to protest without ending up with a rap sheet. In reality, he liked her. At least she had convictions, as tedious as they might be. His more "realistic" students bored him. For them, their professional lives as lawyers would center about running outrageous time sheets for outrageously wealthy corporate clients. For Ms. Clausen—assuming she would learn how to stay out of jail— someone with a small budget and a large, worthwhile cause would benefit from her fire and legal training. At least he hoped so.

The phone in his cramped office rang at three-thirty.

"Hello," he said.

"Mac. This is Wendell Tierney. Sorry to bother you at work, but—"

"No bother, Wendell. This isn't work. I teach.

We get summers off. Annabel was delighted with her first board meeting. She said you run a smooth ship."

Tierney drew a deep, audible breath. "Mac, I need to talk to you. Something dreadful has happened."

Smith pushed half-glasses up on his forehead and leaned back in his chair. "I'm listening."

"I received a call an hour ago from the police. Pauline has been . . . she's been murdered." There was a momentary break in his voice.

"Your assistant? Pauline Juris?"

Forced breathing on the other end steadied the voice. "Yes. Her body was found this morning on Roosevelt Island."

"You're sure it was murder? *They're sure?* MPD, I mean."

"That's what they told me."

"How was she killed?"

"I asked, but they wouldn't say. Mac, I'll get straight to the point. I would be extremely grateful if you could find time for us to get together today."

"I don't understand," Smith said.

"I need some clear thinking," Tierney said. "I don't know what will come of this—legally, I mean—but there's no one in this city whose judgment I trust more. Will you? I'll make myself available any time, any place."

"I suppose so, Wendell, although I remind you that I am not a practicing attorney."

"That doesn't matter. I'm not seeking legal representation. Just some smart thinking. Will you?"

"Of course. An hour from now?"

"Will you come to the house?"

"Five?"

"I'll be waiting."

He called Annabel at her gallery.

"Pauline Juris murdered? I was with her last night at the board meeting."

"I know. Tierney says they found her body on Roosevelt Island."

"I don't believe this," Annabel said.

"I'd rather not believe it. Wendell did seem desperate to talk to me, and he is . . . well, sort of a friend."

Her silence said much.

"Something wrong?" he asked.

"A woman with whom I spent last evening has been murdered. I'd say that represents something wrong."

"Whoa, wait a minute," Smith said. "I'm not talking about being upset over the fact that she's dead. You seem angry with *me*."

"Angry with you? No. Concerned? Yes. I suppose you're doing the right thing by responding to Wendell's call. I also know it frightens me. Another murder. Is it going to start all over again?"

He didn't hesitate with his answer. "No, it isn't," he said. "I'll be home for dinner. Any preferences?"

"Somehow, I'm having trouble thinking of food at this moment."

"Your gastric juices will say something else by the time I get there. Chinese? Salads from American Cafe?"

"Whatever. Please tell Wendell how sorry I am about Pauline."

8 Five O'Clock That Afternoon

The Tierney complex sat majestically on a ridge in McLean, Virginia, over-looking the Potomac River. A long set of gray wooden steps zigzagged down through woods and boulders to the river's edge where Tierney's personal marina had been dredged and built years ago. Anchored at it were four boats: his 105-foot luxury yacht, *Marilyn;* a Cigarette racing boat belonging to his adopted son, Sun Ben Cheong, that carried the name *M.O.R.,* which was translated beneath in Chinese symbols; an Aquasport utility fishing boat; and a fully fitted-out bass boat.

The complex itself centered on a huge Georgian Revival–style home that had been expanded over the years into a series of wings that jutted out at odd angles. Some wings, depending upon the architect, approximated the main house's architectural theme. Others did not, taking a more contemporary approach. A columnar porch ran the width of the front of the home, affording excellent vistas of the river and beyond. To the rear of the house, which was what you approached as you entered along a winding tree-lined drive, was a cluster of small gardens, one Japanese, some distinctly British, another an obvious vegetable patch. Outbuildings included a barn and a six-car garage with living quarters above.

A dozen cars were in the circular gravel drive, two of them marked police vehicles.

Smith parked his navy-blue Chevy Caprice at the end of the line, got out, and looked up to the sky. It was gray overall, with heavier clouds approaching from the west. He stepped up onto a farmer's porch containing potting materials, a barbecue, and three bicycles, and knocked. The door was opened by Tierney's son. "Mr. Smith. Hello. My father said you were coming."

"Hello, Chip. I'm on time, I think. Sorry about the news."

"It was quite a blow to all of us. Come in, please."

Because the main entrance was on the river side in front, and since there wasn't automobile access to that side of the house, visitors entered through the back door into a large mudroom—for lack of a better word—that had been spruced up to function as a foyer. Still, the prevailing feeling was mudroom.

It was a home in which an active family obviously lived; the vestiges of young men were in ample evidence. Baseball bats and gloves, a lacrosse stick, fishing rods, and skis littered corners of the foyer—mudroom—where they had been carelessly tossed. A row of wooden pegs acted as hangers for an assortment of outerwear.

Smith knew from previous visits that the rest of the house was not so casual. It was sprawling and splendid, each large room filled with enough antiques to excite Sotheby's. At the same time, Tierney's love of electronic gadgets was ever in evidence. You didn't have to move more than a few feet to put your hand on a telephone. The house's security system was state-of-the-art. Large TV projection screens dominated many rooms, and the main stereo system, with speakers throughout the house, had enough wattage to amplify the Kennedy Center.

"Dad is in his study. The police are here."

"So I noticed," Smith said.

He followed Chip up a wide curved staircase to the study on the second level where Tierney sat in a large red leather chair facing the door. He sprang to his feet, crossed the room, and extended his hand. "Right on time, Mac. But no surprise there. Come in, come in."

Smith said something noncommittal; to say he was pleased to be there would have misrepresented the truth. Tierney led him to where the others now stood. "Mac Smith, let me introduce you to these gentlemen, and lady, from the police department." The two men wore discount-store suits of an undefined color and sported requisite short haircuts. They were detectives Winters and Casale. The woman was introduced as "Detective Darcy Eikenberg. The lead investigator in this tragedy."

As Smith took her outstretched hand, he was aware that it was exquisitely manicured: Long red nails, more like talons, seemed distinctly at odds with her job.

"Detective Eikenberg and I have met," Smith said. "You were a student of mine not long ago."

"I certainly was. You gave a night course on the law and contemporary urban ills. A requisite course, I believe. I'm a thesis away from my Ph.D. at GW in urban studies."

Smith smiled. "And I attended one of *your* lectures," he said. "About a year ago. You spoke to a criminal-justice class on new forensic techniques. I had some free time and dropped in. I was especially interested in that electrostatic detection equipment. What did you say? It can analyze indented writing as many as twenty pages down in a pad of paper?"

She'd held his hand throughout the exchange. Now she withdrew it, smiled, and said, "You have a good memory, Professor. And I should tell you that your class was the highlight of my Ph.D. program."

"I hope not," he said.

As he sat next to Tierney, he thought that of all the detectives with whom he'd come in contact during his long career as a criminal attorney, none looked like Darcy Eikenberg. She was tall—five-eleven, he guessed—had a head of thick, luxuriant brown hair that was more a mane and a face shaped by a master craftsman who'd had an uncanny sense of symmetry and proportion.

Her tall, lithe body was no less carefully crafted. Most female detectives Smith had known (their numbers grew at an astounding rate) tended to dress in the same uncaring way as the majority of their male counterparts. Not Detective Eikenberg. She looked ready to present takeover plans to General Motors' board. The black linen suit said it had come from the most expensive rack in an expensive shop. The white silk blouse featured a large bow at the neck, and it said: Woman. A detective? If the old game show *What's My Line?* were still on TV, she'd be certain to stump the panel.

With everyone seated again, Smith asked Eikenberg to fill him in on Pauline Juris's murder.

"Not much to tell you," she said, one shapely leg crossing over the other. "The body was found early this morning by a park ranger on Roosevelt Island. Positive I.D. on Ms. Juris. Blow to the head with a heavy but clearly defined object."

" 'Clearly defined'?" Smith said. "Like the head of a hammer?"

"It wasn't a hammer. Body was partially submerged along with debris on the shoreline, just below the pedestrian causeway to the island."

"Fully clothed?" Smith asked.

Eikenberg laughed and looked at her male assistants. "Do you have the feeling *we're* being investigated by the learned professor?" She said it in such a way that Smith would not take offense. Which he wouldn't have no matter how she'd said it.

."Sorry," Smith said. "Can't get out of the habit."

Eikenberg said coyly, "Teasing."

Smith turned to Tierney. "Wendell, I'm not sure why I'm here. Could we go into another room?"

Tierney looked to the detectives for the answer. "Are you through with me?" he asked.

"I think so, Mr. Tierney," Eikenberg said, recrossing her legs. "Obviously, we'll have more questions for you. I trust you don't have travel plans in the near future."

Tierney smiled, a perfect set of white teeth made more so by the tan of his face. "As a matter of fact, I do. Are you telling me I'm not to leave town?"

"That would be a good idea," she said.

Tierney asked Smith, "What do you think of this, Counselor?"

Smith shrugged. "I'm not your attorney, Wendell."

"Maybe we should rectify that."

"I'm afraid that's impossible." Smith spoke to Eikenberg: "You aren't really suggesting that Mr. Tierney cancel important business travel, are you? Is he a suspect?"

"Mr. Tierney is important to the resolution of this case, just as others are," she answered. Diplomatic, Smith thought, to not confirm suspect status. He stared at her. She smiled and said, "Mr. Tierney—who is not your client—is free to travel, provided he lets me know in advance of his plans."

"No problem," Tierney said. "Nothing extensive. Just one, maybe two, overnight trips."

Tierney showed the officers out of the house. When he returned, he came up behind Smith and kneaded his shoulders. "I loved it, Mac, the way she backed down about me traveling when you confronted her."

Smith winced, not at the pressure exerted by Tierney's fingers but because he didn't like people who gave massages without invitation. He slid out of the chair and went to a window overlooking the river, watching a small red boat moving fast downriver. He turned and faced Tierney. "Well, here I am, Wendell. What can I do for you?"

"What you just did a few minutes ago. Keep me out of this."

Smith shoved his hands in his pockets and leaned against the sill. "There is no one who can, as you put it, keep you out of it. You and Pauline worked closely together for years. It's my understanding that she was like a member of the family. As pleasantly as Detective Eikenberg put it, you are a suspect."

"Nonsense," Tierney said, touching a spot on a paneled wall that caused doors to open. Behind was a fully stocked liquor cabinet. "Drink?" he asked without looking back.

"Thanks, no," Smith said. "I really should be going."

"Not yet." Then, as though realizing he was in no position to make demands, he added, "Please. Just a few more minutes."

"A three-minute splash of bourbon on the rocks."

Seated across from each other, Tierney leaned forward, elbows on knees, and fixed Smith in a compelling stare. "Mac, let me level with you. Pauline's murder is going to have a dreadful impact on a lot of people, including me."

Smith said nothing. Silently, he wondered at Tierney's coldness. His closest aide and family

friend had been found murdered only hours earlier. Yet he mentioned it only in terms of its potential impact upon him.

Smith's silence prompted Tierney to continue.
"Pauline's long tenure with me has naturally
brought her into close contact with everyone with
whom I deal, including my family. There have
been occasional problems over the years where
they're concerned."

"Your family?"

"Yes."

"What sort of problems?"

Tierney sat back and thought before replying.
"Nothing major, Mac, but there have been times
when Pauline's—how shall I say it?—when Pauline's curt, abrasive manner rubbed people the
wrong way."

"Marilyn?" Smith asked, referring to Tierney's
wife.

Tierney nodded. "The point is," he said,
"Marilyn and I have been traveling a rocky road
these days. That's between us, of course. To compound that, I'm involved in some sensitive deals
that could be crucial to the future of Tierney Development. They demand my full attention. I
can't afford interruptions."

Smith considered whether to say it, then decided what the hell. "Wendell, I'm hearing you
voice concerns about a lot of things. I haven't

once heard you talk about the tragedy that occurred last night."

His message prompted a change in Tierney's otherwise consistent expression. He closed his eyes as though to shut them against the unpleasant truth he'd just heard and slowly shook his head. When he opened his eyes, he said, "Mac, you should have been here when I received the call about Pauline. I was devastated, damn near broke down. But I happen to be a man who believes that life is a series of problems to be solved. That takes clear, unemotional thinking. I *had* my emotional response. Now it's time to meet any resulting problems head-on." A smile. "As a lawyer, I'm sure you agree."

Smith said nothing.

Tierney slapped his hands on his thighs and stood. "Will you represent me?" he asked.

"Represent you? For what? You haven't been accused of anything. I no longer practice law. And unless you've forgotten, you have enough top-notch lawyers on retainer to make up another Supreme Court. Maybe a better one. No, you don't need me."

"Perhaps not in an official capacity, but as a friend and adviser? Sure, I have lawyers at my disposal, but none with your experience, Mac. We're talking *murder* here, and I'm aware of your previous experience with *that* nasty business. All

I ask is that I be able to confer with you if things get too complicated."

"You know you can always talk to me, Wendell. Let's leave it at that. What plans have been made for Pauline's funeral?"

"Haven't even thought about it. I suppose I'll end up burying her. There isn't anyone else. She hasn't had any contact with her ex-husband, and as far as family goes—"

"Pauline was married?"

"Years ago. It lasted less than a year. That's all I know. She wasn't big on discussing personal matters. At any rate, the police are doing an autopsy. Will slow things up, I suppose."

"Undoubtedly." Smith stood. "I think I should go."

He extended his hand to Tierney, who took it in both of his and pumped it. "Thanks, Mac. You know, the way you handled Eikenberg was a joy to behold. Spectacular woman, isn't she?"

"And bright. I remember her as a student. An ability to clamp down hard on a concept, chew, digest, and understand it."

Tierney put his hand over Smith's shoulder and walked him through the house to the rear entrance. "Before I forget," he said, "that private investigator of yours still in business?"

"Tony? Tony Buffolino? I wouldn't call him my

investigator. But yes, he is. Still in business. Why?"

"I may call on him again to beef up security around here and at the office."

"You really feel you need additional security?"

"You never know, Mac. Maybe someone did this to Pauline to get at me. I have a family to protect, and I intend to do that. Your friend Buffolino did a good job last time I used him."

"He usually does. Well, Wendell, we'll be in touch."

"Of course. See you and Annabel on Saturday?"

Smith frowned. "The cruise? I assumed it would be canceled, considering what's happened."

"No. Been scheduled for months. There's no reason for people to have to alter their plans, especially since most of them really had very little to do with Pauline. Life goes on, Mac. So does the Saturday cruise."

"I'll talk to Annabel about it. Thanks for the drink."

Smith reached his car, opened the door, and looked back at the house. Marilyn Tierney stood in a second-floor window, her face pulled down into an expression that was at once sad and angry. Smith waved. She closed the drapes.

9 An Hour Later

Annabel was rearranging a kitchen cupboard when Mac returned carrying duck pâté, salad, and a baguette from the French Market. She had to stretch to reach the top shelf, which caused her dress to ride up her legs. "Lovely sight," Smith said, touching her hip. "Lifts your skirt and my spirits."

"Watch it, mister," she said, returning to a flat-footed posture and accepting his kiss. "Oh, you have a message on your machine, Mac." Theirs was a his-and-her answering-machine household.

"Who?" he asked as he emptied the bags.

"A Detective Eikenberg. Actually, the message was more for me. She wants to interview me regarding Pauline's murder."

"Why you?"

"Go listen."

He went to the study and hit Play. It rewound, then Darcy Eikenberg's voice came smoothly from the small speaker like an all-night disk jockey playing "Misty."

This is Darcy Eikenberg, Professor Smith. Seeing you today brought back fond memories, reminded me how much I'd learned from you. At any rate, I understand your wife was present at the board meeting of the National Building Museum the night Pauline Juris was murdered. I would like an opportunity to speak with her as soon as possible, and for you to be present as well, if that doesn't pose too much of an inconvenience. Again, it was wonderful seeing you.

She left the number of her direct MPD line.

Annabel entered the study as Mac was resetting the machine. "Routine," he said. "They'll interview everyone who knew her."

"Of course. What did she mean, 'fond memories'?"

Smith laughed. "She was at Wendell's this afternoon questioning him. I had her in a class not long ago. She's close to her doctorate in urban studies, or something like that. And I caught a lecture she gave at the university on forensic police techniques."

"You didn't tell me about that," Annabel said.

"Nothing to tell," Smith replied. "When do you want to get together with her?"

"Whenever."

"I suggest you do it quickly, get it over with. Call her back."

"I thought you might want to do that. She made a point of wanting you present."

"Can't imagine why, but okay. What's good for you?"

"I have to be at the gallery late afternoon to-morrow. Any time before that will be fine. How did it go with Wendell?"

"He's upset, of course. Maybe that's not the right word. He's concerned what kind of impact Pauline's murder will have on him. Maybe the family."

"That sounds cold."

"Probably sounds colder than he means it to be. He hinted that all isn't exactly pure romance with him and Marilyn."

Annabel said over her shoulder as she headed for the kitchen, "I sensed that the first time I met them. He's a cold man who tries to be warm. Wants to be diplomatic, but being blunt comes easier."

Smith followed. "Pauline was killed with a blunt instrument," he said.

"The detective told you that?"

"Yeah. Wendell's a prime suspect, of course. Can't go out of town without prior notification to the police."

Annabel began unwrapping the packages

Smith had brought from the market. "What do you think she'll ask me?"

"The detective? What you might have observed the night of the board meeting. Did you notice anything unusual with Pauline?"

"No. She was businesslike as usual. And pleasant."

"Seem upset about anything?"

"No."

"She say anything to anyone that might . . . ?"

"Mac, I appreciate being prepped, but it gives me the chills."

"Sorry. Force of habit." He laughed. "I did the same thing with Darcy, asked a lot of questions. She didn't appreciate it, either."

They enjoyed a quiet dinner. During it, Mac fell into a prolonged silence. "Something wrong?" Annabel asked.

"I was thinking of that kid who drowned up at the falls. It keeps coming back to me like an out-of-control VCR. Actually, when I see that little child down there in the water, I think of Geof." Geof was Mac's son who died at the hand of a drunken driver.

When her husband slipped into that dark mode, Annabel knew there was nothing she could say or do to help it pass. It simply would, and did, a few minutes later.

Dinner dishes cleared, they settled in for an

evening of reading. First, Mac said, "Want me to call now and set up an appointment? She might still be at MPD."

"Sure."

Eikenberg answered on the first ring.

"Mac Smith here. I spoke with my wife, and she'll make herself available to you any time to-morrow morning." He listened, placed his hand over the mouthpiece, and said to Annabel, "Ten?"

"Ten is fine," Annabel said.

Mac confirmed it with Eikenberg. "Yes, I'll be here," he said, "unless you prefer that I not be. All right. Fine. See you then."

10 The Next Morning

Anthony A. Buffolino, private investigator, gasped as a sharp pain stabbed him in the back. He was on the floor of his office on G Street, between Fourteenth and Fifteenth. He grimaced and rolled onto his side. "Al!" he yelled.

The door between the office and reception area opened, and his third and most recent wife—one half of what was undoubtedly his most successful marriage—stood in it. "What's the matter?"

"I pulled something," he groaned, trying to arch his back into a less painful position. He wore a purple-and-white polyester sweat suit. Beneath him was a red-white-and-blue starred-and-striped plastic exercise mat.

The phone rang. Alicia disappeared into the reception area. "Al, for Christsake, I'm dyin' here," Buffolino moaned.

She returned. "You'd better take this, Tony. It sounds like a client."

"Take it? I can't even get up." He painfully rolled himself into a sitting position.

Alicia came to him and helped him to his feet.

"You'd better take it," she repeated, supporting him with the aid of the desk. "It sounds like business. We haven't had a new client for weeks."

He slumped into his desk chair, picked up the phone, and said, "Hello."

"Mr. Buffalino?"

"That's right. Anthony Buff-OH-lino."

"Mr. Buffalino, I was recommended to you by Walt Symington. I believe you handled a case for him last year."

Tony flipped through his Rolodex, which was entirely mental. Symington? He had done work for somebody with that name. A matrimonial. The guy, a bank big shot, as Tony recalled, thought his wife was cheating on him and wanted proof. The husband had been right. There was an overabundance of proof. Tony delivered a surveillance log and photographs and collected his check. What Mr. Symington eventually did with the information was his own business. You never ask about those things.

"All right," Buffolino said, adjusting himself in his chair. The pain had subsided. "What can I do for you?"

"I'm not sure we should discuss this over the phone. Is your line secure?"

Buffolino frowned. Secure? What does he think this is, the CIA? "We can talk," he said.

"I believe my wife is having an affair with my best friend. My former best friend."

"Sorry to hear that. So why are you calling me?"

His blunt question caused the caller to pause before saying, "I would like you to prove my suspicion for me."

Buffolino didn't dare look up at Alicia, who now stood at the desk, hands pressed into it. "Sorry," Tony said, "but Buffolino and Associates don't do matrimonials."

The responses from both ends—through the phone and on the other side of the desk—were instantaneous.

"T-o-n-y!" Alicia hissed.

"But Walt told me you did that sort of thing and were very good at it."

"Look, thanks for calling, but we don't do matrimonial cases. Me and my staff strictly do corporate security and espionage, government assignments. Minimum fee is three hundred thousand." He hung up.

"What is *wrong* with you?" Alicia shouted. "We're behind on the rent again, the bills are piling up at home, and—"

Buffolino waved her off. "I told you, Alicia, doing matrimonials is lowlife. I told you that if we're gonna make a score here in D.C., we have to take the high road. Class. Image. Be politically correct, I think they call it. That's where it's at."

She slapped her hands against her sides. "Some high road," she said. "Tell that to the phone company when they yank the phones—Mr. Class." She stomped from the room, her feet hitting the floor for emphasis like a sumo wrestler.

Buffolino sat back and closed his eyes. She was right. But he had to stick to the decision he'd made recently to take only cases that enhanced his reputation. All he had to do was hold out. How long he could do so was the big question.

The phone rang. Buffolino stared at it until Alicia opened the door and said, "It's the high road calling. Wendell Tierney."

Buffolino sat up straight and adjusted a tie that wasn't there. He cleared his throat. "Hello," he said in his deepest voice, then picked up the phone and repeated, "Hello, Mr. Tierney. How nice to hear from you. What a pleasure . . . Yes? . . . Of course we can meet today. . . . At your home? . . . My sincere pleasure, Mr. Tierney. I'll be at there at two sharp—I was sorry to hear about the untimely death of your associate. Terrible tragedy. Like in a Shakespeare play. . . . Yes, sir. Two this afternoon."

He hung up.

"So?" Alicia asked.

"So everything's cool, Al. Tierney has a big

assignment for me. You know what that means. I get to meet more of his big-shot friends like I did last time, only that assignment didn't last long enough for me to score. This time, I get a feeling it might be long term. See what I mean, babe? You stick to the high road, you don't get stuck in the mud. Run my suit down for a quick clean and press. Please. I'm going out to get a haircut."

"How's your back?" she asked.

"My back? Never felt better."

That Same Morning

"... and you say you observed nothing unusual about Ms. Juris at the board meeting."

Annabel, Mac, and Detective Eikenberg sat at the Smiths' kitchen table. Darcy Eikenberg had been late for their ten o'clock interview. She'd arrived at 10:12; it was now 10:20.

Annabel reaffirmed what she had said moments earlier. "I noticed nothing unusual," she said. "But that in itself was not unusual. Pauline was not what you would call a terribly open person. At least that was my evaluation of her, bearing in mind that I didn't know her well. But no, she seemed to do what I suppose she always did at those meetings, took notes and occasionally reminded Mr. Tierney of business to be raised."

"The relationship between them?" Eikenberg asked. "Between Mr. Tierney and Ms. Juris."

"Professional, as far as I know. I've always understood that she was a trusted assistant. Her behavior with him—and his with her—suggested nothing else."

Annabel glanced at Mac, who sat opposite her,

hands folded, gaze fixed firmly on the tabletop. He looked up, knew what she was thinking, and asked Eikenberg, "Do you have any reason to suggest a more personal relationship between Wendell Tierney and Pauline Juris?"

Eikenberg smiled. "Yes, I am looking for that. Guess you've seen through me, Professor." Another exchange of looks between Mac and Annabel. *How nice to have a fan club.* Her silent message was eloquent.

The detective leaned back in her chair, smiled, and shook her head. She said to Annabel, "I must admit, Mrs. Smith, that I'm slightly overwhelmed sitting here with the two of you."

"I can't imagine why," Annabel replied.

"Well, here you are, both former successful attorneys, your husband a professor of law and highly respected in every quarter of the city, and you the owner of an important art gallery *and* on the board of the National Building Museum. Those are pretty heavy credentials to be contained in one household."

"That's kind of you to say," said Annabel, "but the only thing we attempt to overwhelm, or control, at any rate, is our dog, Rufus. Usually, he won't stand for it and prevails."

Eikenberg laughed. "I do appreciate Rufus not joining us this morning," she said. "From the way you described him, he'd overwhelm me, too." She turned to Mac with her next round of questions. Annabel sat back, folded her arms, lowered her chin, and listened.

"You know Wendell Tierney pretty well, don't you, Professor?"

Smith shook his head. "I wouldn't say that. We're certainly friendly and have been for a number of years. But not close friends. I think the distinction is important."

"I understand," Eikenberg said. "Mr. Tierney is one of your many friends in high places."

"If you wish, although 'high places' doesn't quite define it. Successful and rich? Absolutely."

"But you were the one he called to be at his side."

"His reasons for doing that had little to do with the depth of our friendship."

"What *were* his reasons?"

"He considers me to be knowledgeable in criminal law. And I suppose he wanted advice from an unbiased observer."

"As opposed to?"

"As opposed to those who have a stake in saying the right thing to him. His own lawyers, for example. I don't."

"But you know him well enough to be aware of—well—to be aware of any affairs he might have had outside his marriage."

Smith, too, leaned back in his chair. Then he leaned forward. "Detective Eikenberg, I have no interest in anyone's personal life aside from my own, nor do I have any knowledge of how Wendell Tierney conducts his . . . personal life."

Eikenberg lightly touched his arm. "You understand where I'm going with this, Professor Smith. I have to. That's my job."

Smith knew, of course, where she was leading. She had asked the questions knowing it was unlikely he would have the details, or, if he did, was unlikely to volunteer them. She would ask the same question of as many people as possible, hoping that someone would inadvertently let something slip. There were seldom touchdown bombs thrown in the business of criminal interrogation. The answers were dug out one muddy yard at a time.

Smith said, "I don't know of any relationship other than professional between Wendell Tierney and Pauline Juris."

"Others?"

"Pardon?"

"Others in Mr. Tierney's sphere who might have been romantically involved with Ms. Juris?"

"Sorry."

Annabel stood. "If you won't be needing me anymore, I'll tend to some other things."

Eikenberg looked up. "Of course, Mrs. Smith. You've been very gracious to give me this time. Thank you."

"A pleasure meeting you," Annabel said without excessive warmth, extending her hand, which Eikenberg took without standing.

With Annabel gone, Eikenberg continued her questioning. "What do you know about the Scarlet Sin Society?"

"Probably the same thing you know about it. A fund-raising organization that recreates historical Washington murders."

"It was started by Mr. Tierney, wasn't it?"

"Yes. A special interest of his."

"The term I hear used is 'obsession.' An obsession of his."

Smith shrugged. "Call it what you will. I wouldn't know how to define obsession with Wendell Tierney. He has many interests."

"So I understand. But Tri-S is particularly important to him. At least that's what I'm told."

"Then it probably is."

"Are you involved with Tri-S? That is what they call it, isn't it?"

"Yes."

"You are?"

"Yes. No. I mean, it is commonly called Tri-S. But no, I am not involved with it."

"Do you know any of the people in it?"

Smith thought of his professor friend, Monty Jamison. "A few," he said.

"Seymour Fletcher?"

Smith frowned, drumming his fingers on the tabletop. "He's their director, I believe."

"Correct. Ever meet him?"

"No, I don't believe I have."

"He was the last person to see Pauline Juris alive."

"I didn't know that," Smith said.

"That's our information. They fought, arguing loudly at the church where a rehearsal was taking place for their next production. Familiar with the drama?"

"Only from what I read. The murder of Philip Barton Key by Congressman Sickles."

"I've been reading about that case, too. A lot of fascinating overtones."

"I'll take your word for it."

"Mr. Tierney sent Pauline to confront Fletcher the night she was murdered."

Smith said nothing.

"Another member of the board I interviewed overheard a conversation between Tierney and Juris at the conclusion of the board meeting."

"And?"

"That board member was certain your wife overheard the same conversation."

"Uh-huh."

"I wonder why she didn't tell me that."

For the first time that morning Smith felt uncomfortable. He was sitting with a shrewd interviewer who'd done her homework. But her questions up to this point had been innocuous. Now she seemed to be questioning Annabel's veracity. Enough, he decided. "I have no idea whether Annabel overheard any such conversation. If she did and failed to mention it to you, it was because she'd forgotten about it. Would you like her to come back in so you can ask directly?"

Eikenberg pursed her lips and stretched her arms above her head, straining the fabric at the front of her blouse. She'd been sitting with both feet flat on the floor beneath the table. Turning in her chair, she faced Smith and crossed her legs. She wore a short beige linen skirt, a black blouse with the top buttons unsecured, and a white jacket cut safari-style. Smith had recently purchased such a jacket from Banana Republic in Georgetown, but Eikenberg's was cut for a woman and had obviously cost a great deal more than his version.

"May I ask you a direct personal question, Professor Smith?"

She'd caught him looking at her legs. As he snapped his eyes up to meet hers, a smile crossed her lips. "Sure," he said.

"Who do you think killed Pauline Juris?"

"That's personal?"

"I think so. I mean, I'm asking you for your personal gut opinion as opposed to what you might *know*. Understand?" She wet her lips.

"Sorry, Detective, but I haven't the slightest idea who might have killed her."

"Pardon me for being skeptical, Professor— would you be offended if I called you Mackensie?"

"Mac."

"Oh, yes." She laughed. "Mac. Pardon me for being skeptical, Mac, but I can't believe you don't have some instinctive feel for who might have killed her."

Smith's eyes went to the door, then back to Eikenberg's face. "Sorry to disappoint you, Detective, but—"

"Please. Let's not have our relationship informal one-way. Darcy."

"Have you interviewed her former husband?" Did she know that Pauline had been briefly married years ago?

She did. "Not yet," she said. "He's in New York, and we've contacted him. We expect him here in a day or two. Why do you ask?"

"Just curious. I never knew she was married until Wendell told me yesterday."

"Kept it a secret, huh?"

"Yes. Well, she evidently didn't talk about it to many people."

"Tierney's sons? Daughter?"

"What about them?"

"You know them?"

"Yes. They're evidently good citizens."

"Citizens, maybe. But the daughter, Suzanne, has been at war with her father for years."

"I wouldn't know about that."

"Anything else you might *know* about?" she asked.

"Not at the moment. But if I think of something, I'll certainly call. More coffee?"

"Thank you, no, but it was delicious. Where do you buy it?"

"Various places. I mix it myself, a little of this, a little of that, some decaf, some regular. What you're drinking this morning has a hint of amaretto."

She laughed. Even her teeth were perfect, he thought. "More than a hint, I'd say," she said. "What a wonderful flavor. And what a wonderful side to you."

"Meaning what?"

"To care that much about coffee."

"I'm a coffee snob."

"I like that in a man. Little pockets of snobbery, but not the whole person."

Smith got to his feet in the hope that it would signal an end to what had become awkward. Eikenberg didn't move. "Anything else you wish to ask me?" he said.

"Lots of things, but not at the moment. I would like to get together with you again. I promise not to unduly intrude. Is that all right with you?"

"Why, yes—I suppose so."

She stood, straightened her skirt, which had developed wrinkles across her thighs, and bent to pick up her briefcase from the floor. "I wish all my interviews were this pleasant."

"Nothing pleasant about any interview when it involves murder," he said.

"Well, as you know from all your years of criminal law, Mac, you find pleasantness where you can. You and your wife have been extremely co-operative this morning. I hesitate . . ."

His expression invited her to continue.

"I'd like to spend more time with you, pick your brain a little—a lot."

"Fine."

"Don't be so quick to agree. I'm known in the department for my ability to reach pest status once I get started."

"I'll let you know when you get there. Become a pest."

"Fair enough. There are elements of this case that I really can't go into at the moment, but that

I'd like to discuss with you in a less formal setting."

Smith looked left and right. "You call this formal? My kitchen?"

She laughed. "You know what I mean. I
need—and I won't be coy about it, I need—I'd
appreciate being able to run things by you. Not
necessarily specifics of the case but . . . more your
general thinking about it. Maybe about murder in
general."

"You should consider joining Scarlet Sin," he
said pleasantly.

"That's always a possibility. . . ."

"Or taking another of my classes. That's what
I'm paid for at GW."

"Maybe we could consider lunch a seminar of
sorts. An extension course. Could we?"

"Well, maybe."

"I'll call. Where's your wife? I'd like to say
good-bye."

"I'll find her," he said.

"Not necessary. Just thank her for me. She's a
very nice woman."

"I'll pass along the compliment."

As he opened the front door for her, she said,
"Please ask Mrs. Smith whether she overheard
that conversation at the board meeting between
Mr. Tierney and Ms. Juris about Seymour
Fletcher. It had to do with budgets, I believe."

"I will."

He watched her descend the few brick steps in front of the house, turn left, and stride confidently up the street until out of sight. When he turned, he faced Annabel. "You snuck up on me," he said with a smile.

"You know I wouldn't do that. How did it go?"

"I think Wendell might be in for a long, tough run. He's made a lot of enemies over the years, people who wouldn't mind taking him down. By the way, why didn't you tell her about a conversation between Wendell and Pauline at the end of the board meeting?"

"Conversation?"

"Something to do with budgets."

"Oh, right. I did hear them talking. He wanted her to confront someone about money. I never gave it a thought—until now. Sort of like Leona Helmsley."

"Who's like Leona Helmsley?"

"Wendell. She crossed a lot of people, made a lot of enemies. Just as he has. That's why she ended up in jail."

"She's a convicted felon."

"People didn't like her. Nice doctors get sued less than nasty ones. Did she get what she wanted from you?"

"Leona?" He laughed. "Oh, Detective Eikenberg. Probably not. I don't have anything to give her."

"Hmmmm."

"Are you upset about something?"

"You asked me that yesterday. I told you I was upset about Pauline's murder."

"And I also asked if you were upset with me. I'll ask that again, too."

"No." She smiled and said, "She's an impressive woman. Hardly the stereotypical cop."

"I suppose so. I'm sure you're glad this morning is over with."

"I certainly hope it is, Professor Smith."

12 The Next Day

When Mac Smith walked into the faculty cafeteria the following morning, he found Monty Jamison, hidden behind the morning newspaper. The history professor suddenly realized Smith stood over him, glanced up, grunted a greeting, and went back to reading. Smith took a seat across the small table.

"Damn shame what happened to that young student last night," Jamison said.

"But fortunate it turned out the way it did."

A freshman at the university had been attacked on a side street on the fringe of the campus. Using a can of mace she always carried, she'd subdued her attacker and attracted the attention of a passerby, who called the police.

"No young woman is safe these days unless armed," Jamison said. He put down the paper and stared at Smith through Coke-bottle glasses. "Another example of society gone to rot. Have you read the story this morning about poor Pauline Juris?"

"Most of it. I was interrupted. Excuse me."

Smith returned from the serving line with a

lightly buttered bagel and cup of tea. His feeling for coffee was sufficiently strong to preclude, unless the circumstances were dire, drinking coffee brewed anywhere but in his own kitchen.

"Here. Finish it," Jamison said, turning the paper and sliding it on top of Smith's plate. Mac retrieved his bagel from beneath the paper, bit in, rearranged things, and quickly finished the article. It was primarily a profile of Pauline Juris culled from various sources, including interviews with several people who'd requested anonymity. A significant portion was devoted to her former husband, Lucas Wharton, a thoracic surgeon in New York City. According to the reporter, Lucas and Pauline had met while undergraduates at Johns Hopkins University in Baltimore, Wharton's hometown. The marriage had lasted eleven months. No children. Dr. Wharton, the article said, had been contacted by the police and would be questioned in Washington. Pauline's relationship with Wendell Tierney was also explored. In the best tradition of innuendo journalism, it hinted—but only hinted—that the bond between Tierney and Pauline Juris might have exceeded the boundaries of business.

Smith folded the paper, sighed, and took another bite of bagel.

"I find the name of her former husband interesting," said Jamison.

Smith looked up. "How so?"

"Wharton. I think I'll do a little research into his family background."

Smith couldn't help but laugh. "Why?"

"To see whether he might be related, no matter how tangentially, to the infamous and stylish Elizabeth Wharton."

Bagel poised halfway between plate and mouth, Smith said, "Someone I should know?"

Jamison's chuckle was mildly scolding. "There you have it, Mackensie Smith, a prime example of what you miss by not joining Tri-S."

Here we go again. Smith sat silently; the bagel proved a useful shield.

"Surely, Mac, you must remember Elizabeth Wharton."

"Not personally. Yes, in fact I do know a little about her. Sort of Washington's early 1870s Lucrezia Borgia."

"Exactly. That's why you should join us. A remarkable story. Mrs. Wharton was a society lady from Philadelphia who settled in Baltimore—interesting coincidence that Dr. Lucas Wharton hails from that same city—and glided easily through the upper strata of Baltimore and Washington. Problem was, she had a habit of borrowing money and not paying it back."

"That doesn't make her unique," said Mac.

"It does when coupled with a tendency to murder those who asked for it back. Their money, that is. Those unfortunate souls would visit Mrs. Wharton at her home in search of repayment, be served tea, and die mysteriously."

"Black or . . . ?"

"No, they were white. Upper crust."

"I meant what kind of tea did she serve, black, green, or oolong?"

This time Jamison's laugh was defensive. "Kind of tea? How would I know that?"

Smith shrugged and smiled. "If you were a modern French historian, you'd know that everyday details are important. Or a detective. Go on, Monty. Just kidding."

"I should say," Jamison said. "Where was I? Oh, yes. Well, it seems Mrs. Wharton eventually befriended a famous Civil War general, W. S. Ketchum of Georgetown, and borrowed twenty-six hundred dollars from him. She never repaid it, not even the interest. When he learned she was planning an extended European stay, he and a lady friend paid her a visit, a kind of reminder about the I.O.U. Became weekend guests, as a matter of fact, and were elegantly entertained. But after breakfast and a cup of Mrs. Wharton's tea, the general fell ill. A few days later, after he'd been served a large glass of lemonade in the same house, he took to what would be his deathbed."

"Lemonade?" Smith said.

"Yes, lovingly prepared by Mrs. Wharton herself." Jamison stopped talking to finish his scrambled eggs.

Smith said, "And Mrs. Wharton was accused of murder. The case is coming back to me."

"She certainly was. One of the most celebrated trials of Washington. Of course, it would be more than a vague memory for you if you were with us at Tri-S. We've devoted a considerable number of evenings to discussing Mrs. Wharton and her lemonade."

"I see what I've missed."

Jamison leaned on the table. "You do?"

"Yes. Go on, Monty."

"She was judged innocent by a jury of her peers. It was one of the first cases in which forensic medicine was used in a trial."

Smith nodded. "You're absolutely correct. There was confusion over whether the general died of a dose of tartar emetic or some natural disease like meningitis."

"Exactly. Both produce the same symptoms. The autopsy on General Ketchum revealed a large amount of tartar emetic in his stomach, certainly enough to kill him. And it was proved that Mrs. Wharton had purchased a supply of it just days prior to the general's visit."

"Open and shut, you might say."

"Not in that era, Mac. There were only two

types of woman back then, weren't there? A virtuous lady or a whore. Everyone knew that virtuous ladies did not go around serving poisoned lemonade to distinguished generals."

Smith dabbed at his mouth with a paper napkin and pushed back his chair. "I really have to run, Monty. This was fascinating."

"I've only skimmed the surface, of course. There are myriad provocative details. Perhaps one night when you attend a meeting of Tri-S, I'll reopen a discussion of this case. Say, how come you know so much about this, when you said you didn't?"

"A good lawyer searches for precedents, Monty. And conveniently forgets cases, as well."

As Smith was about to walk away, Jamison said, "Oh, Mac, I understand you were summoned to Wendell's house the day Pauline's body was discovered."

Smith frowned. " 'Summoned' isn't the word I would use. I did meet with him that afternoon."

Jamison's arched eyebrows asked, And?

"Wendell is naturally concerned about the ramifications of this. He asked my advice."

"Cherchez la femme," Jamison said.

"Why look for the woman? What woman?"

"Mackensie, you sly devil. You aren't fooling me one bit. You are going to become directly involved in this case, most likely as Wendell Tierney's legal counsel. And I have a feeling that when all is said and done, it will be a woman who takes front-and-center in this tragic melodrama. Will make for a tremendously interesting case for a future Scarlet Sin session—say, in the year 2500."

"My class is waiting," Smith said.

"So are we, Mac."

13 That Afternoon

Sun Ben Cheong left Gary's Restaurant on M Street NW, where he had lunched with a large pension fund's investment manager. It had been pleasant enough. Although the manager, whose name was Barrenstein, seemed enthusiastic about the investments Cheong had outlined for him, Cheong instinctively knew: Nothing would come of it. He judged Barrenstein to be a man who enjoyed being wooed but who would act upon only the most conservative opportunities. What Cheong had suggested—using money from the fund to buy and rehabilitate a block of downtown buildings that had fallen into decay—did not fall into that category.

Outside and away from his lunch guest, Cheong enjoyed the sun on his face. The day had started gray. When he'd arrived at the restaurant, cool, moist air was one step removed from outright rain. But a front had arrived during lunch, dragging behind it a broom of cool, sunny weather.

He looked at his watch: ten minutes past two. Lunch had lasted too long, but the Norwegian salmon had prospered at the hands of the anonymous chef.

He adjusted the lapels of his black Armani double-breasted suit and watched a tall, statuesque blond woman walk past. Well, saunter by, to be precise. As his eyes lingered on the seductive sway of her body, a smile of appreciation formed on his lips. Cheong's face seldom displayed thoughts and feelings. When describing him, friends and colleagues often said, "Not very expressive." One said to him, "You ought to enter the World Poker Championship. You'd win hands-down with that face of yours."

He checked his watch again. Almost an hour before the call would come. He walked at a leisurely pace, stopped to admire offerings in the windows of men's shops, bought a vanilla frozen-yogurt cone from a sidewalk vendor, and eventually reached Judiciary Square, yet another Washington monument, this to the nation's law-enforcement officers who'd fallen in the line of duty. The square sat between D and F streets, a Metro entrance in its center. Lining the D Street side were courthouses: the United States Court of Military Appeals, the Superior Court of the District of Columbia, and other granite halls of justice and otherwise.

At the opposite end, on F Street, stood the

redbrick National Building Museum, its three-feet-high, twelve-hundred-feet-long facade of buff terra-cotta frieze depicting Civil War forces. Pension records were once kept secure there. The facade was a perpetual stone parade of Union infantry, navy, medical units, artillery, cavalry, and quartermaster personnel returning from battle.

Behind the museum was the General Accounting Office. And beyond that was the beginning of Washington's "Chinatown," small by San Francisco or New York standards but home to five thousand of the some thirty thousand Chinese-Americans living in the area.

He paused in front of the Friendship Arch that marked its official entrance at Seventh and H streets. Three hundred garishly painted dragons mauled each other across its top. Cheong knew the arch had important meaning for Chinatown's citizens, but it had no significance for him. He'd decided long ago that symbolism, like religion, only mattered to the poor, who needed something mysterious to ease dreary lives. "Dreary" was not a word Cheong would use to describe his life since coming to America.

He walked another block, pausing occasionally to inhale the pungent odors wafting from small produce shops. Some things you never outgrew. Two elderly Chinese men argued on the sidewalk over a transaction gone sour. Something to do with a wristwatch. Cheong didn't listen long enough to learn more details.

He stopped again, this time to read a plaque affixed to a historical landmark—THE SURRATT BOARDING HOUSE. According to the Chinese-American Lions Club, which had placed the plaque, it was here conspirators had plotted the abduction of President Abraham Lincoln in 1865.

Obviously before it fell into the hands of the Chinese, Cheong thought.

A few doors from the plaque was a restaurant. Cheong peered through the front window. Someone inside waved. He looked left and right, then entered, returned a greeting without breaking stride, went to the rear of the dining room, swung open doors into the steaming kitchen, slid past sweating cooks, and disappeared through another door, behind which was a narrow flight of wooden stairs.

He exited two floors up into a carpeted corridor lighted by recessed ceiling fixtures with low-wattage bulbs. A series of doors lined the hallway. Cheong stood in front of one on which black Chinese symbols announced the business and its purpose: import-export. He inserted a key, entered, and locked the door behind him.

Three men and one woman were in the room. She greeted Cheong in Chinese. The others glanced up, said nothing, returned to their desk-top tasks. The room's windows overlooking the street were covered by heavy draperies. The only light in the room came from powerful halogen lamps illuminating the desks of the four people. Two of the men wore jewelers' loupes. Familiar fragments of Chinese music played from a small tape recorder.

Cheong stopped at each of the four desks. The powerful, focused light from the halogens caught the dazzling multiple facets—dozens of diamonds spread out on soft green cloths, the effect kaleido-scopic.

He left the room and entered another, a small office as tastefully decorated and furnished as the outside room was sparse. The windows in this room, too, were draped against outside light—and eyes. It was a study in blacks.

A large black lacquer desk with a white marble top. A high-backed black leather chair separating the desk from a long black lacquer credenza, its surface bare except for an elaborate telephone system that included a black tape recorder, an-swering machine, speakerphone, and earphones. A second, plain phone sat next to it—but red. A large circular black-and-brass clock displaying time zones around the world dominated the wall above.

On the opposite wall was a white plastic chart. Written on it with erasable pen were the names of a dozen American cities. A series of columns following each name were filled with Chinese notations.

Cheong picked up the red phone and dialed a private number. "Is Ricky there? This is Sun Ben."

A minute later Ricky, a host for special customers, came on the line and said with extreme pleasantness, "Sun Ben. Great to hear your voice. How are you, my friend?"

Cheong's voice was humdrum. "I'm fine, thank you. I have to be in Philadelphia tomorrow. I would like to stay with you tonight."

"Terrific," said Ricky. "All the usual?"

"Yes."

"What time?"

"Eight-thirty."

"Dinner in your suite?"

"Yes. Broiled skinless chicken, no sauce, a salad, one roll."

"You got it, my friend. We'll welcome you again to Atlantic City. See you tonight."

Cheong carefully hung his suit jacket on a hanger behind the door and returned to his chair. He sat back, propped his feet on the edge of the desk, and closed his eyes.

Until the larger, more elaborate phone rang.

He slowly swiveled, picked up the receiver, and spoke in Chinese, as did the caller.

CHEONG: How are you?

CALLER: Fine. Just fine. You have an order to place?

CHEONG: Two-hundred fifty.

CALLER: At the prevailing rate?

CHEONG: Yes. Has it changed since last week?

CALLER: No.

CHEONG: Good. The money will be wired in the morning. All is well with your family?

CALLER: My family is fine. Your . . . family?

CHEONG: We are all in good health.

CALLER: We must see each other again one day.

Cheong dangled the receiver over the cradle and lowered it until it clicked. The clock on the wall said it was 3:15 in Washington, 9:15 the following morning in Hong Kong.

He sat motionless in the room's dim light until 3:30, when a buzzer indicated someone had entered the outer office. Cheong got up from behind his desk, put on his jacket and buttoned it, returned to the chair, and sat ramrod straight. Someone knocked. "Come in," Cheong said in Chinese.

One of the men wearing a jeweler's loupe stepped aside to allow another man to enter. He was fat; his straining suit had been purchased many pounds ago. He carried a canvas Hecht's shopping bag, bulging like his suit.

After exchanging the briefest greetings, the visitor came to the desk, lowered the bag to the floor, nodded, and left. Cheong waited until he heard the buzzer again. He came around the desk, picked up the bag, placed it on the desk, and examined its contents. It was filled with thick envelopes, each secured with a rubber band. He plucked one from the bag and ran his fingers over it, as though his fingertips could determine its contents and worth like a bar-code reader at a supermarket checkout counter. He dropped the envelope into the bag and went to the paneled wall next to the clock where he gently pressed the lower corner of one section. A portion of the wall swung open. Behind it was a safe. Cheong dialed the combination, opened the door, and dumped the contents of the canvas bag on top of dozens of other envelopes.

Process reversed, he went to the larger outer room, dropped the empty shopping bag on a table in the corner, and left.

He walked to his office at the Tankloff Investment Advisory Group, picked up a briefcase and overnight bag he'd left there that morning, and told his secretary he would be in Philadelphia the following day for a meeting and would not be reachable that night. He checked his messages—

nothing that couldn't wait until he returned, including a call from Suzanne Tierney.

He retrieved his red XJS Jaguar convertible from the parking garage beneath the building and turned on the radio. At 107.7 was an FM station that played middle-of-the-road oldies. And not Chinese oldies. He smiled his slight smile, positioned Porsche sunglasses on his nose, and checked himself in the rearview mirror. With James Taylor's "Your Smiling Face" playing a little too loud, he headed out of the city. It was good to get away.

14 Saturday Morning

If recent events in Wendell Tierney's world could have affected the weather appropriately, there would have been a torrential downpour accompanied by tornadoes. It was the Saturday of his cruise up the Potomac. But such a link didn't exist except in the minds of mythologists. The day dawned sunny and breezy, perfect for mildly nautical meanderings on a peaceful river. Turbulence was all in the mind.

Guests for the cruise were played on board by a bagpiper in full Scottish regalia, a tip of Tierney's hat to his heritage, as well as to a departed friend, publishing tycoon Malcolm Forbes, whose cruises on his yacht, *The Highlander,* had been as passionately coveted by business movers and shakers as dinner invitations to the White House were to those seeking political favors.

Mac Smith took his wife's arm as they climbed the gangplank to the *Marilyn.* Tierney's yacht wasn't as large as the famed Forbes ship, but it was no dinghy. The *Marilyn* was a 105-foot beauty with a twenty-three-foot beam, whose draft of only four feet made it possible to navigate relatively shallow portions of the Potomac. Built in 1989 by Derecktor Shipyards of New York and christened *Lady Frances,* it was bought by Tierney the following year through the Bertram Yacht Company of Miami and renamed. "She'll do over thirty knots," he'd told Mac and Annabel during their last cruise together. "Double most yachts her size. Cruise at twenty-four. Susan Puleo did the interiors." The name meant nothing to the Smiths. Keeping up with the world of international designers was not one of their many interests.

They declined a uniformed waiter's tray of mimosas and Bloody Marys and made their way to the large, open aft deck where other early arrivals had congregated. Sarah Walters spotted them immediately. She was chairwoman of the National Cathedral's chapter, the equivalent of a board of directors at secular institutions. "Mac, how delightful to see you," she said, extending her hand. "And Annabel. Wendell certainly has good taste when choosing shipmates."

Walters's husband, Fred, a tall, overweight, jowly man with the veined cheeks and watery eyes of a heavy drinker, was an undersecretary in the Defense Department. He lifted his drink in salute.

The Walterses had been standing with two other couples. The black man, Joe Dorsey, headed the D.C. Urban League. His wife,

Tammy, extraordinarily attractive, seemed to receive a great deal of press attention and was one of the city's most vocal pro-choice advocates on the abortion issue.

The white couple, both small and wiry, looked remarkably alike considering they were simply married. They were introduced as Victor and Buffy Morrissey. "Victor," Sarah Walters told Mac and Annabel after introducing them, "owns half of Virginia."

"Impressive," Smith said. "Who owns the other half?"

Buffy Morrissey giggled, exposing a set of yellowing teeth that were interchangeable with her husband's. "Who else? The government," she replied.

Fred Walters motioned for a waiter to bring him another drink. Annabel decided to have a mimosa. Others joined them, prompting Mac to touch Annabel's arm as a signal to leave the burgeoning group. They went midship and looked down at the waters of the Potomac. "Peaceful," Annabel said, drawing a deep, contented breath.

"When we're alone," Mac said.

The sound of an outboard motor caused them to look to their right. Inching along the length of the yacht was Tierney's twenty-two-foot Aquasport. Mac narrowed his eyes and leaned farther over the rail as he thought he recognized the man at the smaller vessel's center console. "Tony?" he said loudly.

Anthony Buffolino grinned broadly and tossed Smith a sharp salute. He wore a double-breasted blue blazer with oversized brass buttons, teal turtleneck, gray trousers, and a small-billed black yachting cap with too much gold braid for its size. The cap sat at a jaunty angle. He guided the Aquasport closer to the *Marilyn* until it was directly below Mac and Annabel. "What are you doing here?" Smith asked over the rumble of the idling outboard.

"On the case," Buffolino replied. "Mr. Tierney hired me to provide beefed-up security. I'll be riding shotgun today."

"Shotgun?" Annabel asked.

Buffolino laughed. "Just tagging along and keeping my eyes open. Like they do with political bigwigs when they're out on the water."

"You know how to drive that thing?" Smith asked.

"Me? Sure. I spent a couple 'a years with MPD Marine Division." He hit a brace, tossed another crisp salute, and said, "Captain A. Buffolino at your service, sir." He looked down at his watch. "I'd better move. Maybe we'll catch up later."

As Buffolino increased power to the outboard and moved away, Annabel said to her husband, "He never ceases to amaze me."

Smith grinned. "Tony's the kind of guy who's always marching up to the brink of disaster but pulls back at the last second."

"He's gone over the brink three times," Annabel offered, referring to the investigator's marriages.

Smith chuckled. "Sometimes you learn late. I think he's finally found the right woman in Alicia. Don't you?"

"I hope so. At least she doesn't have horns like the last one."

"Neither does he, though Tony's no angel. As we both know."

One time that Tony Buffolino failed to pull back in time had led to his dismissal from the police department.

He'd been an exemplary officer, his file filled with commendations, a cop who wasn't afraid to put everything on the line, including his life. But then a son from his first marriage was diagnosed with leukemia, and the medical bills mounted rapidly. Desperate, Tony took money from a Colombian drug dealer but was caught in an Internal Affairs sting. That's when he met attorney Mackensie Smith, who worked out a deal for criminal charges to be dropped in return for Buffolino's resignation from MPD.

Since those dark days in his life, Buffolino and Smith had worked together on a number of occasions, Mac giving him work, and getting him work, to help with his rehabilitation. But it wasn't all from the goodness of Mac's heart. Mac Smith had worked with plenty of private investigators over the course of his legal career, but none had the instincts of Tony Buffolino. It was street smarts plus a way of looking at things from an offbeat, sometimes skewed perspective that often proved right. He was different, and that was his edge.

A friendship of sorts had also developed between the two men, an unlikely one, perhaps, but satisfactory to both. It wasn't that they socialized. Each predictably moved in his own circle. But Smith liked the savvy, tough-talking ex-cop, and Buffolino liked and respected his friend "the prof." Which was good enough.

Wendell and Marilyn Tierney boarded. Wendell, in the best tradition of a ship's captain, barked orders to the crew. Minutes later, the *Marilyn* left the dock and slowly headed downriver toward the capital and points beyond.

Once they were under way, Tierney abandoned his role of captain and became gregarious host to his thirty guests. The murder of Pauline Juris, less than a week old, was unofficially off-limits as a topic of conversation, at least when Tierney was within earshot. When he wasn't, guests whispered about it. Many expressed admiration for the way he was holding up. Electing to go forward with this cruise was, they felt, an example of what the man was made of, a backbone of steel, a determination that life went on no matter whose life had not. And, of course, a few questioned where backbone ended and insensitivity began.

As the *Marilyn* continued downriver, Smith noticed two men aboard who did not appear to be guests or members of the crew. Security personnel provided by Buffolino? he wondered. Tierney might present a front of strength and business-as-usual, but he was obviously concerned enough to have hired protection. Which Smith did not entirely understand. Did Wendell *know* something about an outside destructive force that played a role in Pauline's death and that might be unleashed on him and his family? Probably not. Wendell Tierney was a man of excesses, Mac knew. Never one boat when four would do.

The yacht's real captain used the P.A. system to point out landmarks on shore: Glen Echo, billed as a utopian community in 1889 and wiped out by a malaria epidemic in 1892; Cabin John, named after an early settler who'd struck gold there and now the site of the Cabin John Arch, the largest stone arch in the Western Hemisphere, across which the Washington Aqueduct flowed; the Clara Barton House, built in Mississippi Riverboat style by the founder of the American Red

Cross; famed Fletcher's Boat House and its mill, closed in 1870 after years of turning out Evermay Flour, currently a popular place for renting canoes and rowboats; and Little Falls Skirting Canal, a 2.2-mile canal now part of the C&O.

They cruised beneath the Chain Bridge, one of the oldest bridges to span the Potomac. After they had sailed seven miles, Teddy Roosevelt Island came into view.

Then a woman, dropping delicacy after several drinks, wondered aloud whether they would pass the actual spot where Pauline Juris's body had been found. An athletic-looking man, an inveterate boatsman and guiding light of the prestigious Washington Canoe Club, laid that speculation to rest. Boats did not ply that side of the island, he explained. Too shallow. They would pass through a channel at the northern end, far from the scene of the park ranger's gruesome sunrise surprise.

While the captain's earlier running commentary was interesting, history was not uppermost on the minds of most guests. Show tunes performed by a piano-bass-drums trio filled the air with a sense of here and now as waiters in short white jackets and long black bow ties moved with precision, their trays ladened with lobster hors d'oeuvres and drinks. There would be cold salmon, lobster, and crab for lunch, with champagne and iced vodka to accompany a czar's supply of beluga caviar.

The one person who didn't seem to have been caught up in the festive spirit was Marilyn Tierney. Annabel commented to Mac that Marilyn looked the part of a dutiful, professional hostess who would rather be some other place, preferably alone and without the need to smile on demand. "I ache when I see someone like that," she said into Mac's ear.

"As I told you, they have their problems," Smith said.

"Problems I hope we never have."

"No chance."

"Don't be so smug," she said, squeezing the muscle of his arm. "It can happen—unless we work hard to make sure we won't."

Smith's frown turned into a smile. "And that's exactly what we are, Annabel. Two people working hard. Nice work if you can get it." He kissed her, took her hand, and they settled back into yellow canvas deck chairs at the yacht's stern.

Their solitude didn't last long. Alabama congressman Wells Montgomery and his wife, Tricia, he the white-haired, red-faced House whip, she with the bouncy style and pert looks of the perpetual cheerleader, joined them. They were accompanied by the founder and principal fund-raiser for the Coalition for a Better D.C., Amanda Cole, and her husband, Richard, the successful owner of a string of suburban mall multimovie theaters.

"Gives me the creeps," Amanda Cole said, suddenly and uncharacteristically serious, as they looked at Roosevelt Island. The yacht had begun to swing north through the narrow Georgetown Channel that would traverse the island and bring them out into the more open waters of Washington Harbor.

"Inconceivable," Congressman Montgomery said.

They uttered a few more sober sentiments before walking away from Mac and Annabel to join other guests on the starboard side, where the spires of Georgetown University, and Three Sisters Islands, provided less troublesome visual interest.

"I know what you're thinking," Annabel said.

Her voice startled Mac. The comments of the others had caused him to focus on a vision of Pauline Juris's body tangled in weeds and branches along Roosevelt Island's shoreline. He snapped his head in Annabel's direction. "You do? Yes, of course you do. I was thinking of Pauline Juris."

"And of Wendell Tierney wanting you to help him."

Smith shook his head. "No, I wasn't thinking

about that. There's nothing I can do for Wendell, except what I did—lend an ear."

A bell announced that lunch was served in the main cabin.

"Mac, stay out of it."

He looked at her.

"Please."

He glumly nodded. "Hungry?"

"For lobster? Lobster creates appetites."

And so they filled their plates, balanced them on their knees, and allowed the sun and crisp air and succulent tastes to replace grim thoughts. That pleasant reverie lasted all the way to Point Lookout at the entrance to the bay, where Tierney's captain made a large, languid circle and pointed the yacht home.

Lunch had been cleared by the time they reached Breton Bay, and fresh glasses on serving trays had taken on a more distinct hue of white and amber. Mac and Annabel now stood near the bow, their faces raised to capture the invigorating breeze caused by its movement, and to enjoy the fading rays of a sun heading west. Wendell Tierney, who'd spent little time with them that day, came up behind and asked, "Enjoying yourselves?"

"Very much, Wendell," Annabel answered. "It's a lovely day, lovely event."

"Marred only by what's on everyone's mind, I

suppose," Tierney said. "What scuttlebutt have you picked up today, Mac?"

Smith was surprised by the question.

"I'm sure that in spite of all this nice-nice, everyone is talking about Pauline," Tierney said. He leaned on the railing and looked straight ahead.

"Very little of that kind of talk," Smith lied. "Too nice a day to think about murder." Which was more nearly true.

"Not if you're a suspect."

"No, I suppose not. Anything new from your end?"

Tierney shoved his hands in the pockets of his white slacks and peered down at the deck. "They finished the autopsy."

"When?" Smith asked.

"Last night. Detective Eikenberg called this morning as I was leaving the house."

Smith's face reflected his puzzlement. Why would she call Tierney with that information?

Tierney continued. "Nothing surprising, I suppose. Murdered with a heavy object with a defined edge during the hours following the board meeting." He said to Annabel, "Hell of an introduction for our newest board member."

She said nothing.

"Mac, any chance of stealing you away from your bride for five minutes?"

Smith glanced at Annabel. She replied, "By all

means." To Mac: "I'll be here when you get back."

Smith followed Tierney through the master suite on the main deck, with its Jacuzzi and queen-sized bed, and into the smallest of three additional guest quarters that had been configured as an office. "My favorite getaway," he said. He indicated a small couch to Smith. "Sometimes, when I really have to think something out, I rustle up the crew, and we go out on the river. I hole up here and let my mind wander. I'll probably be doing a lot of that these days." He perched on the edge of a desk and continued. "Eikenberg didn't call just to give me the autopsy report. She told me they'd found letters in Pauline's apartment."

"What kind of letters?"

"Love letters."

Smith's face asked for further explanation.

"The detective said I'd written them to Pauline."

"I see," Smith said. There was silence in the room except for the steady throb of the *Marilyn*'s powerful engines. Smith asked the obvious question: "Did you? Write them?"

"Of course not."

"Then why would such letters be in her apartment? I mean, did Eikenberg say the letters had been signed by you?"

"Yes."

"And you say you didn't write them. Someone else did and signed your name?"

"I suppose that's the logical explanation. But will she buy it?"

Smith didn't like Tierney wondering whether the police would "buy it." He asked, "Did Darcy Eikenberg tell you anything else about the letters? Specific language?"

Tierney shook his head. "All she said was that they were intimate in nature and could be called love letters."

"Why are you telling *me* this, Wendell?"

Tierney's eyes widened; animation returned to his face. "Because I don't know who else to turn to, Mac. I obviously can't discuss this with my family. I've got a slew of attorneys I pay a fortune to who wouldn't mind the fees, and one or two who wouldn't mind seeing me sink in some kind of scandal."

Smith stood, twisted his torso to manipulate his spine against a fleeting spasm in his lower back, and sat again. "Wendell, I suppose I should be flattered that you've trusted me with this information. But, frankly, I'm at as much of a loss today as I was coming to your house the day they found Pauline. There's nothing I can do for you except what I've done—offer my friendship and a willing ear."

Tierney didn't hesitate. "Mac," he said, "I was hoping you'd use your connections to find out more about these letters, maybe even get hold of them for me."

Smith looked at Tierney quizzically, then laughed a little. "What makes you think I could do that?"

"It's my understanding," Tierney said, "that Mackensie Smith can do damn near anything he wants in this town. It's called connections."

"You need better sources of information, Wendell. I happen to be a law professor who leads a cloistered, unconnected life these days."

"Come on, Mac. You don't spend years as Washington's top criminal attorney without having plenty of strings to pull, chips to call." He pushed himself away from the desk and slapped Smith on the shoulder. "Besides, the police arrive, and you arrive, and the head cop learned her trade from you. And I saw the way the lovely lady detective looked at you. Obviously infatuated. Maybe you could trade on that infatuation. I'd be eternally grateful. Name your price."

"It has nothing to do with price," Smith said, his good nature now roughened up by Tierney's sandpaper style. But he reminded himself that this was, after all, Tierney's manner. He was a man used to getting his way, hiring and firing, spreading money around, an archetypal D.C. power broker. Second nature to him.

"Will you, Mac? I mean, at least take a shot at it for me? I don't expect miracles, but I would appreciate the effort. Just a few phone calls." Tierney sat on the couch next to Smith, glanced at the closed slatted doors through which the faint sounds of the party could be heard, and lowered his voice. "What I really want, Mac, is for these letters to not be made public. I don't want some son of a bitch leaking them to the press. You can imagine what that would do to Marilyn, to my children. It would be devastating."

"Not if you didn't write them," Smith said.

"What does it matter if I wrote them or not? If the police say my name is on them, the seed is planted. Please, Mac. I know I've been imposing upon you since Pauline's death, but I'm pulling out all the stops to keep my family together. If I ever needed family, it's now. I don't think I can survive this without their support."

The new sincerity in Tierney's voice had its intended effect. Smith had known a lot of men like Tierney—arrogant, self-assured, yet with the magical ability to draw you in and make you want to respond.

Tierney continued. "I don't care about business," he said. "I don't care about myself. But I do care about my family. Whoever wrote those letters and put my name on them is out to destroy me. Whether it's a business competitor or someone with a personal grudge doesn't matter a hell of a lot. All I know is that I'll do anything to keep my family out of it. One call, Mac. Just see what you can do. That's all I ask."

Smith stood, sighed. "Let me think about it, Wendell."

Tierney said, "I can't ask more than that. By the way, Mac, introducing me to Tony Buffolino was a real favor. I've hired him until this mess is resolved. You don't think I'm paranoid, wanting security beefed up, do you?"

"Better safe than sorry."

"He's a real character. But you know something? He's changed since the last time he worked for me. I wouldn't call him refined, but he's smoothed some of the rough edges."

Smith smiled. "I hope he doesn't lose too many of those rough edges. That's part of his charm— and his effectiveness."

When Smith returned to the deck, Annabel had left the bow and joined a group aft. Her eyes asked the obvious. Smith's expression said, "I'll tell you when we get home."

And so it was left until they pulled up to Tierney's private dock, the gangplank was lowered, and the guests filed off, each woman carrying a souvenir of the trip, a sterling-silver music box in the shape of balustrades that adorn the National Building Museum.

Mac and Annabel didn't say much on the drive home. But once inside the house, and after Annabel had placed the music box on the mantel—"What a beautiful gift," she said—they sat in the kitchen, where he told her of his conversation with Tierney.

"What do you think?" Annabel asked.

"I don't know what I think," was his response. "Somehow, I believe him. I don't think he wrote those letters. On the other hand, maybe he did. If he didn't, somebody not only wants to link him to Pauline's murder, they're out to destroy him personally."

"Will you make the phone call?" she asked.

"Yes. It's a small thing. I doubt if I'll learn much, but I'd like to be able to say I tried."

"Who will you call?"

"MPD."

"Detective Eikenberg?"

"She's the lead detective on the case and the one who told Wendell about the letters."

"Do what you think is right. Now excuse me. I brought home the account books from the gallery to reconcile this weekend. I think I'll get started."

Smith intercepted her on her way out of the kitchen and embraced her. "How about extending a perfect day on the Potomac? Just the two of us."

He nuzzled her ear with his nose and attempted to kiss her neck. She disengaged. "Let's save your ardor for another day," she said.

"Tomorrow?" he asked.

"Call me in the morning."

He stood in the kitchen and heard her go to the den and wind the sterling music box—the tinkle of "Sailing, Sailing, over the Bounding Main . . ." drifted from the room—and then to the bedroom, where she had a small desk. She closed the door behind her.

Smith sat at the kitchen table and glanced at mail they'd brought in. Rufus placed his oversized gray head on his master's lap and looked up with wet, soulful eyes. Smith scratched behind the dog's ears. "I think the lady of the house is upset, my hairy friend, because she thinks I'm going to end up in the middle of another murder. She's wrong, Rufus. Not Guilty." He cocked his head and said, "You look skeptical, Rufus. Careful. Remember what they say about biting the hand that feeds you."

Rufus continued to stare at him.

Smith sighed. "All right. All right. I change my plea, Your Honor. Guilty—but with an explanation." He took a leash from where it hung from a wooden peg and slipped it over the dog's head. "Walk time," he said.

15 Monday Morning

"Professor Smith."

Mac turned at the mention of his name. "Good morning," he said. "What brings you to these hallowed halls?"

"A meeting. I've been named adjunct professor of economics," Sun Ben Cheong said. He *sounded* pleased with his announcement. His face said nothing.

"Well, welcome. And congratulations." They shook hands.

"Nothing like a real professor," Cheong said. "Just one class a semester on investment banking."

"I can't think of a better person to teach it. And anyone who can teach well is real—and rare. Missed you on the cruise Saturday."

"Couldn't make it, Professor Smith. I was out of town on business. I understand it was a typically pleasant day on the *Marilyn.*"

"Extremely."

"Well, nice to see you. I'm honored to be on the same faculty."

"The honor is all mine."

Smith caught up on an hour's worth of routine administrative details in his office before leaving Lerner Hall and heading for Twenty-fifth Street. He was early for his lunch date at the Foggy Bottom Cafe and considered taking a walk to kill the minutes. Instead, he entered the restaurant, sat at the bar, and had a Bloody Shame, a Virgin Mary renamed and disarmed—in England, he seemed to remember—to appease Catholic waiters who balked at placing the more familiar order.

Smith sipped the spicy, reinforced tomato juice and thought about bumping into Sun Ben Cheong at the university. From everything Smith had heard, Cheong was a financial genius. Which didn't, of course, necessarily translate into being a good teacher. Time would tell.

The pretty young barmaid was in the middle of a story about how her car died the previous night when someone tapped Smith on the shoulder. "Am I late?" Darcy Eikenberg asked.

Smith glanced at his watch. "Right on time," he said. "The punctual detective."

"And the early professor."

"Preferable to being the late professor. Drink?"

"I may not look it, but I am on duty. A rain check? Sometime when I'm off duty?" She wore a properly fitted beige sweater and knee-length brown leather skirt.

Smith tossed a few bills on the bar and indicated to the host they were ready to be seated.

A club soda with lime in front of her, Smith's mild Mary in front of him, they bantered about the weather, sports, the day's political headlines.

". . . I really think he'll win in November," she said. "And I'm delighted you took me up on my offer to have lunch."

"At first, I didn't think I could. Have lunch. No, I don't think he'll win."

"Small bet?"

"Sure. Then I realized a previous lunch date had been canceled. So, here we are, Detective. Tell me how the Juris case is progressing—if you can."

"First, the bet. Ten dollars?"

"I'm a lowly professor. Make it a dollar."

"You've got it. The Juris case? Of course I can discuss it with you. I can do anything. But—I may choose not to. Let me see. You called about the letters to Ms. Juris written by Mr. Tierney. Yes, we found letters in Ms. Juris's apartment. They came from him."

"So sure?"

"No reason not to be. They were very intimate and contained material only he was likely to know."

"How many letters?" Smith asked.

"A half-dozen."

"More than he led me to believe."

"The number doesn't impress me. One would be enough."

Smith cocked his head. "Enough for what?"

"Enough to convince me that Mr. Tierney and Ms. Juris were having an affair."

"Somehow that strikes me as too large a leap in assumption."

She smiled, reached across the small table, and placed her manicured fingertips on top of his hand. "You're right, of course. It is just that, too large a leap. At least at this juncture."

"Wendell denies having written the letters."

"What does he have to say about having had an affair with her?"

"We haven't discussed that. I don't believe he did. Have an affair, that is."

"An unusual man."

"I don't think so." Smith started to exclaim that he hadn't had an affair since being married to Annabel, or during his longer marriage to his first wife. He didn't. Not having an affair outside of marriage was as private a matter as having one. " 'Tain't nobody's business if I do," as Billie Holiday once explained musically. Or don't, Smith added to the lyric.

"You will show the letters to Wendell," he said, his tone saying he expected an affirmative answer.

She disappointed him. "Maybe, maybe not. Depends on how they fit into the overall investigation."

"I see." He looked up at the young waiter who stood over the table, order pad and pencil at the ready. Smith would have his usual chicken Caesar salad but asked for a menu for Eikenberg. She chose a grilled shrimp salad.

The order in, Eikenberg said, "I suppose you read about the deceased's former husband, Dr. Wharton."

"Yes. I understand they were married only briefly."

"About as long as my husband and I lasted."

Smith draped an arm over his chair's back. "I have to admit a certain curiosity about marriages of extremely short duration," he said. "The people in them must not have known each other very well."

"I suppose that would represent the majority of cases. It wasn't true in my marriage. My husband and I knew each other too well. We went through undergraduate school together."

Smith was happy the service was unusually swift this day. He didn't want to go any further with this phase of their conversation. He speared a chunk of chicken.

"Go ahead," Eikenberg said. "Ask me all the

questions you want about why my marriage ended with the speed of a single bullet."

Smith glanced up and grinned. "No," he said. "No questions. But free-associate if you'd like."

"Okay. He was a handsome devil. Still is. The juices flowed fast and furious. God, I thought, this is a miracle. Everyone I knew was going with guys who were okay, but this was different. This was heaven-sent. Meant to be." She giggled. "And so we got married the minute we graduated and settled into our 'adult' lives."

"Sounds like it followed the script," said Smith.

"Oh, it did. Except whoever wrote it started changing the lines. Nick, my husband, who always said he wanted to start his own business, settled instead for a job with the Census Bureau. That's what brought us here to D.C. He became a bureaucrat, and I joined the force."

"How did he react to his wife becoming a cop?"

"Hated it. Thought all women cops were lesbians. At any rate, we started to go our separate ways, living together sometimes, living apart more often than not. Modern. We're good friends."

"He still with Census?" Smith asked.

"Sure is. A big shot."

"And you climbed the ladder at MPD."

She laughed. "Too quick for Nick. This lesbian

was accused of using her sexual wiles to gain favor with the male brass. Meet the original androgynous woman." Her laugh was more throaty this time.

"An interesting tale," Smith said, digging into his salad. "I'm glad you're still friends."

"How long have you and Mrs. Smith been married?"

"Not long enough," he replied.

"Nice," she said. "How long is that?"

"Three years."

"Second marriage for both?"

"For me. My wife and son were killed by a drunk on the Beltway."

"I know," she said. "I'm sorry."

"Needless to say, I contribute to MADD," Smith said. "You mentioned Dr. Wharton, Pauline's former husband. I read that he was coming to Washington to be questioned."

"Already has. He came, and we questioned him."

"Anything come of it?"

"First, let me ask: Are you serving as Tierney's attorney?"

"More like a friend in court—in this case, out of court."

The pretty detective said, "Wharton happened to have been in town the night she was murdered, met with her briefly, at least according to his story. It seems they owned a piece of land together in West Virginia and got together to discuss whether to sell it."

"Ah-hah," Smith said with exaggerated flourish. "A suspect."

"Along with everybody else. No shortage here."

"Was he the last person to see her alive?" Smith asked.

"Not sure. She also met late that night with the director of the theater group that puts on those historical murders for Mr. Tierney's Scarlet Sin Society."

"Seymour Fletcher," Smith said.

"Yes. You know him?"

"You asked me that at the house. No, I don't. By the way, I asked my wife about having overheard that conversation between Wendell and Pauline. She had but forgot about it."

"Fine."

"What brought about this late-night meeting between them?" Smith asked.

"Money. According to Mr. Fletcher, Ms. Juris was dispatched by Tierney to lay down the law about budgets. Evidently, the theater group has a habit of exceeding them."

"Par for the course in this town—and in Hollywood. I take it there was animosity between them."

"Mr. Fletcher's hatred of her drools out of both corners of his mouth every time he mentions her name."

"Another suspect."

Eikenberg laughed softly. "As I said, the whole world is suspect at this point, Mac." She touched his hand again and drew a deep breath. Smith couldn't tell whether it was in preparation to say something difficult, or a sigh of contentment.

Her next comment failed to answer the question. She said flatly, "You'd like to see the letters."

Smith was surprised that she even raised the possibility. "Yes," he said. "I would."

She leaned forward, and her face lightened. "Then you *are* Tierney's attorney."

"No, I am not his attorney. Are you offering to show me the letters?"

Her expression was that of a mother deciding whether a child had been good enough to receive a reward. They locked eyes. "No," she said. "But that's today. There's always, as you've heard, tomorrow."

Smith said gruffly, "Sometimes tomorrow doesn't show up for people in trouble. Okay, you've been forthcoming about the letters, although you really haven't told me any more than you told Wendell. I suppose I can't blame you for that. I like people who play by the rules. But maybe you'll tell me just how intimate the letters really are."

"Do you mean were they filled with prurient, erogenous memories of intense sexual encounters between them, replete with loving descriptions of bodies and passionate moans? No, not that bad. They are—and I think the term I used originally is apt—they are love letters. Letters from a man to a woman with whom he is very much in love."

Up until that statement, Smith had been neutral about whether the letters had been written by Tierney. Now he had doubts. Tierney might have been involved with Pauline Juris sexually, but the pragmatic businessman would not have fallen in love, and certainly wouldn't have gushed poetic on paper. Smith didn't say what he was thinking. He waited for Eikenberg to say more.

She did. "I think it only fair to tell you, Mac"— the use of his first name continued to be, at once, unsettling and pleasant—"that someone has leaked the letters."

Smith straightened in his chair. "Leaked them to whom? The press?"

She avoided his eyes by focusing upon her half-eaten lunch. "I'm afraid so."

His anger showed.

She looked up and shook her head in a gesture of sadness. "They'll be in the papers tomorrow morning."

"Do you mean to tell me that you can't release those letters to Wendell Tierney, yet they end up in the goddamn newspapers?"

She held up her hands in a gesture of defense. "Don't say 'you.' I had nothing to do with it."

"Then who did? Who had custody of them within MPD?"

"The evidence unit."

"Some unit," Smith said.

"I know, I know," she said. "I've demanded an internal investigation to find out who leaked them."

"After the horse is gone."

"Yes. But I didn't know the barn door was open."

"The actual letters have been given to the press?"

"Oh, no. The letters are still in the Juris file. My understanding is that someone told a reporter what they contained."

Small comfort, Smith thought. As angry as he was at the news, he realized there was nothing to be gained by beating up on her. He sighed in resignation. "Okay," he said, "I appreciate being told this. I'll pass on the information to Wendell. It's going to be devastating to him and his family."

For the first time since walking into the River Inn, Darcy Eikenberg seemed flustered. She started to say something, stopped, then said, "I am sincerely sorry, Mac, that what should have been a pleasant lunch has ended up this way. All I can do is assure you of one thing. I am as angry and indignant as you are about what has happened. I just hope you'll transmit that to Mr. Tierney."

"Sure. I really should be going." He motioned for the check. Eikenberg grabbed it. "My lunch, my suggestion, my check."

"Can we do this again? Soon?" she asked outside, extending her hand.

His determination to say, "I don't think that would be a good idea" turned into, "Perhaps. Thanks for the lunch—and the information." He shook her hand.

Smith had gone straight from lunch to the Yates Field House at Georgetown University for a mind-clearing workout. He'd been a member for years. Although he had free access to facilities at his university, he preferred to stick with the familiar—at least where a gym was involved. He exercised vigorously for almost two hours, culminating with enough laps in the pool that he thought he might drown from exhaustion.

He returned home at four-thirty after picking up two pieces of swordfish and salad makings for dinner. He called Wendell Tierney and was informed that he was away overnight on business. He pressed for a way to reach Tierney and was given the name and number of the Waldorf Astoria. He left a message with the hotel operator to have Tierney call him as soon as he got it.

Annabel arrived home as he was preparing the swordfish for grilling on a hibachi on their patio. She spent a few minutes at her desk in the bedroom before changing into a sweatsuit and joining him outside. They kissed. "How was your day?" he asked.

"Basically hectic but nonproductive," she replied. "Yours?"

"I suppose the same could be said for me, although I did manage to get in a good workout this afternoon."

"Did you follow up with Detective Eikenberg?"

"As a matter of fact, I did. Bad news for Wendell. Someone at MPD leaked the contents of the letters to the press. According to Eikenberg, it'll be in the papers tomorrow."

"Oh, God," she said. "That's horrible."

"It certainly is." The sound of a phone ringing was heard through an open window. "That might be Wendell. I called him in New York. Excuse me."

"Anything you want me to do?" she asked.

"Nope, but thanks. Everything is under control. More or less."

16 The Next Morning

It seemed as though everyone was fighting that Tuesday morning.

Private investigator Anthony Buffolino ("with an *O*," he told secretaries) had left the house at five that morning with Alicia's loving words ringing in his ears: "You'll never change. You are an irresponsible, uncaring, insensitive *moron*!"

The words between Tony and his third wife had broken what had been a relatively long period of calm in their marriage. His two previous matrimonial efforts hadn't enjoyed such lulls. Two days of truce were like the span between world wars I and II.

It was different with Alicia. At least *he* was different with her than he'd been with his previous wives. Maybe she knew how to handle him better. Maybe not having kids around the house all the time—his from former marriages were with exwives—made the difference. Maybe—maybe he'd gotten older and more mellow. That possibility occasionally crossed his mind, but he would quickly dismiss it. It had to be Alicia. Or the absence of kids.

This unanticipated blowup had erupted at dinner the night before when he announced he was moving into a spare apartment in the Tierney complex until his assignment was completed. "He wants me close and on duty twenty-four hours a day," he'd tried to explain.

Alicia brought up the obvious. They lived a half hour's drive from Tierney. Tony tried to convince her that it was not his decision. His—their—good-paying client had requested he be on the premises. "What was I supposed to do, Al, blow him off? You're on my back about making a buck. So, I'm making big bucks with Tierney, and I figure you can lighten up a little, huh?"

"Lighten up? While you can go out and screw around? You're a married man, Tony."

And so it went, right up until he left with his bag packed and his temper tenuously in check. His final words to her were, "I'll call."

And her final words were, "Don't bother. I won't be here."

Now, after unpacking in a small, cramped room above Tierney's garage that contained a single bed, a stall shower in need of a scrubdown, toilet, sink, and a metal cabinet that functioned as a closet, Buffolino came down into the courtyard created by the outbuildings and walked the grounds. After chatting with three guards he'd assigned to the overnight detail—one on disability, one retired, and one working the MPD day shift but needing extra money—he came around back again and paused next to a small screen porch directly beneath the master bedroom. The first thing he heard was a woman crying. "Please, get hold of yourself," Wendell Tierney's voice said. Buffolino stood silently and controlled his breathing.

"You have disgraced this family," the woman said loudly, her crying partly under control.

"I can't control what other people do," Wendell Tierney said. "I did not write those letters. And I am furious that they've gotten to the goddamn press. But I can't control that, Marilyn!"

"But you could have controlled yourself with that woman!" A different female voice. Buffolino tried to place it, decided it belonged to the daughter, Suzanne.

"I suggest you shut your mouth," Wendell Tierney snapped.

"And maybe if you shut your fly, we wouldn't be in this embarrassing position," Suzanne said.

Silence. A door slammed. Buffolino visualized the room upstairs and figured Suzanne had left.

"She's right," Marilyn said.

"She's nothing but a little tramp, and you know it."

Marilyn's cruel, strangled laugh. She said, "Speaking of tramps. The least you could have been was discreet. Sleeping with Pauline was one thing. Writing her sophomoric love letters was stupid."

"I told you I did *not* write any letters. And I did not sleep with Pauline. Christ, Marilyn, this thing is hard enough without you jumping all over me. Can't you give me the benefit of the doubt?"

Mrs. Tierney's voice lowered, now barely audible to Buffolino. He cocked his head and cupped one ear. "I have been giving you the benefit of the doubt for years, Wendell. I have put up with your arrogance and your out-of-control libido. I can't do it any longer. I *won't* do it any longer."

The door slammed again. Ear to the sky, he did not hear Chip Tierney approach the porch. The Tierney son cleared his throat. Buffolino turned, grinning. "Good morning, Chip," he said. "Looks like . . . well, it's going to be a nice day."

Tierney said nothing.

"Are your folks home?" Buffolino asked.

A sardonic smile crossed Chip's lips. "I think they are. Excuse me." He disappeared through the back door.

The sound of tires on gravel caused Buffolino to turn to the driveway. A car parked, and two men who were to relieve the night shift got out. There were supposed to be three. Tony asked where the missing guard was. One of them said,

"We swung by to pick him up, but his wife said he wasn't going to work today."

Buffolino muttered under his breath. That was the trouble with taking on security assignments that involved other people. You couldn't trust them. Even cops. Especially cops.

He went to the front of the house and asked the guard who'd been there all night if he would pull a double shift. He groaned, rubbed his eyes, stood, and stretched. "Time and a half," Buffolino said.

"Yeah, okay, Tony."

Buffolino returned to the courtyard and entered the house through the back door. He'd been told he had the run of the house, although he knew that offer came with restrictions. He picked up a telephone and dialed Mac Smith's number. Smith answered on the first ring. "Been sitting there waiting for me to call, huh?" Buffolino said.

"No. I've been sitting here trying to figure out why they've raised the taxes on my house, and reading this morning's jaundiced article about the letters they found in Pauline Juris's apartment. Where are you?"

"At the Tierney residence."

"Any reaction from your client about the letters?"

"A little. A lot."

"I imagine. Enjoying your new job?"

"Sure. This is a very nice position, and I figure I can't thank you enough for introducing me to my new client. Only I think it's overkill. The security system here is better than Fort Knox."

"Have you told him that?"

"Whatta ya, crazy? Whatta you have planned for today?"

Smith's conversations with Buffolino were infrequent and usually short in duration. But this morning the private investigator came off like an old friend inviting a buddy on a golf date. "Why do you ask?" Smith asked.

"I thought you might want to take a ride with me."

"A ride? Where?"

"Up the river. I've got all my men in place, so I figured I'd kill a couple hours in the boat. Maybe have lunch up the river at one of the waterfront joints. Restaurants."

He *is* inviting me on an outing, Smith thought. "As it turns out, Tony, I have nothing to do today except a little shopping for dinner, maybe work out at the gym, maybe—maybe—pick your brain about the Pauline Juris case."

It was a Buffolino cackle. "So you are Tierney's attorney."

"Don't be ridiculous."

"I heard."

"Heard what?"

"That you're back in the saddle."

"Where the hell did you hear that?"

"All over town, Mac. You know Washington. Anyway, I would be honored to have you aboard. Meet me at Tierney's house at ten?"

Smith felt like a plate of iron filings being inextricably drawn toward a powerful magnet. He didn't want to go. Somehow, based upon his upbringing, "goofing off" in the middle of what was a workday for most people was anathema to him. He often vowed that one day he would go to an afternoon movie but never had. It didn't matter that he might spend the time napping in his La-Z-Boy recliner, or killing an afternoon thumbing through catalogs and newsletters. For some reason, those activities seemed justified. But a movie in the afternoon? A trip up the Potomac with Anthony Buffolino?

Why not?

Suzanne Tierney stormed from the house and sat in her car for what seemed a long time. She hated her father, but not the car, a 1992 Chrysler LeBaron convertible he'd bought her two months ago. He was so controlling, so domineering. How could her mother have put up with it for so many years? His insistence that everyone in the family toe the line and do things his way was bad enough. Now there were the letters to Pauline Juris.

She was glad they'd surfaced. It was about time the sham was exposed. Everyone knew about her father and Pauline. You'd have to be blind and deaf to miss it. Which no one in the household was. Her mother put up with it and turned the other cheek because she liked the money and the house and the expensive furnishings and the trips to Europe and South America. She'd sold out. How could anyone sell out that way?

She'd implored her mother to leave her father dozens of times. It wasn't worth it, she'd told her, the humiliation of playing dutiful hostess to his friends and business associates, watching him come home at three and four in the morning without explanation of where he'd been or with whom. In moments of candor her mother would tell her that the family was more important than her individual pain. Crap! She loved her mother but knew the woman was tethered to her husband by money, pure and simple. What a way to live. At least she'd had the gumption to walk away from it. Drive away from it . . . in the latest new car he'd provided.

She slipped the automatic transmission into Low and deliberately spun the rear tires on the gravel as she left the compound. Next to her on the seat was a large, shapeless, empty canvas bag zippered across the top. She parked at National Airport and barely made the nine o'clock shuttle to New York.

The standard surly cabdriver drove her from LaGuardia to the Saul School of Dramatic Arts on lower Broadway. She tipped small, which prompted a string of obscenities—his best English—from the Arabic driver.

She bounded through a door, took a flight of noisy, graffiti-marred stairs two at a time, and stepped into the main rehearsal room where thirty other aspiring actors and actresses awaited the arrival of the school's founder and guru. Suzanne knew many of the young men and women in the room and greeted them, hugged a few, punched a young man in the chest in response to a flippant comment.

And then *he* entered.

Short, face pockmarked, black curly hair hanging in irregular strands from the sides of his head, black eyes glistening behind oversized wire-rimmed glasses, scripts cradled in his arms, Arthur Saul strode past his students and took his customary seat in the center of the makeshift rehearsal hall.

Standing next to him was his assistant, a tall, younger man with white-bleached hair who wore his homosexuality as a badge and who surveyed the gathered like a shepherd choosing the first sheep for slaughter. He hissed a name: "Suzanne Tierney."

"I have to be first?" Suzanne said nervously to those around her. She was about to request that someone else be chosen but remembered the last time she'd done that. It had raised Saul's wrath to an intense level: "Yes," he'd said, leaping to his feet and closing the gap between them, "tell the director you aren't ready, my pretty little rich bitch."

And so she climbed the three short steps to the stage, went to its center, and looked down at him.

He smiled. "And how is Ms. Tierney this fine day?" he asked.

"Fine, Arthur. I'm fine. I flew in this morning."

"On Daddy's private jet?"

Her face turned red. Embarrassment. Anger. She said, "No. On the shuttle like everyone else."

He quietly clapped his hands. "How plebeian," he said. "And how are your rich mother and father?"

She looked left and right, fists clenched at her side. Finally, she came to the stage apron and asked, "Why do you keep bringing up my family? I am here to learn acting. I wish to be a good actress, that's all. Why do you harp upon my background? I can't help where I came from. I only know where I am and where I want to go."

He clapped a little louder. "Breaking the chains

that bind you?" he said, eyebrows arched inhumanly high. "You seem agitated, Suzanne. Trouble at home?"

She drew a deep breath and shoved her hands in the pockets of her jeans. After looking at the floor for a moment, she brought her head up and said, "Yes, I am angry."

"Good," he said. "Can you inject that anger into the scene you've prepared for us?"

"I think so."

Saul leaped to his feet and came to the apron. "Finally, Suzanne, you might have gotten what it is I've been preaching all these months. You have anger *inside* you. You have love, sympathy, bewilderment. But it's all worthless if it remains inside. You wish to act, to assume the role of a character created by a mad artist in a garret. He creates a character who is angry. At what? Politics? His wife? World hunger, surly waitresses, his mother and father? Can you take your anger—and I have no doubt it is directed at your rich and overbearing parents—and bring it to another person, another character?"

She replied simply, "I would like to do a scene from *Glass Menagerie.*"

"Splendid," Saul said. He turned to face the others. "I ask that you give your undivided attention to Ms. Tierney, who obviously has flown here from our nation's capital seething with hatred and disgust for her privileged lifestyle and those who created it for her. How fortunate we are to see this metamorphosis from little rich girl to waif." To Suzanne: "I salivate with anticipation."

Suzanne stumbled through the scene. She couldn't control her nerves; her hands trembled, her voice quavered. Saul and the students were silent. Some winced and squirmed in sympathy. Others took pleasure in her pain. When she finished the scene, a few in the audience applauded. Saul did not join them. He slowly climbed onto the stage and stood next to Suzanne, looking at her with a patronizing smile. "You hate them, don't you?" he said softly.

She looked at him in a puzzled way.

"You hate your parents. If you could only channel more of that hatred into a performance, you might actually succeed in becoming an actress."

All the emotions boiling inside of her that she'd kept from spilling over now gushed out in a torrent of tears. She wrapped her arms about herself.

Saul put his arm over her shoulder and pulled her close. He said to his assistant, "Rehearse the improvisational pairs until I return." He led Suzanne from the stage, out of the room, and to his office, where he closed the door, sat on a small leather couch, and patted the empty space next to him. "Come, sit."

She did. His arm went over her shoulder, and he said in soothing tones, "I know you think I'm too hard on you, Suzanne, but I must be if you are ever to realize your true potential as an actress. I want you to be angry. I want you to cry."

Her crying was now reduced to an occasional whimper. Her eyes were red; a large tear streaked one cheek.

"I also told you last time that it's necessary for me to establish control in front of the others. I also don't want them to think I'm showing favoritism—to one of my best students, someone who will achieve stardom one day but only if she continues to work with me. To listen to me. To believe in me."

She looked into his face with pleading, vulnerable eyes. "You say that all the time, Arthur, but then you're so cruel."

"And you are so talented—and so lazy. And so lovely. Trust me, Suzanne. I know how to bring out the best in you."

He stood, locked the door, and unbuttoned his shirt.

Suzanne did not return to the theater where the other students were being put through their paces. She walked up Broadway, stopped to admire a pair of shoes in a window, bought them, tossed her purchase into the large, empty canvas bag and continued uptown. She picked up a Greek salad from a take-out place and went to the newly renovated Bryant Park, where she ate her leafy lunch. She checked her watch: one-thirty. Just enough time.

She walked farther until reaching a tall office building. In front of it were low marble walls and planters where people sat enjoying the sunshine. Suzanne stood at the corner and waited. A lean young Hispanic man carrying a large package wrapped in brown paper and secured with string entered the corporate courtyard. He sat. Suzanne made eye contact briefly. He waited thirty seconds, then walked away, leaving the package on the edge of a planter.

Suzanne moved to where he'd been sitting and observed those around her. No one seemed to have noticed. She placed the package in the large canvas bag and zippered it shut.

An hour later she was on a shuttle back to Washington, the bag securely wedged beneath the seat in front of her.

17

10:00 A.M. That Same Morning

Tony Buffolino was waiting when Smith pulled into the gravel courtyard at the rear of Tierney's house. He'd abandoned his yachting uniform of Saturday for black slacks, a heavy knit olive-green sweater that might have been snatched from a U-boat commander, and a black beret frequently seen on paratroopers.

"Glad you could make it, Mac."

"What are we going on, a commando raid?"

"When the man hires me for security work, I want to look like security. Makes him feel . . . well, more secure."

"Nice day for a ride on the river," Smith said.

Buffolino led them to the front of the house and down the long set of wooden stairs to the Tierney dock where the four vessels—the *Marilyn,* the Aquasport utility boat, the bass boat, and *M.O.R.,* the sleek red-and-white Cigarette racing craft—bobbed gently, a small flotilla.

"Are we taking the yacht?" Smith said, smiling.

Buffolino did a double-take. "Don't think I could handle it?" he asked.

"Just kidding, Tony. Besides, you're not dressed for it. What *are* we taking?"

"The Aquasport." Buffolino pointed to the twenty-two-foot, center-console craft rigged with canvas to provide shelter.

"Pretty snazzy," Smith said, indicating the Cigarette.

"Ain't that a beauty?" Buffolino said, shaking his head in awe. "Do a hundred wide open."

"The Aquasport will be fine."

Buffolino noticed a small point-and-shot camera hanging from a strap around Smith's neck. "You taking up photography?" he asked.

Smith thought of an obvious wisecrack, said instead, "I thought I might snap a few." He raised the camera to eye level. "Let me get one of you, Captain."

Buffolino grinned. "Sure." He started toward the Aquasport, but Smith suggested he stand in front of the Cigarette. "More befitting your soldier-of-fortune look," he said.

"I probably look more like there was a sale at the army-navy store." Buffolino posed, and Smith pressed off three shots. They climbed into the boat, and Tony started the larger of two outboards attached to the transom. He neatly coiled the mooring lines inside the boat, then steered it away from the dock and out into the center of the river. Smith stood next to him at the console and drew a deep breath. He was glad he'd decided to take Tony up on his offer. Although he hadn't been especially busy these past few weeks, he'd been busy thinking about being busy. So it felt good to be away from such burdensome thoughts, from daily routine, from the classroom and the grading of papers at home, from anything that might be considered a typical day. Buffolino glanced over and smiled. "Nice, huh?"

"Better than that," Smith replied. "You look like you're enjoying this assignment."

"Hell, yes, only Alicia isn't happy. Tierney wanted me to move in, so I did. She figures I'm out messing around, which is the way I guess women always figure. But she should know me better than that. Right?"

"Right, Tony."

Tony advanced the throttle. "Want to take it?" he asked.

"Sure," Smith said, pulling his GW windbreaker around him as the boat's increased speed created a parallel pickup in the wind.

"Just keep us going in this direction," Tony said. While Smith held course, Buffolino pulled out a nautical chart and studied it.

"Where are we heading?" Smith asked, raising his voice over the wind's whistle.

"I figured maybe we'd go by Roosevelt Island. Interested?"

Smith nodded. Somehow he knew that would be on their itinerary.

Tony laid the chart on the console, and they rode without speaking until reaching the Key Bridge. The island was visible beyond it. He pointed to an area of water on the chart between the island and the mainland, spanned by the pedestrian bridge. Smith noticed that the section of the map under Tony's index finger was blue. The deeper channel that ran the other side of the island was white. Numbers in the white section indicated considerable depth. FOUL was printed on the blue side.

"Yeah, real shallow, Mac, but this baby rides high in the water. I think we can inch in close enough to take a look. Game?"

"You're the captain, my friend. But, remember, this isn't your boat. It belongs to Tierney."

"Not to worry," Tony said, placing his hand on the throttle and pulling it back to barely above Idle. With just enough rpms to maneuver, they drifted beneath the bridge. Buffolino gently turned right, his eyes shifting between the chart and the water ahead of them.

"You sure this is a good idea?" Smith asked.

Buffolino didn't answer; his attention was riveted on his task. As they continued their slow movement in the direction of the pedestrian walkway, Smith looked over the side. The water was brown, but he could see rocks just below its surface. He looked up. A log sat in their path. Buffolino killed the engine until the log drifted away, then advanced the throttle to its previous low setting.

They eventually reached a spot thirty feet from shore. "Right about there they found her," Buffolino said. He throttled back and allowed the Aquasport to respond to the river's natural flow, which nudged them closer to shore.

"How do you figure the body ended up there?" Smith asked.

Buffolino shrugged. "I got to figure it drifted in."

"Why?"

Buffolino looked at the pedestrian causeway. "It doesn't make sense to me that anybody would bother hauling a dead body all the way across that thing—hell, look how long it is."

"Unless killer and victim walked here together," Smith said.

"I don't think so, Mac. Besides, the gate's locked at night. That's what I read."

"I heard it hadn't been locked that night."

"Yeah, but who would know that except the park ranger? Nah. Doesn't add up."

Smith observed the movement of the boat. "If the body were dumped in the water, it would move the way we are, toward shore. Right?"

Buffolino nodded.

Smith grunted and said, "From everything I've read, she was pretty well covered with debris. But she wasn't murdered many hours before she was discovered."

Buffolino looked back in the direction from which they'd come. "They've done a pretty good job of cleaning up this river, Mac. They got rid of the PCBs, ABCs, whatever the hell those things are called. The fishing's pretty good now. But the water runs twenty miles down from Great Falls and picks up lots of debris." He returned his attention to the shoreline. "I don't figure it would take more than a couple of hours to get covered up pretty good with twigs and leaves and stuff the yahoos toss in."

Smith didn't look convinced.

"Tell you what," Tony said. He went to the rear of the boat and untied an orange plastic bumper used to keep the craft from hitting the dock.

"What are you going to do with that?" Smith asked.

"Experiment." Buffolino tossed the bumper out onto the water, and both men watched it begin to drift. It was headed, slowly, toward shore. "Pretty good aim, huh?" Buffolino said. "Looks like it'll land right where the body was."

Smith nodded.

"Here's what we do," Buffolino said. "We get

out of here, go up through the channel, and grab some lunch. Got a preference? There's good seafood joints up around Maine and Seventh. You know. What's your pleasure?"

"Your call," Smith answered. "I've eaten in all of them."

Buffolino maneuvered the Aquasport so that its direction was now reversed and gave the engine a boost. "Lunch should take us a couple hours," he said. "By the time we get back, we'll see whether that bumper's got a ton a' garbage on it."

Over two flounder specials at Hogate's, Smith brought up Buffolino's assignment. "The Tierney job going well?"

"Yeah."

"So, who killed Pauline Juris?"

Buffolino shook his head. "Could have been anybody. Somebody she worked with. Maybe somebody she was sleeping with. Somebody out of her past. Could even be somebody in Tierney's family."

"How well have you gotten to know the family?"

"Well enough. More tension in that house than in my own. I pick up on things just by hanging around. I got big ears, Mac. Mr. and Mrs. Tierney do not engage in what you would call marriage bliss. At each other's throats all the time. And then there's the kids. They're not kids anymore, but they are their—kids. The daughter, Suzanne, she's whack-a-ding-hoy."

Smith's eyebrows went up.

"Flaky," Buffolino explained.

"You've been taking Chinese lessons?" Smith asked, laughing.

"Nah. Just a word I heard someplace. She's an actress, and you know how they are. The artsy-craftsy crowd. Very dramatic, high-strung. Takes acting lessons up in New York, works for some booking agent in D.C. I know one thing. She's no fan of her old man."

"What about her relationship with her mother?"

"Okay, I guess."

"Chip Tierney? How does he get along with the rest of the group?"

"Depends on who you're talking about. He and his father are close. Real close. The kid is like a clone of the old man. Mr. T. can do no wrong in Chip's eyes. Even treats his mother the way the old man does. Scorn. No patience with her."

"An unhappy woman," Smith said.

"Very unhappy. They treat the daughter, Suzanne, the same way. Mr. Tierney is unhappy with her, that means Chip is unhappy with her."

"Sun Ben?"

"He and Chip seem to hit it off okay. Chip's one of those guys should be in politics. Or front a fancy restaurant. Real pleasant, but I read it as all show. What you see ain't necessarily what you get."

Smith sipped his coffee. "While you're doing psychological profiles, give me your read on Sun Ben."

"Strange cat, but he's got to be different from the rest of them. Hell, he's Chinese."

"You noticed."

"I miss nothing, Sherlock. He's *cold,* Mac. Never smiles. Not friendly." Buffolino leaned forward and motioned for Smith to do the same. He said in a stage whisper, "I ran some checks on him, too."

"*Too*? Who else did you run checks on?"

"Everybody."

"Why?"

" 'Cause I wanted to get a handle on them."

"Does Tierney know?"

"No."

"You're overstepping your boundaries, Tony."

"Come on, Mac. Get real. I like to know the people I'm protecting. Am I right?" Smith said nothing. Buffolino continued. "Mr. Sun Ben Cheong-Tierney is a high roller in Atlantic City."

"I heard he gambled."

Buffolino laughed softly. "I heard he loses."

"So?"

"He must be paid big bucks by Sam Tankloff."

"I assume so. He's considered a financial genius. Did you know he's teaching a course at GW?"

"Yeah. But that's not exactly big bucks."

"What else did you find out about him?"

"That's about it—so far. Except a hunch. I think he and his sister, Suzanne, might be getting it on."

Smith's expression was skeptical.

Buffolino nodded, smiling. "Just a hunch, Mac. I've never seen them in the sack, but I have this feeling."

They argued over the check. Buffolino won, insisting he owed Smith for having gotten him the lucrative assignment with Wendell Tierney. They returned to the Aquasport, which was docked just outside the restaurant, and headed back.

They came around the channel side of the island and went to where Tony had released the bumper. He'd been right. There was considerable debris clinging to it. Tony retrieved it with a boathook and, without striking the rocks that kept Mac on edge, returned safely to the Tierney dock.

"Thank you for a pleasant day on the water, Tony. You didn't have to buy lunch."

Buffolino shrugged and grinned. "Hey, for you, no limit. Anything else I can do for you?"

"Sure. Deliver those love letters Wendell supposedly wrote to Pauline Juris."

"Deliver?"

Smith laughed. "Just a little fantasy of mine," he said. "Simple curiosity. I'd love to know what they really said."

As they ascended the wooden stairs to the front of the house, Smith said, "Watch yourself, Tony."

"How so?"

"You've been hired to protect Tierney and his family, not to investigate Pauline Juris's murder. I know it's almost automatic for you, after your years on the force, but I'd go easy checking into the background of anyone in the family."

"I suppose you're right, Mac. But like I said, I like to know who I'm protecting. But, yeah, I'll go easy. You coming inside?"

"No. Things to do. Thanks again. Keep in touch. And keep your head."

18 Simultaneously

Mac Smith had no sooner left the house for his cruising date with Tony Buffolino than the phone rang in his study. The machine took the message:

> *In case you try to reach me, I'm on my way to an eleven o'clock special meeting of the finance committee at the museum. I got a call from Don Farley. No idea what it's about, but it sounds important. Call you later. Love you.*

Annabel arrived at the National Building Museum at 10:45 and browsed the book and gift shop just off the lobby. As she admired architecturally significant puzzles and games, she heard high heels clicking outside. She looked at the open door as Detective Darcy Eikenberg walked by.

Annabel went to the lobby and saw Eikenberg turn left and disappear up a set of stairs. She followed, her crepe-soled shoes silently striking the floor. She reached the first landing. Eikenberg entered the executive offices. Annabel looked at her watch. Time to get to the meeting.

Others were seated at a small round table, in what had once been the pension commissioner's suite, when Annabel entered. She poured herself coffee from a service in a corner and joined Hazel Best-Mason, Sam Tankloff, and three other members of the committee. Donald Farley chaired it. Farley, well into his seventies, was energetic and alert. Slender and fit, his face a series of briery angles and lines, he owned radio stations in Maryland and West Virginia. He got to the point. "The reason for calling this meeting is anything but pleasant," he said. "Frankly, Hazel and I had hoped we could resolve it quietly without involving the committee. It initially seemed to be nothing more than a bookkeeping error, an administrative snarl. But it now appears that the problem is greater than that."

Expressions on the faces of other committee members indicated they were as much in the dark as Annabel. "I think it best if Hazel lays out the dimensions of this problem for us," Farley said.

Best-Mason, dressed in a coffee-colored suit with subtle white pinstripe, frilly off-white blouse that could have been created of gardenias, and her usual assortment of rings, necklaces, and earrings, opened a file folder, studied it, then took in each person. "Money is missing from the museum," she said.

Annabel's immediate thought went to Eikenberg. Was that why she was there that morning? She hoped not. You didn't have to be trained in public relations to know that such matters were best handled internally. A nonprofit institution tainted by financial scandal invariably finds it more difficult to raise funds, at least in the short run.

"How much is missing?" a board member asked.

Hazel referred to her notes. "To date, approximately a hundred and eighty thousand dollars."

Another board member whistled.

"You said the money was missing," Annabel said. "Was it stolen?"

"That's what I'm focusing on at the moment," the controller said.

Tankloff met Annabel's eyes and shook his head sadly. "It appears Pauline might have been responsible," he said.

"Pauline Juris?" Annabel said. "That's shocking." She waited a beat before adding, "And unfortunate."

"Extremely," Farley said.

"I mean it's unfortunate because she's dead. Not here to defend herself."

"I don't think that's the issue," Best-Mason said sharply. "The important thing is to determine the extent of the theft and how it was accomplished. Then we can decide whether to attempt to recover any or all of it."

"Recover?" Tankloff said. "Wendell is Pauline's executor. He told me she had virtually nothing in her bank accounts at the time of her death."

"Which doesn't mean she didn't have bank accounts not in her name," said Best-Mason.

"What proof do we have that Pauline stole the money?" Annabel asked.

"These," Best-Mason responded, overtly annoyed at Annabel's questioning. She slid a stack of vouchers across the table, and Annabel flipped through them. They were receipts for cash disbursements, each signed by Pauline Juris.

"What dismays me is that she had free access to this account," said Farley to Best-Mason. "No check-and-balance, no oversight procedure."

"Are you accusing me of negligence?" the controller asked.

Farley smiled. His smile was sweet, but his meaning was otherwise. "Of course not. But it does seem that allowing easy access to such sums of money represents a lapse in our accounting procedures."

His words angered Hazel. She responded coldly. "I suggest you talk to Wendell Tierney about that. The fund Pauline drew from was established by him personally. Most of it came from cash receipts from the bookstore and gift shop, and from tours. Only he and Pauline had authority to access it. I pointed out to him that it was an unusual arrangement. I suggested the money not be segregated into a separate account but be included in the general revenue fund. But he insisted. Talk to *him,* Donald."

Farley was taken aback by Hazel's clipped defense. He managed, "Yes, I will."

The door opened, and museum director Joe Chester stepped into the room. As he did, and before he could close the door behind him, Annabel heard the click-click-click of high heels. The tall, graceful figure glided by.

"Sorry I'm late," Chester said, not sounding as though he meant it. "I was with a detective."

"About this?" Tankloff asked, his face reflecting displeasure.

"This? Oh, you mean the missing funds. No. She talked to me about Pauline's murder. It's the third time." He pulled up a chair.

"Anything new?" Tankloff asked.

"No," Chester said, "but I wish they'd solve the damn thing. I'm beginning to feel like a suspect. Someone told the detective that Pauline and I didn't get along. You know that's not true."

No one replied. It was common knowledge that Chester and Wendell Tierney and Pauline were not members of a mutual-admiration society. It was also known that while Tierney disliked the young man, he appreciated his talents, even coming to his defense on occasion when other board members questioned Chester's actions.

Chester sank low in his chair. "And now this," he said. "How far have you gotten with your audit?" he asked Best-Mason.

"Far enough to know the funds are missing, and that they were taken by Pauline."

Annabel spread her hands in the air. "I'm sorry, but I just don't understand. Pauline could simply sign a voucher for any amount of cash she wished and walk out with it?"

"Some system, huh?" Chester grumbled.

Annabel added, "And she didn't have to indicate to anyone what she intended to do with it?"

"Sometimes she did, sometimes she didn't," Best-Mason replied. "She usually said she was drawing money to make cash payments to suppliers. She'd scribble something on the vouchers about who was supposedly getting paid." The vouchers still sat in front of Annabel. She thumbed through them again and saw what looked like hieroglyphics—a few letters of the alphabet followed by the word "services."

"Isn't it unusual to pay bills in cash?" Annabel asked.

Best-Mason sighed. "I don't think this will help us get to the bottom of it," she said curtly.

"Frankly, I would have preferred to resolve this on my own without the need for a meeting. But Donald overruled me."

Farley said quickly, "I think it's of sufficient magnitude for the board to be involved."

Tankloff concurred. "My only concern is that the more people who know about it, the greater the chance of leaks to the outside. We don't need some creative reporter linking the missing funds with Pauline's murder. If that happens, it will be all over the front page and on the nightly news."

Annabel was thinking the same thing, but her concern was not publicity. Why shouldn't the possibility be raised that the missing funds could be linked to Pauline's murder? Maybe the motive for killing her had to do with the funds—and whoever they went to.

"And there's a question of bringing criminal charges if someone else was involved with Pauline," Farley said.

"I have to leave," Tankloff said. "I have to go to another important meeting downtown. My suggestion is that Hazel be allowed to pursue this quietly, using her own considerable expertise. Unless there is a compelling need to know, I suggest we not meet again. People who contribute money to this institution won't be happy hearing that one of its own walked away with some of it."

"I second that motion," Joe Chester said.

Tankloff was not his usual polite self this day. He walked from the room without another word and closed the door with more force than necessary, as if the door were the final vote.

"Are we adjourning?" a board member asked.

"We might as well," Farley said. "Unless anyone has something else to offer."

No one did. The meeting was over.

Annabel and Farley were left alone in the suite. He said, "Sorry your early days on the committee involve this sort of thing."

"That's all right, Don. I just feel terrible that this has happened to the museum. Mind if I ask something that's probably none of my business?"

"Of course not. If it has to do with the museum and the finance committee, it *is* your business."

"If this thing happened the way Hazel says it did—Pauline drawing cash from the museum for her own use but with Wendell's blessing—it means that he bears considerable responsibility."

"You're right, of course. I don't know how many boards you've served on, Annabel, but—"

"One," she said, smiling. "This one."

He returned her smile as he explained. "Some boards are relatively balanced. No individual dominates policy and decision making. With others, there *is* a dominant force. That's very much the case with Wendell. Don't misunderstand. Besides being an extremely forceful leader, he has almost single-handedly turned the fortunes of this museum around. He not only has the contacts from which to generate considerable money, he's always been willing to use them. I remember when he announced the creation of the special fund. I objected. So did others. But he brushed our objections aside. I can't even remember the reasons he gave, but as you know, he can be, ah, extremely persuasive. Our revenues have increased twofold since he assumed the chairmanship. Who were we to argue over a fund that amounted to only a few thousand dollars?"

"A few thousand dollars? Hazel said the theft amounted to almost two hundred thousand."

"That's right. But when the fund was established, it didn't amount to much. Increasingly large amounts of money were eventually funneled into it. I didn't even know how large it had grown until this happened. I suppose that makes me responsible, too."

"Well, I just wish it hadn't happened, which is as weak and innocuous a comment as I can come up with at the moment. If there's anything I can do, please call."

"I certainly will, Annabel. And, as Sam emphasized, we've got to keep this in-house."

"I understand."

But Annabel had not said she would.

19 That Night

For those who didn't know better, Darcy Eikenberg and Nick Penna might have been a happily married couple. They once were. Now they had dinner together at least once a month, and there were occasional long weekends at the Maryland shore, or the Homestead in Hot Springs. A modern, civilized divorce, the sociologists would term it. A "relationship," others might say. For them, it just seemed natural.

This night they met for dinner at a Greek restaurant, Mykonos, on K Street NW. Usually, Darcy would meet Nick wearing whatever she'd worn that day to work. But she'd left the MPD earlier than usual and had run home to change into peach crinkle-cotton pants, an oversized raspberry blouse, and an oyster-white sweater vest. He wore a trim gray suit and a pale green-and-red-striped shirt with white collar. It was Darcy's favorite type of shirt; she'd bought a number of them for him over the years. "How's things at the head-count factory?" she asked pleasantly.

"As bureaucratic as ever. The political pressure

is on again to beef up the count in certain areas so they can redistrict. But we're remaining true to our mission." He laughed softly. "I've been offered an interesting assignment."

She touched his hand. "That's wonderful, Nick. Another promotion?"

"Not exactly. They want an updated history of the bureau written. I might head up the research."

She sat back and looked impressed. "I'm impressed," she said. "I never should have left you."

"You didn't leave me. We left each other. A draw. Remember?"

She leaned forward and smiled warmly. "Yes, I remember."

"It's an interesting history, Darcy. Our first census was in 1790. Of course, taking a census goes back a lot farther than that, as far as 3800 B.C. in Babylonia. They used it to determine who should pay taxes." He stopped, smiled, and said, "All of which pales when compared to the life of a homicide detective. How are things at MPD?"

"Insanely busy. I was afraid I might have to cancel tonight. But then I realized it's been three weeks since we had dinner. That's too long. How's your love life, Nick? Are you seeing anyone?"

"Of course, but no one special. You?"

"Ah, the joys of bachelorhood in the nation's capital. Ten women to every man."

"Remember, you're talking to a big shot in the Census Bureau. You have your numbers wrong."

"Nine-to-one? Me? I get by."

His laugh was knowing and wicked. "Who's the lucky man this week?"

"It just so happens there isn't anyone in my life these days, although I have been spending time with a fascinating gentleman."

"A cop?"

"An attorney. And professor."

The words spilled immediately out of his mouth. "Mackensie Smith."

Her eyes opened in mock shock. "How rumors spread in this town."

"Come on, Darcy, give me a break. A lawyer and professor? You've been talking about him since you took his course at GW."

"It was that bad?" He didn't reply. "I mean, my infatuation with him was that obvious?"

"All over your sleeve."

"He was a good teacher." Her smile indicated she was only letting half the cat out of the bag.

Nick looked up at the ceiling as though retrieving distant memories. " 'Handsome.' 'Urbane,' " he said. "You'd just learned the word 'urbane' and used it a lot when referring to Smith." His eyes went up again. " 'Ruggedly handsome.' 'Brilliant.' 'Sensitive.' 'Worldly'—"

"Was I that obvious?"

"Worse than that," he said. "Hey, Smith is married."

"News from the front. I know he's married."

"And that doesn't bother you?"

"I didn't say we were sleeping together, Nick. As I recall, I said I was spending time with him lately."

"On the Juris case."

"Exactly. He's—he's Wendell Tierney's confidant and attorney."

"I've met Smith's wife. Her name is Annabel."

"Oh?"

"I needed a gift for a friend's birthday. Actually, a woman I was seeing. She's crazy about pre-Columbian art, and I stopped in this gallery in Georgetown to see if I could pick up something inexpensive. No luck there. Everything is just slightly below the national debt. But Annabel Smith owns the gallery, and we got talking. Lovely lady. A knockout."

"In a matronly way."

He'd just taken a sip of wine. Her comment caused him to laugh; it took all his lip strength to keep the wine from splattering on the table. " 'Matronly'? You call that matronly?"

"Prefer 'middle-aged'?"

"Like us."

"Speak for yourself. I'm not there yet."

They ordered: *imam baldi* for two—slices of

eggplant baked to almost the melting point and topped with tomato, pine nuts, garlic, and onions.

Penna's face turned serious. "Mind some advice from somebody who cares about you, Darcy?"

"Depends. If you're going to lay moral judgments on me, keep them to yourself."

"Why would you think I'd be passing moral judgment? You are romantically involved with Smith, aren't you?"

She thought for a moment. "No. Would I like to be? Definitely."

"Is he interested in you?"

"Don't say it as though it's inconceivable. As a matter of fact, I think he is. He's been married for three or four years. That's a long time for a man like Mackensie Smith. He's the restless type, never content with something—someone—for very long. That's one of the things I admire most about him, Nick. He was this city's most famous and successful criminal attorney but gave it up to teach law. That takes guts."

"So how come you didn't think I had guts when I gave up dreams of owning my own business to take a job with the government?"

"I guess I mean character. Anyhow, you did it backward. If you'd started your own business and then decided to become a bureaucrat, I would have said that took guts. No matter. Mac Smith excites me. Is there something wrong with a woman being excited by a man?"

"Depends upon the man. You're making a mistake."

"And you have just issued a moral judgment."

They got off the subject and back on their careers. Penna had little to report. But she had stories to tell because she was a cop. That was one thing she loved about being around cops. They might hate you, but they always had a story to tell.

"Any closer to solving the Juris murder?" he asked.

"Maybe, maybe no."

"How juicy were those letters I read about?"

"The ones from Wendell Tierney to Pauline Juris? Not juicy at all. But there's been a new development with them." He raised his eyebrows, waiting for more. She said, "But I can't discuss it. We interviewed Juris's former husband again, the surgeon from New York."

"Why?"

"Because he's looking more like a suspect every day."

"Care to elaborate?"

"No. I mean, I care to, but I can't. Juris lived a more interesting life than I was initially led to believe."

"You like that, don't you? People who live interesting lives."

"Of course."

"How was she interesting? I mean, beyond the normal."

"Had a dark side like we all do. Only hers was darker. Keep a secret?"

"Of course. I work for the government."

"I think Ms. Juris might have been an embezzler."

"That does make her interesting. Who'd she embezzle from, her boss, Tierney?"

"No. From the National Building Museum, where Tierney is chairman of the board. Just a rumor I picked up today. Does that qualify as 'juicy'?"

He nodded. He enjoyed listening to his former wife talk about her career as a police officer. But at these times their decision to separate and divorce was reinforced for him. She loved, in fact had a need for, action and intrigue, things he was incapable of providing. But he liked her tales of life outside the mundane, routinized life he led. Maybe he enjoyed gossip and intrigue more than he was willing to admit.

And she knew he enjoyed hearing her tales of life in Washington, her life, anyhow, stories of murder and rape and incest and fraud and political skulduggery. If he'd showed such interest when they were married, they might still be together, she sometimes mused. But that thought was always fleeting. They belonged to that increasing tribe of odd couples, better friends than spouses.

Over cups of strong coffee, and *galaktobouriko* for dessert—custard in the delicate pastry called phyllo leaves—she said, "The Juris case becomes thicker every day. Juris might have embezzled funds from the museum. And Tierney's best friend, the investment banker Tankloff, Sam Tankloff—who's also Tierney's biggest source of capital—could come up for indictment any day."

"Who did he screw?" Penna asked.

"I don't know yet. Scuttlebutt out of Justice. Financial fraud, maybe IRS trouble. But here they are, some of D.C.'s rich and mighty writing love letters to secretaries, stealing money from public institutions, and defrauding each other." She smacked her lips. "I love it!"

He had been right. But his suggestion that they spend the night together was wrong. She declined. She was tired and had to be up early. They brushed lips outside the restaurant, like cousins. Then she threw her arms around him and kissed him hard. "Call me?" she said, looking at him in a manner that said, Do it! She didn't want him to go. She never wanted an evening spent together to end. The marriage, yes. But not these occasional evenings when she talked and he listened. Nick was the best listener in her life. And that was important, after all. What good were all the intriguing stories out of her life if there was no one to tell them to?

"Sure, Darcy. I'll call. I always do. And, Darcy. Stay away from married men. There's no future in it. No moral judgment intended."

"You're absolutely right," she said. "That's what I like about you, Nick. Always a fountain of clear, conservative thinking."

"You should have taken me up on my offer," Nick said. He'd been asleep when she called at one; they'd been talking for almost an hour.

"I know. I miss you."

"Loneliness passes, Darce."

"I know. I wish I still smoked. I only get lonely once in a while. Been months since I woke you up."

"It's okay. Sure you don't want me to come over? I will."

"Thanks, no. I just needed to talk, Nick. Didn't know who else to talk to."

He laughed. "Didn't know anybody else who wouldn't mind being woken up in the middle of the night. Get some sleep, lady."

"Yes, sir. Good night."

20 The Following Morning

Over bowls of blueberries, raspberries, and fashionable high-fiber cereal, Mac and Annabel discussed the previous day.

"I agree with you," Mac said. "The missing money could have bearing upon Pauline's murder. Then again, it might be pure coincidence, mean nothing. And they're convicting her without a trial."

Annabel took the last spoonful before saying, "Sam said Pauline died without funds to speak of. Wendell was the executor."

Smith nodded. "Does he know about the missing money?"

"I assume he does. After all, he's chairman."

"Which means he might be the last to know. Could be embarrassing to the museum if it gets out."

"That was Sam's concern. Oh, I forgot to mention that Ms. Eikenberg was there while the meeting was going on."

"There? Because of the missing funds?"

"Not according to Joe Chester. He came into

the meeting late, said she'd been questioning him again about the murder."

"Hmmm," Smith said, rinsing the empty bowls in the sink. "What's on your agenda today?" he asked over the noise of running water.

"Meetings," Annabel said.

"More? At the museum? You're busier than the National Security Council."

"You mean that shadowy bunch who keeps the president secure in his job? And democracy safe until our next election? No. Has to do with my trip to San Francisco."

Smith turned off the faucet. "Your trip to San Francisco? When?"

"Didn't I tell you?"

"No, you didn't."

"Weekend after next. The Smithsonian and Dumbarton Oaks are cosponsoring a conference out there on pre-Columbian art. Private collectors and small museums from around the country will be attending. Someone on Dumbarton's Harvard Advisory Committee called and invited me. I'm excited."

"I can imagine. How long will you be gone?"

"Four days. Leaving Friday night, back Wednesday. I'm sorry if I forgot to mention it. I thought I had."

"You probably did. Shame your trip isn't this

weekend. A good excuse to skip Tri-S's extravaganza."

Annabel laughed. "Sorry I can't provide that
for you. Lighten up, Mac. You might even enjoy
it."

"That's always a possibility."

The re-creation of the murder of Philip Barton
Key by Congressman Dan Sickles was to be presented on Saturday in Lafayette Park, across from
the White House. Later that evening, a black-tie
dinner-dance would be held at the National
Building Museum. Smith would have preferred to
avoid the theatrical production and attend only
the dinner, but Annabel had pointed out that it
was bad form, like attending a wedding reception
but skipping the ceremony.

"You?"

"Me what?"

"What are you doing today?"

"Same thing you're doing, attending meetings.
The dean has been pushing for a curriculum
change, and we're huddling about it. I don't like
what he's suggesting, but he is the dean. My boss.
And I am a good soldier."

"But only after you make your objections
known in your usual loquacious style."

"Wrong word," Smith said. "I prefer to think I
persuade through a minimum of carefully chosen

words. But no matter. Yes, the dean will know my thoughts."

It was a day of meetings all over town.

Darcy Eikenberg faced four of them at MPD Headquarters at 300 Indiana Avenue.

She was late for the first because she'd spent more time than planned interviewing employees of Tierney Development Corporation. Her tardy arrival didn't set well with the head of the Forensic Unit, the crusty veteran Wally Zenger. He said as she came through the door, "I hate to break the news, Darcy, but the Juris case isn't the only one we're working on."

Eikenberg brushed off his comment and took a chair at the table. In the middle of it was a fourteen-by-twelve black typewriter case. "Canon" was printed on its cover. Inside was a Typestar 6 battery-powered typewriter that used the ink-jet principle of printing.

"Well?" Eikenberg asked Zenger.

"No doubt about it. The letters found in her apartment were typed on this thing."

"On this type of machine, or this one specifically?" Eikenberg asked.

Zenger raised large, bushy eyebrows and muttered something under his breath. He fixed her across the table and said, "If I say the letters were typed on this typewriter, I mean *this* typewriter. We bought four others. They all look pretty much alike except the T and M tend to bleed a little on this one. The others didn't. On top of that, this unit is set to the same specifications as the letters, margins left and right, top and bottom. It's the one."

"Okay," Eikenberg said, taking in faces around the table, including two detectives who'd produced the typewriter and who were assigned to Eikenberg on the Juris case, and three cops from Forensics. She said to the detectives, "Get back to the National Building Museum and find out who had access to this typewriter and where it was kept most of the time."

"We took it from the room they call the commissioner's suite," a detective said.

"Is that where it was always kept? Run it down before the day is out."

The Second Meeting
MPD's Evidence Unit had been a source of embarrassment for years. Its job was seemingly simple and straightforward—to catalog and file evidence in criminal cases so that it was available in its original form for presentation during trial. But evidence sometimes disappeared. Illegal drugs seized in raids occasionally vanished. In one case, Internal Affairs built a case against cops

who'd confiscated the drugs and sold them back to the same dealers from whom they'd been taken. Weapons had occasionally flown the coop, too. And sensitive documents to be used to prosecute certain government officials seemed to have been lifted aloft by breezes through open windows and floated to a kinder, gentler place.

Such incidents did not occur with regularity. To the contrary, materials generally stayed in Evidence until prosecutors called upon them to build their cases. It had been at least six months since any controversy had arisen over MPD's handling of evidence.

But the leak of the letters purportedly written by Wendell Tierney to Pauline Juris had broken that string.

The officer in charge of Evidence, eighteen-year veteran Frank Chester, had spent most of his MPD years behind a desk and pushing papers. His early years on D.C.'s streets had been relatively uneventful, and his performance reports never rated him higher than average. The word was that Chester didn't have the heart, or guts, to be a street cop.

When he was offered a job in Evidence after four years, Chester took it and never complained. It suited his style. A nine-to-fiver. In it for the pension. Two years to go.

Seeing Detective Darcy Eikenberg come

through the door was not destined to make Frank Chester smile. He had little use for all detectives, with their swagger and boast, but had a particular dislike for female cops. Women didn't belong in fire trucks, patrol cars, or the military. He wasn't terribly original in his rationale—"There's always that time of the month," or, "They just end up quitting to have babies." He'd never married.

Eikenberg was aware of Chester's chauvinistic attitudes and knew he wasn't unique. Many of her male colleagues felt the same. She also knew that Chester was not a man to seek confrontation or conflict. He kept such thoughts to himself. Watery blue eyes and weak lips said more than any words.

When confronted with men like Frank Chester, Eikenberg invariably presented herself at her female best. She knew it made them squirm and took pleasure from their discomfort. Instead of choosing a chair, she perched on the edge of his desk and slowly, provocatively crossed her legs. "Well, Frank, whodunit?" she asked, flashing a winsome smile.

He looked at her quizzically.

"Who leaked the letters?"

"I don't know," he said.

"Leaking the contents of those letters put me in one hell of an awkward position. Ever hear of Mackensie Smith?"

"Yeah."

"He's Wendell Tierney's attorney. He's a professor at George Washington University. And he's one unhappy camper. When I told him some inefficient, ineffectual, stupid member of the Evidence Unit blabbered to reporters about those letters, he—well, he looked like he'd just eaten a rotten egg." Before Chester could respond—if he'd even intended to—she added, and stopped smiling: "And that makes *me* very angry."

"Look, Darcy, lots of people saw those letters. Why are you looking at me like I leaked them?"

"I'm not looking at you as though you personally leaked them, Frank. But you are the head of Evidence. Ever hear of an old presidential expression 'The buck stops here'?"

"Truman. Harry Truman."

"A history scholar, too," she said. "IA is serious about this investigation. When they find out who leaked those letters, bye-bye pension."

"Yeah, okay," Chester muttered.

"I talked to your brother this morning," she said.

His response was a blank stare.

"I asked Joe Chester whether *he* had some reason for those letters to be made public."

"So?"

"So, he told me he didn't. But I figured maybe he had a reason to hang Wendell Tierney out to dry. Maybe he called his brother at MPD and said, 'Hey, Frank, give me some stuff on what Tierney wrote to his mistress.' "

"I don't have to listen to this," Chester said, standing. "My brother and I don't talk. My brother and I haven't talked in ten years. So get off my case, awright?"

Eikenberg stood, straightened her skirt, and checked her reflection in a window. "I know I'm wrong," she said, continuing to study herself in the pane. "At least I hope I'm wrong." She turned and looked down at him—she was inches taller. "I assume those letters are secure in the safe."

Chester walked out.

The Third Meeting
Eikenberg had been assigned three more detectives for the Juris case. They met in a basement room. With them, she was all business. "Dr. Lucas Wharton, former husband of the deceased, claims he had dinner with her to discuss land they jointly owned in West Virginia. He claims he never went near Roosevelt Island that night. Maybe he did, maybe he didn't." She pushed photocopies of paper across the table to each of them. "Here's the information he gave us on the car he rented. Find it, bring it in, and let the lab go over it."

"Chances are the rental company cleaned it

up," one of the detectives said. He was an obese older man with a breathing problem.

"When's the last time you drove a truly clean rented car?" she said. "Check it out and do it fast."

The Fourth Meeting
Chief of Detectives Joe Horton was known as a cop's cop, seasoned by D.C. street wars, steel-eyed, taciturn, and with a generous blessing of balanced cynicism. He'd gone bald at twenty but hadn't tried to do anything about it. A point for him. His head was a series of craters and hills, a lunar landscape. He still wore knit ties—maroon this day—and had framed pictures of his children and grandchildren all over his office. A good guy, everyone knew. But don't cross him. Eikenberg made sure she was on time.

"Fill me in," Horton said.

"Making progress," she said, pulling a steno pad from her purse and referring to it. "I've got people checking out the rental car the deceased's husband drove the night of her murder. That's Dr. Lucas Wharton, big-shot surgeon from New York. We've interviewed him twice. Talks a good story, but I have my doubts."

Horton's reply was to place a folder in front of her. She opened it, read, glanced up with a knowing look. "This was fast," she said.

"I put a priority on it," he said. "That's valuable land Ms. Juris and her ex-husband owned."

"Only they didn't own all of it together," Eikenberg said. "Not from what I see here."

"Right. Juris bought the adjacent parcel a month before she was killed. Down payment in cash. A hundred-and-fifty grand."

"But she didn't have any money," Eikenberg said. She decided to not mention the rumor of missing funds from the National Building Museum. Not yet. She'd run that down herself. No sense giving up what it might produce to another cop.

"So she has a friend," said Horton. "The land they jointly held wasn't worth a hell of a lot. But when you add what she brought to the deal, it's suddenly worth a lot more. Tierney Development is going in there big time. Condos, shopping mall, the works. Worth a lot if you put the two parcels together. And she owned the big slice."

"I want to think about this," Eikenberg said, placing the folder in her briefcase.

"Yeah, I figured you would. Looks to me like the doc got screwed by his ex-wife."

"Don't you love it when we're drowning in motives?" she said. "Want to hear another?"

"Sure, only make it quick. The commissioner and I have a date in a few minutes."

"I interviewed people at Tierney Development

again this morning. I asked them about rumors that Wendell Tierney might have had a thing going with Pauline Juris."

"And?"

"And I got these noncommittal stares. Nobody knows anything, of course."

"Of course."

"Except that two people I talked to didn't completely dismiss the notion of an affair between Tierney and Juris."

"That's progress," said Horton.

"I thought so, Joe, especially since the Tierney they pointed to wasn't Wendell Tierney. It was his son, Chip."

Horton removed half-glasses that had been perched on the end of his prominent nose. "Son? Sleeping with Pauline Juris?"

"That's what I read into what I heard this morning."

"So how do you figure this?"

"Like everything else, I have to think about it. But if Chip Tierney and his father's personal assistant were sleeping together, it means he might have had a reason to do her in. Lovers' squabble. Threats to tell his father about their affair. Or—"

"Or what? I have to leave."

"Or Chip Tierney's fiancée, Terri Pete. I talked to her, Joe. Hate to be old-fashioned, but she defines gold digger. She's got Chip Tierney all twisted up around her finger—and body. Claims she only met Pauline Juris once or twice and had no feelings about her one way or the other. Right! She could have found out about her sweetie's fling with Daddy's aide and done in the competition. Certainly adds to the suspect list."

Horton stood, stretched, buttoned his suit jacket, and came around the desk. "You're really into this, aren't you?"

She looked up. "I guess you could say that."

"Gotten to the point where you want somebody brought in and charged?"

"Brought in, not charged. Held as long as we can get away with," she said.

"Who?"

"Dr. Wharton."

"We have enough on him?"

"No, but I'd like Tierney—make that plural—the Tierneys to think the pressure is off them."

"All right, but let's wait until they check the rental car. I'd feel better having caught him in a lie."

"Fair enough. By the way, Joe, I need a bigger expense account."

It was his first laugh that day.

"Tierney runs with a well-heeled crowd," she said. "I've gotten to know some of them and want to get to know them better. That means lunches, dinners, hanging out, getting them to trust me, forget I'm a cop and view me as a sympathetic listener. Not big expenses, Joe, but I don't want to feel guilty picking up a tab."

He smiled and patted her shoulder. "Okay, but don't overdo it. IA tells me they haven't come up with who leaked the Tierney letters."

"No surprise," she said. "Just as long as it doesn't happen again."

"If it does, heads will hang on these walls along with the shots of my kids and grandkids."

21 That Same Night

Suzanne Tierney entered the Grand Hyatt Hotel on H Street and headed directly for the Grand Slam. The Slam was a popular bar where sports of every stripe and season were projected on huge TV screens. She snaked her way through the crowded room.

Sun Ben Cheong looked at her but said nothing, returning his attention to the screen. He'd placed a sizable bet on a baseball game and was unhappy his team wasn't covering the spread.

Suzanne, whose annoyance level was always close to the surface, tapped his arm. "Hey, I have a life, too. Tear yourself away from the game. I need to talk to you *now*."

Cheong ran fingers over his nose and scowled at what was on the screen. No need to watch any longer. He was a loser and knew it. "Over there," he said, indicating an unoccupied corner of the room.

"Okay," he said. "What's so important?"

"The money you owe me."

Suzanne had rehearsed a number of lead-ins on

her way to the bar, but Cheong's cold, unsympathetic demeanor rendered smooth opening gambits difficult. He had that effect on people. Because he was direct, it brought out directness in others.

He stared at her, unblinking, then glanced at another television set at the sound of the crowd's roar. They had scored again; his bookie in Tyson's Corner would want his money in the morning.

"Sun Ben, please don't play games with me," Suzanne said, her earlier toughness replaced by a pleading tone. "It isn't fair."

Cheong returned his attention to her and knit his brow as though running through a complex series of calculations. "How much?" he asked.

Toughness to pleading to frustration. "You *know* how much. One hundred thousand dollars. What we agreed on."

"Just like that," he said.

"No, not just like that. I've been putting my neck out for you for months now. Every week that I pick up a package in New York, I feel like a criminal, like the FBI is going to jump out of the bushes and arrest me."

His smile was a slight imperfection. "You're being dramatic again, Suzanne."

"The hell I am. Look, I don't care what kind of

scam you're involved in. That's your business, and maybe Sam Tankloff's. Should it become Daddy's business, too?"

There was no smile now. His face was granite. "You aren't threatening me, are you?"

"Call it what you will. I want my money. It's that simple. I promised Arthur Saul in New York that I'd have it. He's going to put me in a play. Damn it, Sun, I want it now."

"I don't have it now."

"What did you do, drop it all in Atlantic City?"

He didn't respond.

"Please, Sun. It's my big chance. I've been writing this one-woman show for a year. Arthur says he'll produce it and turn it into a real showcase for me. You know Daddy won't give it to me. I asked him six months ago, and he laughed. He just looked at me and laughed. What do you think that did to me, made me feel? When I told you—"

They were interrupted by a young man who asked Cheong how he was doing. "Fine," Cheong responded. The young man slapped him on the shoulder and continued to the bar. "When I told you, you seemed to understand," Suzanne continued. "So I started doing the pickups for you in New York, when you told me it would be worth a hundred thousand dollars for me."

His black eyes darted back and forth. Confident that they weren't being overheard, he leaned closer. "I don't want to argue with you, Suzanne. I'll give you the money, but it will take me a week or two. I'm going to the Cayman Islands with Sam on business. While I'm gone, I expect an infusion of cash. When I get back—and if the cash is there—I'll give it to you. I can't do more than that."

Her face brightened. She placed a small hand on his chest and smiled. "That's all I wanted to hear. I'll call Arthur and tell him it's set so he can get the ball rolling. What else can I say except thank you? I knew you wouldn't let me down the way Daddy has all these years."

"I have to go," he said. "I have an appointment." He strode purposefully from the room and into the hotel lobby, leaving Suzanne alone with her thoughts—and dreams.

She went to a public phone and dialed Arthur Saul's number in New York. His assistant answered and told her he was busy.

"Put him on," she said with conviction. "I have very good news for him. For us."

22 The Next Morning—Thursday

Because Mackensie Smith was obsessive-compulsive when it came to office neatness, he seldom had the courage to visit the office of his friend Professor Monty Jamison, whose office of solid toxic waste was infamous at the university. "Monty will die in there, and we won't know for days and won't be able to find him for a month," a colleague liked to say. One thing for certain, Mac thought, he won't be found under *J.*

Jamison's office was twice the size of Smith's but seemed considerably smaller because of its immense clutter. Most of the space was taken up with books and papers in what seemed to be leaning towers, some reaching from floor to almost ceiling. A narrow path wandered from door to desk, with an even narrower black hole circling the desk to allow Jamison access to his chair. He claimed to be able to put his finger on any document there, and Mac Smith didn't doubt it. A psychiatrist at a party once told Smith that people with organized minds didn't need external order to function. Translation: Smith's need for external order meant that his mind was disorganized. Just another flawed Freudian theory, he told himself after finding an excuse to escape the shrink. He'd once heard Dr. Joyce Brothers on a TV talk show explain that men who needed to arrange throw pillows in a neat row on a couch had a breast fixation. The pillows on Smith's couches were *always* neatly lined up. He'd asked Annabel about it, and she'd assured him that his appreciation of the female breast was well within normal limits.

Jamison had multiple research projects going at once. Few were completed because his initial enthusiasm usually waned when a new idea captured his sizable imagination. Recently, he'd told Smith that he was in the process of studying the background of Amila Bloomer, a nineteenth-century leader of the temperance movement and inventor of women's "bloomers"; George Washington Plunkitt, a New York politician at the turn of the century who'd proudly differentiated between honest and dishonest graft and who claimed that the sort of "honest" graft he practiced was good for society; and, of course, there was always another Washington murder in the past to which the American history professor was lending his insatiable curiosity.

Smith knocked on Jamison's door that morning, heard a gruff "Come in," and pushed open the door as far as it would go, which wasn't far because of books piled behind it. Jamison was leaning back in his chair reading.

"Bad time?" Smith asked.

"Never for you, Mackensie. Come in, come in. Sit down."

"Where?" Smith asked. Night-vision goggles were needed to find the furniture.

"Over there." Jamison pointed to a straight-back chair that had miraculously avoided becoming a repository for books and papers.

Seated, Smith apologized for barging in. "I thought you might have some material on Clement Vallandigham."

Jamison's eyes lighted up. "Of course I do. The original Man Without a Country." He got up from his chair with considerable difficulty, stood on tiptoe to reach a book buried under papers on a high shelf, almost fell into a pile of documents, steadied himself by grabbing the windowsill, and handed the book to Smith, who'd jumped to his feet when Jamison had begun to topple.

"Lost my balance," Jamison said.

"Yes." What Smith was thinking was that Jamison had, indeed, put his finger on the book Smith sought.

"Sad case, Vallandigham," Jamison said. "Shot off his mouth too much about Lincoln being a despot and was banished to the Confederacy. But they had no use for him and sent him back. Wandered about till he shot himself."

Smith browsed the book as Jamison capsulized the life of its subject. It was exactly what Smith needed to prepare a class, offering Clement Vallandigham as a possible example of excessive punishment for loyal opposition.

Jamison returned to his chair, picked up what he'd been reading when Smith arrived, and held it up. "Fascinating story here, Mackensie," he said.

Smith looked up. "What is it?"

"A biography of sorts of Pauline Juris."

"Where did you get *that*?"

"From Wendell, last night, at his house. We were going over some last-minute details for Saturday's production. When the others left, he handed this to me. You can imagine how I responded, being a journal keeper myself."

"It's her journal? A day-to-day account of her life?"

Jamison's laugh was a low rumble. "No, nothing like that. Pauline's family goes back to the Revolution, and she'd evidently assumed the role of family historian. Nice assortment of characters. Soldiers, rogues and criminals, merchants large and small, even a woman from her father's side of the family who was a labor organizer in Massachusetts textile mills."

"Another Mother Jones," Smith said.

"Exactly."

"Why did Wendell give it to *you*?" Smith asked.

"He thought I might be interested from a historical perspective, hopes I'll volunteer to edit it and seek a publisher. It was very touching, Mac. Wendell had tears in his eyes. He said he thought its publication would be a fitting tribute to Pauline. I certainly agree."

"Is it good enough to be published?" Smith asked.

"Not in its present form, as much as I've read. But with an astute editor's touch it could be. Care to look at it?" Smith took it from where his friend plopped it on the desk and was surprised at its heft. It had been his experience that people who threatened to write family histories usually quit after page twenty. Pauline's efforts had resulted in more than three hundred pages.

He fanned through the manuscript. "Funny. Pauline didn't seem the sort of woman who would be interested in history," he commented. "I perceived her as strictly here and now. And Wendell, moved to tears?"

"Exactly my perception. What a pleasant surprise to see another dimension to her."

"Have you read much of it, Monty?"

"No, and don't think I will for the next few days, not with the Sickles-Key reenactment this weekend. You and Annabel will be there?"

"Yes. I'd be interested in reading this."

"Ho-ho," Jamison said. "The professor of law about to intrude on the history professor's turf."

Smith laughed gently. "Wouldn't think of it, my friend, but I do have more free time than you do." And more air, Mac thought, claustrophobic in the overwhelming office.

Jamison squared his chair and leaned elbows on the desk. "Nothing in there, Mac, that will shed light on her murder. History pure and simple. I read the last few pages. She brings the history only up to 1921."

"I'm not looking for clues, Monty. I'd just enjoy a leisurely stroll through someone else's family."

"Then take it. It's yours."

Smith considered handing the manuscript back. Tierney had given it to the professor, not to him. "Sure it's okay to have me read this?" he asked.

"Of course. Wendell considers you family."

Hardly what Mac Smith aspired to. "I'll tell him I've read it," he said.

"By all means," said Jamison.

"Everything shaping up for Saturday?"

Jamison's sigh was big enough to threaten a paper earthquake. "Yet another miracle if it goes off as planned," he said. "This is the biggest production we've ever mounted. So many things to go wrong, so many people to appease." He said with gravity, "It was the Bard who first suggested we kill all the lawyers. Correct?"

Smith smiled. "Yes, although I have a problem with that, despite Shakespeare's many followers."

"Well, I say, Mackensie Smith, first kill all the actors and actresses. They are the most self-centered, difficult, whining, infuriatingly frustrating people on earth."

Smith stood and tucked the manuscript and book beneath his arm. "Time to leave, Monty. I have a dentist's appointment in half an hour. I'm sure everything will go splendidly on Saturday. Thanks for these. I'll return both on Monday."

As Smith turned to leave, Jamison said, "Terrible what happened to that dental student last night."

"What dental student?"

"The one who was killed. Incredible coincidence. I just sent out a Tri-S flyer in which . . ."

"Another time, Monty. My dentist has a rule. If you're late, you get root canal whether you need it or not. See you Saturday."

Dr. Bernard Kirshbaum, Mac and Annabel's dentist, maintained elaborate offices in the Watergate complex. His patient roster read like a Washington *Who's Who* list. It included familiar names from the Pentagon, State, the CIA, media, and the Washington Redskins. The hallways were lined with autographed pictures from patients, Kirshbaum's personal rogues' gallery: "Worst impacted wisdom tooth I've ever seen"; "Took three bullets in Nam but freaks out when the needle comes out"; or "Spends most of the time in my chair taking calls from NATO and the White House." He'd been after Smith to provide a photo, but Smith had balked. For Smith, cavities, like domestic quarrels, political preferences, and Oreo-cookie binges at midnight, were private affairs.

Smith settled in Kirshbaum's high-tech chair. An assistant secured a bib around his neck. Smith did not have an undue fear of dentists. What bothered him most was that he invariably sat with mouth filled with cotton, plastic strips, and metal bands while the dentist chattered on about everything from Madonna to *Monday Night Football*. It wasn't fair. The most Smith could manage was a grunt or a hiss, neither of which contributed to the conversation.

This visit was no different. Mouth chockablock with paraphernalia, he listened to a detailed accounting of Kirshbaum's recent fly-fishing expedition to Nova Scotia. He held some photos from the trip in front of Smith, who did a lot of nodding, hoping the movement of his head wouldn't disturb what was going on inside his mouth. Dr. K. worked, and rambled on.

"Read about that dental student being murdered last night?" Kirshbaum asked as he mixed a gooey substance on a glass plate.

"Uh-huh," Smith managed.

The dentist continued mixing his potion with his right hand as he picked up a piece of paper from the counter with his left and handed it behind his back to his patient. Because he wasn't wearing glasses, Smith had to hold the paper at arm's length. It was a newsletter that had obviously been created on a computer. Across the top in blood-red letters was THE SCARLET SIN SOCIETY.

Dear Dentist:
Crime buffs don't often think of dentists as being involved in the nasty business of murder and mayhem. But they're wrong. Over the years there have been a number of murders associated with the field of dentistry. The Membership Committee of Tri-S wanted to relate but one example as an inducement for you to join the society.

Ah, the joys of modern technology, Smith thought. It was the sort of document that could be personalized—send one batch to area dentists, another with different information to accountants, maybe send some in the hope of recruiting taxidermists.

In 1901, at the Kenmore Hotel, a handsome young dental student, James Seymour Ayres, who also worked as a clerk at the Census Office and who was known to have seduced numerous young Washington ladies, was shot to death in his room. Witnesses saw a young woman dressed in a nightgown descend from Ayres's room via the fire escape and disappear through a second-floor window.

All young women living in the hotel at the time were questioned without result. But there were two anonymous letters. One had been written to Michigan congressman Weeks before the murder informing him that his daughter, who'd been often seen on the arm of James Ayres, was romantically involved with a philanderer of the first order. The second letter, written after the murder, was from an unnamed chambermaid—it was signed "chambermaid"—and suggested that the murderess was a young woman living in the hotel at the time, Mary Minas of Indiana. Subsequent interviews of Miss Minas did not bear fruit.

Clues were everywhere. Ayres had been shot with a Harrison & Richardson .32 revolver whose barrel was smeared with blood. There was also a bloody handprint on his room's window. (This was before the ability to identify criminals by their fingerprints had been developed—the sort of interesting information Tri-S members learn at our regular meetings.)

Eventually, a thirty-four-year-old woman, Lola Ida Hemri Bonine, the mother of two children and married to a traveling salesman who was away all week, was charged with the murder. Numerous witnesses claimed she was a frequent visitor to Ayres's room, as well as to the rooms of other young male boarders. Under intense questioning, she told the police that he'd pointed the gun at her to force her to share his bed. They wrestled, and the gun went off three times, each bullet striking him. Then, she said, she escaped through the window.

It took the jury five hours. Lola Bonine was judged not guilty.

This is, of course, the most sketchy of details about this shocking murder. It will be fully explored at a future meeting of the society, and we urge you and interested colleagues to join us at what will be an intensely fascinating evening.

Montgomery Jamison
Chairman
Membership Committee

Kirshbaum took the flyer from Smith and proceeded to plumb the depths of his patient's gaping mouth. "Some coincidence," he said as he worked.

Smith tried to communicate with his eyes.

"The murder of the dental student last night," Kirshbaum said. "You didn't hear about it?"

Smith wanted to tell him that his friend and correspondent Monty Jamison, Tri-S's membership chairman, had begun to mention it, but Mac couldn't form the words.

"Young dental student murdered in a seedy hotel on North Capital. Heard it on the radio. A witness claims to have seen a woman coming down the fire escape. What goes around comes around, I guess."

Eventually, and through lips numbed to stone by multiple injections of novocaine, Smith was free to get up from the chair and ask, "Planning on joining the Scarlet Sin Society?"

"Yeah, I think I might. Sounds like fun. They have a big event coming up this Saturday, don't they?"

"They certainly do. All for a good cause."

"Sounds like something you'd be involved in, Mac. I mean, being a criminal attorney. Sounds like it's right down your alley, your cup of tea."

"Maybe my cup years ago but not now," Smith replied, curbing the temptation to add that an hour in a dentist's chair somehow seemed more gruesome than simple, quick murder. He paid his bill to the nurse at the reception desk, said hello to the next patient, a young senator from Massachusetts with whom Smith occasionally played racquetball, and headed home, fingertips pressed against his abused jawbone, his mind filled with visions of young women in nightgowns dancing down fire escapes.

What had another psychiatrist once told him? "Tell someone not to think of purple elephants, and that's all they can think of." Young women in *purple* nightgowns.

He pledged not to straighten pillows on the couch when he got home.

23 That Night

"I took it upon myself to read up on my character," the clergyman playing President Buchanan said.

"And?"

"I think I now better understand him."

"Good."

Potomac Players' director Seymour Fletcher started to walk away, but the reverend grabbed his sleeve. "The conclusion I've come to is that if I play him with a soft voice as you insist, it simply gives credence to all the nasty rumors."

Fletcher slowly turned. "What nasty rumors?" he asked.

"Well, from what I've read, President Buchanan is accused by some of being our only homosexual president."

"So what?"

"If not a homosexual, he might have been our only virginal president. But that's just another nasty rumor without substantiation. The fact that he never married and preferred the company of male friends should not be used to support such scurrilous allegations. My concern, Seymour, is that if I play him *sotto voce,* it simply feeds into those allegations. I prefer to think of him as a robust man's man with a big, booming voice."

"I think you're absolutely right, Reverend. I think you should boom it out. Excuse me. I have to get this rehearsal going."

Originally, dress rehearsal was to be held on Friday night, but a series of conflicts with the cast, as well as with the church (the small theater had been booked months ahead for a children's dance recital), left Thursday as the only possibility.

The cast clustered in various parts of the auditorium. Some read that day's newspaper story about the Saturday production. According to the article, it would be the Scarlet Sin Society's largest fund-raising effort to date. Wendell Tierney was quoted: "It should be a splendid day and offer those attending a glimpse of one of this city's most sensational murders. The forecasters promise us perfect weather. It's a historic event all Washington will remember for a long time."

Fletcher stood center stage and clapped his hands. "People, people, listen up. This is our final opportunity to smooth the rough edges and go into Saturday confident that we have a first-rate production. We'll go from the top and hopefully sail right through. Because we'll be performing outside on Saturday, we won't be burdened tonight with too many technical interruptions. But

I remind you that even with the sound system, the crowd will be large and scattered, which means each of you is going to have to project as you have never projected before." He looked at the reverend, who smiled. Fletcher continued. "I have just learned from Mr. Tierney that there is a possibility that the president and first lady might attend. While that would be a feather in our cap, it will also be extremely disruptive." He looked to where Tierney sat with Chip. "Any further word about the president showing up?"

"No," Tierney replied.

"All right then," Fletcher said, "places everyone." He stood next to the prop girl. On a table in front of her were two antique guns of the vintage used at the time Congressman Dan Sickles murdered Philip Barton Key. They'd been donated, as the paper said, "from the vast weapons collection owned by venture capitalist Sam Tankloff." Tankloff, who was away in the Cayman Islands with Sun Ben Cheong, had been the source of weapons for the acting troupe since being enticed into Tri-S by his friend Wendell Tierney. He not only loaned weapons for productions, he had them retrofitted to fire blanks.

There were two weapons on the table because of a last-minute script change. When Madelon St. Cere had first written it, she included only the single gun pulled by Sickles from his pocket. But

Monty Jamison had pointed out that Sickles had carried two weapons and dropped one of them during his initial scuffle with Key. And so a second weapon was added, although this one had not been modified to accept blanks.

The cast took their places for the opening scene. Fletcher sat in the third row of the auditorium in front of Wendell and Chip Tierney. "Let's go!" he shouted.

"Where's Carl?" Suzanne Tierney asked.

Fletcher looked around the room. "Yes, where the hell *is* Carl?" Carl Mayberry was the actor playing the role of Philip Barton Key. Fletcher got to his feet. "Yes, damn it, *where is Carl?*" When no one answered, Fletcher leaped onto the stage and extended his arms in frustration. "Call him," he said to the assistant director. "Wake him up. Tell him to be here immediately."

She called from the church's only public phone and returned with a glum face. "He said he's not coming."

"Why not?" Fletcher bellowed. "Doesn't he know this is dress rehearsal?"

"I told him that, Sy, but he said he didn't care. He told me to tell you to take you, the script, and the play and . . . shove them."

Fletcher's face glowed lobster red. "I can't believe this," he said more than once. "Dress rehearsal and—"

"Chip could fill in," Suzanne offered.

Fletcher spun around to face her. "What?"

"My brother, Chip. He knows all the lines."

From the audience came a laugh, followed by, "Oh, no."

Fletcher came to the apron and leaned forward, his hand positioned as a visor over his eyes. "Chip, my friend, would you? I mean, just come up and fill in so that we can get on with the rehearsal."

"But what happens on Saturday?" Wendell Tierney asked.

"We'll deal with that when we have to," Fletcher replied. "At least let the rest of the cast have their rehearsal. Lord knows, they need it." Again to Chip: "Chip, please. You can carry the script if you wish."

"Go on," Wendell said to his son. "Dress rehearsal can't be canceled because of one irresponsible actor."

Chip would have declined if not for his father's urging. He sighed, slowly rose, and joined the others onstage. The prompter held out a script for him, but he waved it away. "Suzanne is right," he said, a wide grin on his boyishly handsome face. "I know the lines—*everybody's* lines."

Rehearsal commenced and went surprisingly smooth considering the last-minute substitution of Chip Tierney. Sy Fletcher was impressed.

Chip had natural stage presence and delivered his lines with conviction and controlled emotion. His romantic scenes with his sister, which would be played the next day on one of two raised platforms near Lafayette Park, avoided anticipated awkwardness. And, as far as Fletcher was concerned, Chip's dying techniques when gunned down by Sickles were considerably more convincing than Carl Mayberry's had been.

The rehearsal ended at midnight. Wendell Tierney had left at eleven after coming to the stage and congratulating Chip on a superb acting job and telling Fletcher, "Chip will play the role on Saturday if he has to." He didn't bother confirming it with his son.

As the cast and crew stood around and critiqued the evening, the tech director, in real life a computer programmer at Agriculture, asked Fletcher a series of technical questions, most having to do with sound effects that were recorded on tape. Cuing the many cuts had been an ongoing thorn in Fletcher's side. Guns went off when it was supposed to thunder; thunder boomed from speakers when birds were to be chirping. "Do your best," Fletcher said. "Stay awake and anticipate."

"That one mike is still giving me trouble," the programmer-cum-tech-director said.

"Fix it."

"I'll try. Maybe we should test-fire the weapon that Sickles uses."

"No need," Fletcher said, envisioning the pistol being discharged in the confines of the basement, shattering eardrums and putting a hole through a mural depicting the Last Supper. Not that blanks would do such damage. But it was the sort of creative visual that Sy Fletcher often had and convinced him he was in the right business. "It'll work," he said. "Mr. Tankloff's weapons always work."

He asked for final comments. There were a flurry of them, most of which were ignored. "Shouldn't I fit out Mr. Tierney in Sid's costumes?" the costume lady asked. "Just in case?"

Fletcher said, "Good idea," and Chip followed her to a room where he tried on the black cutaway coat and black bowler hat worn by Philip Barton Key in the murder scene. They fit perfectly. He was almost the exact height and build and even head size as Carl Mayberry.

"Drink?" Chip asked his sister after returning to the stage.

"Can't. Have to catch the first shuttle to New York in the morning."

"Another lesson with the guru?"

"Yes." She couldn't decide whether his tone was mocking or questioning.

"Well, don't get weathered in up in New York," he said.

"Little chance of that unless a freak storm hits. By the way, you did a great job. Maybe you should become an actor."

His laugh was hardy and genuine. "That's for you, toots. On a list of a thousand things I'd like to accomplish in my life, being an actor ranks at the bottom." He kissed her on the cheek and left.

The stage was cleared of props and furniture. The two pistols provided by Sam Tankloff were locked in the costume room by the costume lady, who handed the keys to Sy Fletcher.

"Hello, Alicia," Mac Smith said after picking up the phone in his study. "How are you?"

"Fine, Mac. Tony asked me to call you."

"Sounds mysterious."

Buffolino's wife laughed. "Tony's always a mystery to me. He's not here. He called from a booth and asked me to get ahold of you. He wants you to meet him tonight if possible."

"Where? Why?"

"I can answer the first part of the question. The small bar in the Watergate."

"Hmmm. No idea why?"

"Nope. He told me to tell you that it was very important and that it would be worth your while."

"When is this clandestine meeting supposed to take place?"

"In an hour. If you can make it, of course. Tony said he'd wait awhile."

It was eleven. Annabel had gone to bed early; she felt a cold coming on and wanted to nip it in the bud. "Okay," Smith told Alicia. "I'll head there in a few minutes."

He let Rufus out the back door into their small fenced yard for a time, then whistled him inside. He plopped a sausage-flavored dog treat into the beast's gaping mouth—you look like you need root-canal work, Rufe, he thought, I've got just the man—patted him on the head and said, "Don't wake the mistress. Take a nap. I'll be back soon." He scribbled a note on a yellow legal pad, the house stationery, and left it on the kitchen table: *Had to run out for a few minutes to meet Tony. No idea why. It's now eleven. Back ASAP. Love, Me.*

Buffolino was at a table when Smith arrived. He looked exhausted. A heavy day's growth of beard might have been a month's worth. He wore a green-and-black flannel shirt, baggy black pants, and a stained tan windbreaker, not quite appropriate for a D.C. power bar where men in dark suits drank and slapped backs and told jokes while women, Nautilus-sinewy and eyes blazing with ambition to be one of the dark suits, laughed too loudly.

"You look like hell," Smith said, greeting the investigator. "Probably why they gave you this good table between the rest rooms."

"The pressure, Mac. Makin' sure guys show up for their shifts is a royal pain in the butt. And Alicia is drilling away at me like a woodpecker. Too much pressure can kill a man."

"Maybe you need a vacation," Smith offered.

"That's what Alicia says. Maybe when the Tierney assignment is over. Drink?" A bottle of Rolling Rock and a half-filled glass were already on the table.

A waiter appeared, reassured by Smith's shirt and tie. Smith ordered a Remy. "So?" he said.

Buffolino's smile was crooked, smug. "Yeah, right. How come I get you out in the middle of the night like this? Right?"

"Right." Smith lifted his snifter. "Cheers."

"Cheers." Buffolino picked up a manila envelope that rested against his chair and held it above the table like an offering.

"What's that?" Smith asked.

"A present."

"A present? For me? Is that why I'm here?"

"Right on, Mac." Smith reached for the envelope, but Buffolino drew it back. "First, I have to ask you something."

"Yes?"

"Lemme see how to put this." He frowned. "You're a straight arrow. Right?"

Smith shrugged. "Not in all things."

"Legally, I mean. You wouldn't break the law—even bend it a little. Am I right?"

"Go on. I have the feeling I'm about to be placed in a compromising position."

"I'd never do that to you, Mac." A few surreptitious glances around the bar. "I want you to know, Mac, that if you tell me to get lost, I'll understand."

"Why would I do that, Tony? What's in the envelope?"

"Something you want very much."

"A winning lottery ticket."

"I wish, you wish. I have in this envelope copies of some very important letters."

"How did you get them?" Smith asked.

"You don't want to know."

"Wrong. I want very much to know."

"You won't be happy."

"I'm not happy now. They *are* Tierney's letters?"

"Copies."

"I'm listening."

"Okay. I have this nice young lady who does work for me part time. She's also a writer. Magazines, poetry. Not very successful but maybe someday. Anyway, I kind of figured out how the letters got leaked to the press. A cop named Frank Chester. A loser, been in charge of the Evidence Unit for years. I heard stories about Chester, how he'll play with evidence for a buck. So I figured I'd take a shot. I had my friend contact him, say she was writing a story on Pauline Juris and wanted to know what was in the letters. Chester tells her he can't help—until she casually mentions her budget on the story is five grand, with two grand for 'research.' Chester still balks, but my friend is v-e-r-y persuasive, very charming. She keeps talking, and finally Chester agrees to meet her but only to discuss the matter. Well, Mac, they meet tonight for dinner, and when they finish up apple pie and coffee, my friend has copies of the letters, which Chester 'just happened to have brought with him.' "

Smith stared at Buffolino.

"Here they are." Buffolino shoved the envelope across the table.

"You bribed a police officer with two thousand dollars?"

"A grand. It only cost a grand."

"I don't care how much they cost, Tony. You've broken the law."

"I didn't do anything. My friend did."

"On your instructions."

"I didn't tell her to pass out money. But she

knew how much I—you wanted to see the letters and—"

"You mentioned me to her?"

"Not by name. I called you an interested friend."

"I see. You do remember, Tony, that you almost went to jail for accepting a bribe."

"That was for drugs. These are just letters. Nothing got taken. The originals are still sitting in Evidence. Copies. Just copies."

Smith didn't know whether to walk out of the bar or to reach across the table and strangle Buffolino. He did neither. "You laid out a thousand dollars for these?" he asked.

"Yeah. I figured Tierney would be happy to reimburse me. He'd like to see the letters. Right?"

Smith couldn't argue that point. He also asked the logical question: "Why am I sitting here? Give the envelope to Tierney."

Buffolino shook his head. "You give the letters to him."

"Why?"

" 'Cause he won't question you about how you got them. Me, he'll question, maybe even get mad. Like you told me, sometimes I go too far."

"Sometimes. This is one of them."

Buffolino sat back, hurt on his craggy face. "Look, Mac, I'm sorry. Maybe it was a mistake. We all make mistakes, huh?"

Smith picked up the envelope. "Has anyone else seen these?" he asked. "Aside from your lady friend?"

Buffolino's face brightened. "Not even her, Mac. The envelope was sealed just like it is now when Chester gave it to her. I told her maybe she should have checked, but she said she was so happy being given the envelope, she didn't want to queer the deal."

"So maybe what's in this isn't the letters after all," Smith said. Buffolino started to protest but stopped. He knew how Smith's mind worked. He'd take the envelope and check its contents because he didn't know for certain what it contained. A real lawyer, Buffolino thought.

Smith waved for the check. A large man in a gray suit and flushed drinker's face pawed a young woman at the bar. She giggled. Smith paid the tab and walked outside with Buffolino. "Don't ever do this again, Tony," he said sternly. "Don't ever act on my behalf without checking with me first."

"You got it, Mac. You will talk to Tierney about getting me back the grand?"

"Go home, Tony."

"Hey, you, too, Mac. Love to Annabel."

When Smith walked through the door, Annabel was reading in their study. "I was worried about you," she said.

"You got my note?"

"Sure. Why did you have to meet Tony at this hour?"

He held up the envelope.

"What's in it?"

"I'll find out when I open it. Why are you up? You were asleep when I left."

"Got restless, came into the kitchen for a glass of water, saw your note, and thought you might be meeting that mysterious lady on a street corner."

Smith said, "I have some reading to do." He'd been reading Pauline Juris's family history when Alicia Buffolino called. Now there were the letters, too.

"Can't wait?" Annabel asked.

"The reading? Sure it can. Why?"

"Because I think we've forgotten something."

"What's that?"

"A few days ago you made amorous advances to me, which I summarily dismissed. I said that it might be wise to try another day."

Smith struck a heroic pose in the middle of the room and looked down at her. "I take it this is that other day."

"Unless your clandestine midnight meetings have taken it all out of you."

"We'll see." He reached out, took both her hands, and pulled her from the couch. They embraced. He whispered into her ear, his breath sending shivers down her body, "I adore you."

Minutes later they were tangled in bedclothes and each other. It was a night not made for reading.

In Seymour Fletcher's apartment in the Adams Morgan section of the city, he sat staring blankly at an old movie on the television set in his little living room, wearing only boxer shorts. Suzanne Tierney emerged from the kitchen. She was now fully dressed. She'd resisted coming home with Fletcher because she *did* have to catch an early-morning shuttle to New York. And that was the problem. Fletcher had pressed about going to New York. It wasn't the day of her acting lessons with that charlatan Arthur Saul, he'd said.

After the sex that had proved unsatisfactory for both, Suzanne told Fletcher that she'd raised money and was giving it to Saul to mount her one-woman show in New York.

He was furious and felt betrayed, he told her, after having helped shape her show and career. Which was only part true. He had made two suggestions after reading her script and had given her leading roles with the Potomac Players, including Tri-S productions.

"It's New York, Sy," she said, trying to reason with him.

"And you'll be lost there. Do the show in D.C. Then bring it to New York. I know you. That fraud Saul is no director. I know how to get the best out of you."

"You didn't know how a few minutes ago," she said. The argument escalated until, with one toss of a heavy vase into a mirror, he ended it.

"I'm sorry, Sy," she said, standing at the door. "I just think New York is right for me."

"Do what you want," he said, his eyes not leaving the flickering TV screen. "Spend Daddy's money any goddamn way you want."

"It's not my father's money. It's—good-bye, Sy."

Still seething with anger, he dressed to go out for a drink at a neighborhood bar. "Damn!" he said. He discovered the ring which held the keys to the basement rehearsal rooms in the church was not with his other keys. Must have left them at the church, he decided. The hell with them. The hell with everything. "That should have been mine," he mumbled as he left the apartment. He meant the money.

24 That Same Night— the Cayman Islands

The club was a two-story, pristine white building on the grounds of a private resort at the northern end of Grand Cayman Island. In the daytime, sun worshipers who hadn't heard of melanoma, couldn't spell it, or didn't care turned copper on the primeval beach while scuba divers and snorkelers sought the abundant, colorful life beneath the tranquil turquoise water.

At night the water was black except for ripples sent dancing by the moon. Above, palm trees illuminated by powerful floodlights gently danced, too, set swaying in the sweet evening breeze.

The club's dining room was as white as the building's exterior, its starkness broken by carpeting, wall accents, and table settings of the same color as the water in daytime. This night it was virtually empty. Diners were outnumbered three-to-one by waiters and waitresses wearing uniforms so heavily starched they appeared to be made of cardboard. The restaurant's service was seldom criticized by the club's board, although the merits of the wine cellar and quality of the food was constantly debated. A private club, no more, no less.

Sam Tankloff, Sun Ben Cheong, and John Simmons occupied a window table. They'd finished dinner and lingered over coffee, glad of the room's sparse clientele.

"I still don't get it," Tankloff said, referring to the discussion earlier that evening—a bank account established in the islands by Sun Ben Cheong in the name of, and for the benefit of, the Tankloff Investment Advisory Group.

Simmons, a patrician gray-haired lawyer, deeply tanned and professionally manicured, sat in the same steel-rod posture he'd maintained all evening. He smiled brilliantly and said in tones that seemed never to need modulation, "There is nothing untoward about your account here, Sam. When Sun Ben and I set it up, we followed the letter of the law." Simmons had flown in that day expressly for the dinner meeting. He lived and practiced in Miami, specializing in creating off-shore bank accounts for wealthy clients.

Tankloff grimaced, vigorously rubbed the back of his neck, then dug his little finger into his right ear. "If that's so," he said, "why am I being investigated?"

"You aren't exactly being investigated," Simmons replied. "A routine inquiry. Mr. Carvella from Treasury made that clear when he spoke with Bob Chalmers at the bank."

Tankloff turned to Cheong. "I thought one of the advantages of opening an account here was secrecy."

Simmons's laugh was this side of patronizing. "Sam, one of the appeals of banking in the Caymans is still secrecy. Congress, with some prodding by the IRS, has been trying to penetrate that secrecy for a long time. It hasn't gotten very far. Carvella made his approach under the Mutual Legal Assistance Treaty. The treaty gives him the right to do that, but there's no teeth in the law to make anyone here comply. You really shouldn't be so concerned. Things are in good order."

Tankloff finished his cognac, looked up at two waiters hovering at the table, and pointed to his empty snifter. "It isn't legality I'm concerned about, John. It's just that offshore banking and secret accounts go against my grain. Hell, I'm supposed to be pretty smart when it comes to investing money. I see a good deal, and I go for it. Simple. I review somebody's plans for a new shopping center or office building, like what I see, advance the money, and get rich on the payback. When Sun Ben suggested we open an account here to avoid certain taxes—and remember, we opened the London office just to give us an international basis for banking abroad—he said it would reap big rewards for me and the company." Thinking he might be sounding harsh concerning his young financial genius, he gave Cheong a warm, friendly smile. "Not that I doubted you for a minute, Sun, and I'm not doubting you now. But I've wheeled and dealed for years without the government sniffing around. I like it that way. Aboveboard. Doing business in the daylight. But now a probe by the Treasury Department *and* the IRS. I don't like it."

Cheong said, "John is right, Sam. There's no probe. This is just a routine visit by Treasury. My contacts tell me there are going to be a lot more of them in the future. It's already happening in Switzerland, Liechtenstein, even Nauru and Vanuatu. But just routine. If we had anything to hide, you'd be justified in your concerns. But we don't. So my suggestion is that we forget about it and let John handle things." Simmons gave another tiny smile and sipped his coffee.

Tankloff squeezed his eyes shut as though attempting to conjure a final, reasoned decision. He opened them. "I suppose you're right. Hell, John, that's what I pay you for." To Cheong: "Just some irrational worries by an old-fashioned businessman. You're meeting with Chalmers, John, and the guy from Treasury in the morning?"

"Yes."

"Want me with you? I'm booked on the first plane out, but I could postpone."

"No need," Simmons said. "Frankly, it's better when clients aren't present. Like an IRS audit. You never know what a client is going to say to get himself in trouble. Are you flying back together?"

"No," Cheong said. "I'm staying until afternoon. I have other business to tend to."

"What's her name?" Tankloff asked, his laugh a knowing one.

"A favor for my brother."

"I forget you have a brother," said Tankloff. "John. Isn't that his name?"

"Yes."

The three men stood outside beneath the swaying palms and inhaled the fragrant, humid air. "Lovely night," Simmons said.

"Pretty place," Tankloff offered. "Wouldn't mind moving here someday."

"To be close to your money," Simmons said.

"To get away from winter ice storms in D.C.," Tankloff replied. "And other kinds."

They walked together until reaching a point where the fieldstone path forked in three directions. Each had a bungalow on the beach. Simmons wished them a good night's sleep. He said he probably wouldn't see them in the morning but would call from Miami to report on how the meeting had gone. He strolled casually to his cottage. Cheong and Tankloff had adjacent cottages in the other direction.

"Nightcap?" Tankloff asked Cheong. "I have scotch in the cottage."

"No, thank you, Sam. I have a lot of reading to catch up on. This is a good time and place to do it. Not only do I have to keep abreast of what's happening in the financial world, I now have a class to prepare for."

Tankloff slapped him on the back with his large, hairy hand. "I think it's terrific you taking that adjunct professor's job. Share a little of that financial genius with others. Maybe you'll spot a couple of winners and recruit them for us."

"I'll keep my eyes open," Cheong said.

As John Simmons met the next morning with the representative from the Financial Crimes Enforcement Network, a two-hundred-person division of the United States Treasury Department, and with the banker in charge of the Tankloff account, Sun Ben Cheong went to another low white building in Georgetown's financial district. By decree, no building in Georgetown was as tall as the trees. Washington's Georgetown should be so enlightened. Regulations concerning such things were stringent in the Caymans. Rules gov-

erning the islands' major industry—banking—
were less so.

The word "bank" did not appear anywhere on
the outside of the building. The blinding white sun
that washed everything in exaggerated cleanliness
bounced off a small brass plaque next to the door:
A. COLLINS, ESQ. It was a "plaque bank," nothing
more than an office with fax machines, computers, and ledger books.

"All transfers have been made as requested,
Mr. Cheong."

A. Collins, Esq., was a corpulent gentleman of
Eurasian descent. The desk behind which he sat
would have better served a smaller man.

"I don't question that," Cheong said. "Have
you had any inquiries about this account from
American officials?"

"Oh, no. No inquiries."

"Hong Kong?"

Another negative. "Why do you ask?"

"Some of my associates seem to be the subject
of curiosity by government officials back home.
You will let me know if any such inquiry is made
on this account."

"Of course, of course. Will you be needing anything during your stay? Is there something I can
do for you of a personal nature?"

"I'm leaving this afternoon, but I may return
shortly."

Collins stood and extended his hand. "Please feel free to call upon me the next time you are here, Mr. Cheong. Your business is appreciated. I stand ready to serve you in any way I can."

Cheong took a cab to a residential area, told the driver to wait, and knocked on the door of a small yellow house. A woman ushered him inside and to a screened porch at the rear, overlooking a pool. Almost immediately a tall, slender Hispanic man joined him. "Mr. Cheong, good to see you," he said, his accent verifying his heritage. "A surprise visit. Is something wrong?"

"Things are going smoothly?"

The man's smile said he was pleased to be able to answer yes. "Of course. Why do you ask?"

Cheong gave the barest of shrugs. "Feelings I get," he answered. "Some things have a smell about them. No one has questioned the shipments?"

"What is there to question? This is the Caribbean. Scuba diving is popular. Why would they question the importing of dive tanks?"

"I'll stop shipping them for a while."

The man's long, lean face saddened. "That is disappointing."

"You'll continue to be paid. Just a short intermission to take inventory. No problems with Mr. Collins?"

"No. No problems. Everything is—what is the

word?—copacetic? Yes. Everything is copacetic. It goes smoothly. How long for you to . . . take inventory?"

"A month, maybe two. If anyone should approach you and ask about me, the tanks or Collins, you will let me know."

"*Sí. Sí.*"

Cheong looked at his watch. "I have to go. I'll be back in a few weeks." He handed the man an envelope filled with cash and left.

As the taxi took him to the airport, Cheong felt edgy. He didn't like that feeling. Nerves could be a powerful enemy, he knew, in business, at a baccarat table, in any situation. He focused on steadying himself, reminding himself that nothing untoward had happened. Everything was in place and in good order. Questions about Sam Tankloff's Cayman account were as John Simmons had said they were. Routine. Government bureaucrats keeping busy to justify their pay. Tankloff's account was legal. As for his own account, no one knew about it who shouldn't, certainly not the Treasury Department or the Internal Revenue Service. That was the point in opening it after all.

He began to relax, comforted by these reminders to himself. He was glad he'd come to the islands. No harm in checking up on things. Accompanying Tankloff was the perfect excuse to look in on Collins. Better to be on your toes than caught flat-footed. Anticipate. Take nothing for granted and keep tabs on everything and everyone. Good business, it was called.

His thoughts drifted to the conversation he'd had with Suzanne and her demand for money. He would have to give it to her, silly, frivolous thing that she was. Theater. A one-woman show. Pie in the sky. Wishful thinking. All the things Cheong prided himself on being above.

He also thought of the production on Saturday. He'd have to attend or face his adoptive father's anger. He wished he'd thought far enough ahead to have scheduled an extended trip out of town.

By the time he reached the airport, his nerve endings had shut down, and he was again in control. There was nothing to worry about, although it might be time to close shop, all of it, check out of the game when you were ahead. He'd been giving that some serious thought lately.

As he entered the terminal, he thought of Atlantic City and his favorite baccarat table. It was a compellingly pleasant contemplation. That's what he needed. He'd make an appointment with his good Philadelphia client for Monday and go to Atlantic City on Sunday. This time, he'd more than make up his losses. He had that winning feeling.

■ ■ ■

With so much to think about since leaving Washington the previous day for this trip to the Caymans, and despite the constant vigilance of which he was inordinately proud, Cheong had been unaware of his surroundings. One man who might have been a seedy, down-at-the-heels accountant had sat two rows behind Cheong on the flight to the islands. This same nondescript man now occupied the waiting room with Cheong for the return flight.

There had been others—the local in the green-and-black flowered shirt who'd waited outside the resort that morning and who'd followed him to his meeting with A. Collins, Esq., and to the airport; the well-dressed couple across the dining room while Cheong, Tankloff, and Simmons had dinner; the taxi driver that morning who'd offered Cheong the use of the cellular phone in his Toyota minivan.

But Cheong, who was attracted to attractive people, gave little notice to these ordinary people.

25 That Morning

Mac and Annabel's Thursday night had an intensity bordering on the desperate. There seemed to be a need to communicate their love as though it might evaporate unless pinned down solidly to the bed.

At 2:00 A.M. Annabel was blissfully sleepy, but Mac was wide awake.

"Something bothering you?" she murmured.

"How could anything be bothering me after *that*?" he said. "Just not ready for more sleep yet. I think I'll do some reading."

"That's right. I forgot. I interrupted your evening."

"Interrupt me any time you want."

"What are you reading?"

"I'm in the middle of a family history Pauline Juris wrote before her death."

Annabel was less drowsy now. "Where did you get it?"

"Monty Jamison. Wendell gave it to him, thought he might edit it and find a publisher. Monty's tied up with tomorrow's production, so I told him I'd take a look at it."

She sat up next to him against the headboard. "You aren't reading it for that reason," she said. "To see if it's publishable."

"No. I was curious, plain and simple."

"Looking for some hint, some clue in it—that might solve her murder?"

"That crossed my mind," he replied, "although it's not likely. Annabel, that envelope I got from Tony tonight."

"Yes?"

"In it are copies of Wendell's alleged letters to Pauline, the ones the police claim to have found in her apartment."

He'd decided not to tell Annabel about the letters until he'd had time to grapple with the impropriety of having received them. Smith was seldom ambivalent, especially about decisions already made. This was certainly one of those rare times. There was no doubt in his mind that he would read the letters. That decision had been made the minute he accepted them from Buffolino. But he wasn't sure how his wife would react. Correction. He knew how she would react and wanted to avoid the complication her response would create until he'd come to his own conclusions.

But that wasn't how their marriage worked. From the fateful day they'd met there hadn't been any sneaking around, fudging the truth, or avoiding reality, as difficult as it might be, of their reactions to each other's decisions and desires. They often referred to each other as partners— how lawyerly—and were comfortable with their partnership. As a partner, she was as much a part of his involvement with Wendell Tierney and the Juris murder as was he and would want to read the letters, too. She was entitled to that.

But allowing her to read them posed his biggest moral dilemma. Bad enough that he would be intruding into private lives, eavesdropping on intimate communication between a man and a woman. Having Annabel privy to their contents would only compound what was a clear-cut invasion of privacy, even if he decided to do nothing except burn them and forget he'd even laid eyes on them.

But all this soul-searching had proved to be only a philosophical exercise. He'd told her, and she was now wide awake. "I won't ask a lot of questions," she said.

They went to the den where he'd laid the envelope on his desk. They sat on a flowered love seat. He opened the envelope and withdrew its contents. Slowly, he read the first letter, then handed it to her and went on to the second. They read in silence. When they were finished, he turned and asked, "Well? What do you think?"

She slowly shook her head and dropped the pages to her lap. "They're . . . bizarre. I don't know what else to call them. There are certainly words of love, even passion. But I can't see Wendell writing them. Can you?"

"No. What's really strange about them is that they aren't signed. His name is typed on the bottom of each. I don't know about you, but where I come from, you don't *type* your name on love letters."

"No, you don't," she said. "What do you intend to do with them?"

"It depends upon which of the two horns of dilemma I choose to gore myself. Wendell asked me to see what I could do to obtain these letters, and I've done that. Which, I suppose, means I should follow through and give them to him. On the other hand, that could be construed as obstruction of justice, to say nothing of aiding and abetting the illegal act of bribing a cop to get them."

When he said nothing else, she said, "And?"

"And—I think I'll postpone that decision until morning." He touched her cheek with his fingertips. "You look sleepy. Go back to bed."

"Aren't you coming?" she asked.

"No. I think I'll finish reading Pauline's family history."

When Annabel awoke in the morning, she looked down at a sight she had seldom since they were married, her husband asleep beside her. He was usually out of bed early and anxious to get the day going. A morning person.

She got up, turned on the coffee that he had set up the night before, got the newspaper, filled two cups, placed them on a bed tray, and carried them to the bedroom where he still slept. He felt her join him on the bed and came to. "What time is it?" he asked, his voice thick.

"Seven. What time did you come to bed?"

He stretched and rubbed his eyes. "Five," he said.

"I made coffee, but if you want to sleep, I can—"

He pushed himself to a sitting position and said, "No, I want to get up." He sipped from his cup and returned it to the tray. He looked at her. "Annabel, Wendell did not write those letters."

"I know."

"There's more than that. Not only didn't he write them, I think I know who did."

He swung his long legs over the side of the bed. "I finished reading Pauline's family history. It's interesting, and well written. What I'd read before looking at the letters didn't have much meaning for me except for an inherent fascination with the lives some of her family had lived. But once I read the letters, there were phrases from the history that stuck in my mind. I went back and found them, then read the rest of it. Annabel, Pauline wrote those letters herself."

Her laugh was involuntary, the sort of sound people exhibit when they don't know what to say. When she did speak, she could only ask, "You think *she* wrote them?"

"That's exactly what I think." He held up his hand to ward off her next comment, saying, "Like you, I'm sensitive to word choice and usage. Maybe it goes with the lawyer's mind. I have another reason for coming to this conclusion. She used different typewriters over the time it took to write various sections of the history. Toward the end, the typewriter she used matches up, at least to this untrained forensic eye, with the typewriter used on the letters."

Annabel drank from her cup before saying, "Okay, a woman writes love letters to herself and signs them with a man's name. Why?"

"Types his name," Smith corrected.

"Yes, types his name. Again, why? Was she trying to implicate Wendell in some way, to create a bogus blackmail situation with his family?"

"Perhaps. It's also possible the reason isn't that logical. It might simply represent the act of a terribly disturbed person, writing to herself and believing they came from a man she loved but who would not return that love."

She picked her robe up from the floor where

she'd unceremoniously dropped it. "I can accept the first, more logical scenario," she said. "The second is beyond my psychological comprehension."

"What I'd like to do with these letters, Annabel, is to show them to Wendell, tell him the conclusion I've reached, and then go to Darcy Eikenberg and tell her the same thing."

"Sure you want to do that with Eikenberg?" she asked, eyebrows raised. "You'll have to explain how you got them."

"Maybe, maybe not. I mean, I'll be asked that. Doesn't mean I have to answer. In a sense, I'm coming forward with new and vital evidence. None of this would have happened if Monty hadn't given me Pauline's family history to read. The police haven't had access to that document. I'll check with Wendell first, of course, but I think they ought to have the history in order to make their own comparison."

Annabel's face had been flushed with animated interest in what her husband was saying. But a sudden sadness crossed it. She went to the bathroom, and he heard the shower come on.

When she emerged from the bathroom wearing her robe and joined him at the kitchen table, he had Pauline's family history and the copies of the letters spread out before him. He'd turned on a tiny television set; their household rule was that breakfast was the only meal during which they would watch TV. A male and female news anchor had just finished a roundup of international events and turned to local happenings. Their voices combined into a background drone in the kitchen until they heard the female anchor say, *"Federal agents announced the arrest last night of Sun Ben Cheong, a prominent Washington investment banker and professor of economics at George Washington University. He was arraigned on charges of money laundering and tax evasion. He pleaded not guilty and was freed on two hundred thousand dollars' bail. Cheong is the adopted son of area developer Wendell Tierney, whose assistant, Pauline Juris, was found murdered a little over a week ago."*

" 'When sorrows come, they come not single spies, but in battalions,' " Smith said grimly. "Not that Wendell was Hamlet or even King Claudius."

"Mac, can we talk?" Annabel asked, sitting across from him and covering his hands with hers.

"The PR people at the university will love this."

"That's not what I want to talk about."

"Sorry. Go ahead. I'm listening."

She chose her words carefully and spoke them deliberately. "I don't know what's going on, Mac. I do know that Wendell Tierney is attracting trouble, and that he's attracted you—us—into the middle of it. You were right, of course, in initially responding to his plight as a friend. But now you've pieced together significant information that draws you even deeper into it. To do that, you've accepted copies of police evidence that were illegally obtained through the bribing of an officer." He started to say something, but she stopped him. "Please, let me finish. I know the kind of man you are. I know you thought long and hard before you accepted the envelope from Tony and chose to open it. I also know that even though you say you're content and happy being a law professor, there's something in your genes, or maybe a need developed when you were practicing law, that prompts you to get involved. I don't like it, but I respect it. Maybe it's even one of the reasons I love you so much. But at the same time I'm frightened."

"Frightened? That something might happen to me?"

She vigorously shook her head. "No, frightened at what this kind of involvement could do to our marriage."

His smile was meant to be reassuring. "Annabel," he said, "I know this sort of thing is upsetting to you, and that it's happened enough times to make you wonder what I really want and need. Maybe I do chomp at the bit now and then, but I don't seek out this sort of diversion, if I can call it that. There's one thing I know for certain. If I ever thought it might ruin this splendid life we've forged, I'd never set foot out of the classroom again. Can you believe me when I say that?"

She grinned. "I believe you mean what you say, Mac. I also know you might not be capable of doing it. Look, I'm sorry I feel this way. I don't mean to be—"

"No, Annabel. You have a right to your fears and feelings. You're right, although—"

Her brow furrowed. "Although what?"

"Well—frankly, I've wondered lately whether you've become bored."

"Bored? Of course I'm not bored."

"You seem restless, that's all, and I can't help but wonder whether I'm the reason."

"You're absolutely wrong," she said.

"Just venting my feelings at this venting session."

"Don't even give it a second thought," she said. "The last thing I am is bored or restless. We'd better get on our way. You're going to Wendell's with the letters this morning?"

"Yes. I called him while you were dressing. He sounded utterly defeated when I asked about Cheong, said he'd discuss it with me when I got there. You? What's on your agenda?"

"Too many things and not nearly enough hours

to do them all. I'll be on the run most of the day, but let's keep in touch through the machines."

"Drop you off somewhere?" he asked.

"No need. I'm not quite ready to leave yet."

As he was almost out the door, he reached in his pocket, turned, and handed her an envelope from a one-hour photo-processing store. "Had these developed yesterday," he said. "A bunch of shots that were in the camera for weeks. I finished up the roll when I went out on the river with Tony."

When he was gone, Annabel poured herself a fresh cup of Mac's great coffee and sat at the kitchen table. A game show was on the TV, and she snapped it off. She needed no TV prizes. A wash of well-being spread over her. How lucky I am, she thought, having Mackensie Smith as my husband. How very lucky. She glanced at the wall clock. Time to be going. She opened the envelope of processed pictures, thumbed through them, laughed at the shots of Buffolino posing in front of the sleek boat, returned them to the envelope, and placed it in her purse.

26 The Next Morning—Friday

Darcy Eikenberg heard about Sun Ben Cheong's arrest on her clock radio at home. Seething, she picked up the phone and attempted to reach Joe Horton. The chief of detectives wasn't available, and she was told to try again later that morning.

She carried her anger with her as she headed for the National Building Museum to follow up on what her detectives had learned about the Canon battery-powered typewriter on which the Tierney letters were evidently written.

"Where was the typewriter usually kept?" she asked Marge Wills, Joe Chester's secretary.

"As I told the other detectives, it was always kept in the pension commissioner's suite."

"Just left there? For anyone to take?"

"Locked up in the kitchen off the suite," Wills replied. She was a slight, older woman with gray hair, a tiny mouth, and a ferocious tic in her left eye.

"Visitors to the museum would not have had the opportunity to take it?"

"That's right."

"What about staff? Who used it?" Eikenberg realized her abrupt direct questions were flustering her subject. She smiled and said softly, "Only a few more questions. I promise."

"No, go on," Marge replied, rearranging papers on her desk that did not need to be rearranged.

"I was saying that the staff must have made use of this particular typewriter. Is that correct?"

"Oh, yes. It's sort of a—what do you call it?—a running joke here at the museum. Whenever anyone needed a typewriter at home, they took it with them."

"Did they have to sign it out?"

"Most times, although I suppose some didn't bother now and then."

"Do you have a log that was used whenever someone took the typewriter home?"

She rummaged through a drawer, pulled out a small blue notebook with spiral binding, and handed it to the detective, who thumbed through it. Notes were handwritten on each page: *Pauline — November 6. Mr. Chester — December 16. Gil Ellis — July 7,* and so on.

"Is this your handwriting?" Eikenberg asked.

Marge nodded and once again shuffled papers, putting them back into their original position.

Eikenberg continued to go through the book until reaching pages for the month preceding

Pauline Juris's murder. Four or five names appeared; Joe Chester and Pauline Juris were most frequently mentioned.

"Did Mr. Tierney ever check out the typewriter?"

"Oh, no," Marge said, chuckling. "I doubt if he even knows how to type."

Eikenberg smiled.

"He has computers and typewriters all over his house. At least that's what I understand. He's quite a gadget fan."

"But he can't use them," Eikenberg said.

"Men in Mr. Tierney's position don't have to know how to use them," she said. "Others do." It was a statement of simple fact, no judgment intended.

"Why would people take the typewriter home with them?"

Marge started to answer, but Eikenberg continued. "I mean, just about everyone owns a typewriter. Why the need to take this one?"

Marge sighed; her expression said she was trying to dredge up an acceptable answer. She finally replied, "Mr. Chester says he likes to use it outdoors. It's battery-powered, you know."

"Yes. I'm aware of that. What about Pauline?"

"She was always complaining about the typewriter she had at home. Said it was filled with gremlins who came out at the worst times. Besides, I remember her saying she liked how quiet it was. It doesn't make noise when it prints."

"Good reason, with all the noise these days." Marge nodded. "These other people in the book. Who are they, and what do they do?"

Marge took a few minutes to go through the notebook, stopping at names and explaining their function at the museum. Eikenberg took notes. When Marge was finished reading off names, she started to put the book back in the drawer, but Eikenberg said, "I'll have to take that." The secretary, who'd visibly relaxed since the interview began, now tensed. Handing over the pad filled with her writing, as evidence in a murder case, unnerved her. "This wouldn't be evidence, Detective. I mean, it's only—"

A reassuring smile from Eikenberg. "Just routine, Marge. We gather up everything we can. Most of it has no value, but we have to do it. Procedure."

Eikenberg stood and extended her hand across the desk. Marge took it tentatively and pulled back quickly. "You say you never saw Wendell Tierney take the typewriter?"

"No, I never did."

"Ever notice him using it while at the museum?"

"He—"

"Right," said Eikenberg. "He couldn't type. But just to write a note, make a list?"

A thoughtful pause. "No."

"Well, thanks so much for all your help this morning. I really appreciate allowing me to barge in on a busy day."

"That's quite all right," Marge said. "I hope you find who killed Ms. Juris. She was a nice person. Very bright."

"I'm glad you felt that way. Did everyone?"

"Did everyone—like her? I suppose not. Pauline could be direct. Hard, maybe, is a better way to put it. Some people were rubbed the wrong way by her. But that doesn't mean she wasn't nice."

"Of course it doesn't."

Darcy left the office, went to her car, and called Homicide. "Is Joe there?" she asked.

"Yes. He said he'd see you anytime this morning."

"I'm heading in now," Eikenberg said.

Horton was on the phone when Darcy entered his office. He glanced up, motioned for her to sit, and continued his conversation, which, Eikenberg soon judged, was with D.C.'s police commissioner.

". . . you can count on it," Horton said. "We'll pull out all the stops. . . . Of course. I'll get back to you this afternoon."

"Good morning, Joe," Eikenberg said, without much good in her voice, when he hung up.

"Good morning to you," Horton responded. "Where have you been?"

"The National Building Museum trying to find out more about the typewriter the Tierney letters were written on. I heard on *my radio* about Cheong being arrested. Why the hell wasn't I informed about it? Jesus, Joe, Cheong is very much a part of the Juris case."

"Complain to the feds. They took him last night when he got off a plane from the Cayman Islands. Money laundering. Tax evasion. What did you find out?"

"What?"

"At the museum. The typewriter."

"Wait a minute. I still would like an answer about Cheong."

"But you won't get it from me. Come on, Darcy, get off it. Nothing new about it. Strictly jurisdiction. The typewriter. What did you find out?"

"All right. Not much. It seems everybody on the staff used it at one time or another. Juris took it home on a regular basis. So did Joe Chester, the director. According to Chester's secretary, Wendell Tierney never took it, only she's dealing from never having *seen* him take it, which doesn't mean he didn't."

Horton sat back and laced his hands behind his head. "Maybe he didn't write them."

"I think he did."

"But what if he didn't? That means somebody else wrote them for one of two reasons—either to cause him problems at home, maybe blackmail him—or turn him into a prime murder suspect."

"Or both," Darcy added. "Until somebody proves to me he didn't write them, I'm assuming he did."

He slid a file folder across his desk. In it was the lab report on soil found in the rental car Pauline Juris's former husband, Dr. Lucas Wharton, had rented the night of her murder. Nothing taken from the car matched soil samples from Roosevelt Island's riverbank.

"I was hoping there would be a match," Eikenberg said. "Disappointing, but it doesn't rule him out. It was a shot. Chances are better anyway that whoever did it dumped her from the pedestrian walkway, or floated her in from a boat."

"You're right. It doesn't rule him out. It doesn't rule him *in,* either. Look, Darcy, I just got off the phone with the commissioner. He got a call from one of Tierney's lawyers who's threatening to sue the department and the city for having leaked the letters. He also got a call from an attorney in New York who represents Lucas Wharton. He's threatening the same thing, only for different reasons. He says that the daily slandering of his client in the press is adversely affecting the doc's practice. The commissioner hasn't taken kindly to either call. He wants us to wrap this up as soon as possible."

Eikenberg's laugh was rueful. "Yes, sir, we should have a confession by sundown."

"Don't pull my string, Darcy. Let's just get the job done. Read this."

Another file folder came her way. In it was a transcript of the latest round of questioning of Dr. Wharton. It wasn't a verbatim transcript. The conversation had taken place between a detective and Wharton when the doctor was back in Washington regarding the examination of the rental car. The detective noted that Wharton was angry with his ex-wife and made no bones about it. He told the detective that she'd bought the land they owned jointly from him for ten thousand dollars and had signed the papers the night she was murdered. According to Wharton, Pauline purchased his share after having already bought the valuable adjacent parcel, which enhanced the package's value tenfold. She'd paid $150,000 for the adjoining tract.

"Mad enough to kill her?" said Eikenberg.

"Maybe. Want some advice?"

"Do I have a choice?"

"No. We have to pour on the steam and do it

now. Have you spoken again with members of Tierney's family? The son, daughter, mother, Cheong?"

"Cheong? Let the feds question him."

"No, Darcy, he has two positions before the law. His status as a murder suspect is still our jurisdiction."

"My people questioned him. He claims to have no knowledge."

"As I remember, he didn't have much of an alibi."

"Nobody does," Eikenberg replied.

"What about the natural son?"

"He's on my calendar for today. I want to see what I can get out about the rumors he and Pauline Juris had been lovers. I also intend to catch up with his fiancée, Terri Pate, to see whether she had any inkling that there was an affair between them."

"Good."

"Money laundering?"

"Huh?"

"Cheong. Is his boss, Tankloff, involved?"

"I have no idea. I've told you what I know, and even what I know didn't come from official channels. Law enforcement in this city is just one big happy family."

"Could have been money then," Eikenberg said.

"What could have been?"

"Pauline Juris was almost certainly killed for one of two reasons. Money. Or passion. She might not have been high on everyone's list of sex objects, at least from what I understand, but loneliness or anger or revenge or simple availability can make any man or woman more desirable. And she was somehow close to nearly everyone in the Tierney household, I gather. Maybe she got wind that number-one adopted son was playing banker for funny money."

Joe looked at her, thinking, You must be number one on a lot of lists, not just the dean's. He said, "What kind of funny money?"

"Just guessing. Money only needs to be dry-cleaned offshore, or someplace else, if it's big enough, like from organized crime, stock market or financial manipulation, maybe embezzlement, big-time blackmail, the casino skim—Mr. Cheong has been known to press his luck, which was usually bad—and drugs, of course."

"Which one of those do you like?"

"Gambling, naturally. He moved in those circles like a roulette ball. Maybe big-business cash; he is supposed to be a financial whiz. Maybe he was whizzing it past everybody until even the federals got wise."

Horton shrugged. "What else?"

"If Juris did know about it and it got her killed,

it's likely somebody else in the household might be aware of it. Chip Tierney. Suzanne Tierney. That could put them in jeopardy."

"If they knew, and if Cheong knows they know, and if Pauline Juris knew and he killed her to keep it quiet . . . Too many *ifs*. Hey, before you go, let me show you something." She came around the desk and looked over his shoulder at a flyer he held in his hand. Across the top in red letters was THE SCARLET SIN SOCIETY. The letter began, "Dear Law Enforcement Professional."

"What is it?" she asked. He handed it to her and said, "Take it home and read it. You're a law-enforcement professional. Maybe you'd be interested in joining these loony tunes."

Eikenberg laughed. "Is that what they want you to do, join?"

"Yeah. And give them a talk some night about police work. They outline a case that's going to be discussed at one of their future meetings. A little ironic. It's about some Chinese students who were in Washington years ago as guests of the government. They ended up stealing funds from the agency that sponsored them and gunning down a couple of the agency's leaders." He snorted. "You know the problem with organizations like this? They stir up the crazies. My dentist gave me a copy of a letter he got asking him to join the group. The case they outlined for him was a dental student who got dead in a seedy hotel years ago. Like the one who was shot the other day."

Eikenberg started to respond, but Horton kept talking. "We've got the scum of the earth roaming these streets at night raping and mugging and murdering, and we end up supplying a hundred cops tomorrow to keep order while these head cases put on an amateur play and *glorify* a murder that happened long ago. Maybe some whack-job decides it would be fun to help re-create old murders, only using real bullets." He muttered an obscenity under his breath, then said loudly, "The pension can't come fast enough. Go on, get moving before this case gets old enough to be history."

27 An Hour Later

It was drizzling when Smith left for the Potomac Palisades and Wendell Tierney's home. By the time he arrived, it had turned to a monotonous rain.

Across the entrance to the estate was an unmarked green sedan. A uniformed guard stood next to it.

Smith rolled down his window: "I have an appointment with Mr. Tierney."

"Name?"

"Mackensie Smith."

The guard consulted a slip of paper. "Okay. You're cleared."

"You from Tony Buffolino's agency?" Smith asked.

"Yup." He climbed into his vehicle and backed up enough for Mac to pass.

Another security man stood at the rear entrance to the house. Smith recognized him from the last time he was there, another of Tony's men. He was waved in and had no sooner stepped into the foyer when Tierney came through the kitchen to greet him. "Hello, Mac," he said. "As usual, my good friend heeds the call. A friendly face. Exactly what I need this morning."

"I imagine you do from what I heard on TV. I see Tony has beefed up security around here. Expecting a frontal attack?"

"Nothing would surprise me," Tierney replied. He looked haggard, as though he hadn't slept much, and was visibly nervous; a tic in his right eye was new to Smith. "I've been up all night," he said. "It may sound paranoid having more security people around, but the way things have been going lately, I could believe there's one hell of a conspiracy against me and my family."

"I hope you're wrong."

"Come on, let's go upstairs," Tierney said. "I'm reasonably certain we can be alone there." He motioned Smith to a high-back red leather chair and sat in a shorter version of it. "I can't believe this thing with Sun Ben," he said. "It's got to be a setup, a goddamn setup."

"Why would the government set up Sun Ben?"

"To get at me," Tierney said without hesitation.

"But why?" Smith asked. "To what end?"

The tenor of Tierney's laugh accused Smith of being naive. "You've been around this town long enough, Mac, to know that when somebody with clout wants to get somebody else, the government's always there to do their bidding provided there's enough money or votes to spread around. Sun Ben involved in money laundering? Tax evasion? Nonsense. I know all about his weakness, that damn baccarat table in Atlantic City and Vegas. So he loses once in a while. Who doesn't?"

Smith didn't respond.

"Sun Ben is a young man who loves this country and what it's done for him. He loves this family and what *it's* done for him."

Smith chewed his cheek. "They arrested him as he was returning from the Caymans. Did he maintain bank accounts there?"

"Sure. For Sam's benefit."

"Tankloff? Is he involved in this?"

"I don't know, but he should be. If Sun Ben had accounts there, it was to accommodate Sam. Sam isn't quite the straight shooter he comes off as, Mac. He's no different than any other guy who makes a bundle and looks for ways to keep it. That's fine. I've done it myself. But if he used Sun Ben to take the fall, I draw the line."

Smith's face said nothing.

Tierney sat back and crossed his legs, a statesman poised to proclaim significant truths to a historian. "I know there are some people you can trust in this world. I also know that when the sun goes down and we retreat into our dark private lives, we aren't always what we've been in the daylight. Follow?"

"Yes."

"Sun Ben is aggressive and ambitious. Very American. He might have made mistakes in judgment. Youth. That's what youth is for, to take great leaps and fall on your face."

"Has he fallen on his face this time?"

Tierney started to answer, stopped, shook his head, and smiled. "Trust Mackensie Smith to ask the right questions. Maybe he has. Know what I did this morning?"

"What?"

"Sent Tony to Atlantic City to check on Sun Ben's gambling losses. The government'll make a big deal out of it, claim he owed the casinos and had to launder money to cover his debts. Tony's there now proving them wrong. I want the facts in front of me before I counterattack."

Tierney continued his monologue about Cheong, conspiracies, and life. He suddenly stopped, fatigued, and said, "Here I am rattling on when it was you who called and said *you* wanted to talk to me. What's up?"

Smith had made a decision while driving. The only person to whom he would give the copied letters was Darcy Eikenberg. But he would tell Tierney that he'd seen and read them. Which he did. The result was a temporarily speechless Wendell Tierney. He managed to ask, "How did you get to see them, Mac? Who gave them to you?"

"It doesn't matter."

"I knew you could do it," Tierney said.

"I didn't *do it*, Wendell. They fell into my lap and, frankly, I wish they hadn't. But they did, and here's the conclusion I've reached. You didn't write those letters."

Tierney laughed heartily. "Finally, somebody who makes sense."

"I know you didn't write them because I also read the family history Pauline had written."

"I gave that to Monty Jamison to read."

"I know, and please don't think poorly of Monty for passing it on to me. He's been up to his neck with tomorrow's Tri-S production and thought I might find the history interesting. He was right. Pauline came from a fabulous family. I guess all families are fabulous, in their own way . . . that is, full of foibles. But that's irrelevant. As it happened, I read the letters and the history in the same evening. The letters are filled with words and sentence structures that appear in the history. Pauline had a convoluted way of expressing things on paper. Phrases are often out of order— 'up the street, the soldiers, they are coming down,' that sort of thing."

Tierney looked puzzled.

Smith didn't bother explaining. "The similarities between the two documents are, at least to me, remarkable. Add to that the fact that she did the last portion of her history on the same typewriter used to type the letters. Of course, that's only my amateur evaluation. No science involved."

"Can you prove it?"

"Not yet. But knowing you're not the author of the letters carries us one step ahead."

Tierney had trouble containing his pleasure at the news. He appeared to be ready to burst from his chair and wrap his arms around Smith, which Smith fervently hoped wouldn't happen.

Smith continued. "The name—your name—that appears on the bottom of each letter, was typewritten. People don't type their names to love letters."

"Of course not," Tierney said quickly. He paused before asking, "Then who wrote the letters?" The meaning of what Smith had said caught up with his question. "Are you saying Pauline wrote those letters?"

"That's exactly what I'm saying."

"That boggles the mind," said Tierney. He stood and went to the liquor cabinet hidden behind the wall. "Join me?" he asked. "I need something."

"No, thank you," Smith said.

Tierney carried a glass of white liquid to his

chair. "The obvious question is *why* she would do that," he said. "Was she nuts, and I didn't know it?"

"It's possible she was disturbed and living out a fantasy. On the other hand, she might have been creating a situation in which she could—well, to be blunt about it, blackmail you with Marilyn, or use the threat of blackmail to entice you into an affair with her. One thing is certain from those letters, Wendell—and this is assuming that she did write them herself—she was very much in love with you."

"That kind of love I don't need," he said. "I mean, from a head case."

Tierney's crude characterization of Pauline made Smith uncomfortable. Even if she had written them out of a warped psychological need, she was to be pitied, not scorned. Mac silently reminded himself, however, that even if Pauline had written the letters, it didn't rule out her having had an affair with Tierney. Nor did it mean that Tierney wasn't aware of the letters even if he hadn't written them. Perhaps he'd already been on the receiving end of blackmail threats from his loyal, smitten assistant.

The drink calmed Tierney. He stood and slowly paced the room, hands on hips, face furrowed. Eventually, he stopped and said, "I would like to see those letters, Mac. I mean, see them for my-self."

Smith shook his head. "Sorry, Wendell, but I think that would be inappropriate. When I leave here, I intend to go directly to the detective, Eikenberg, and tell her what I've told you."

"Do you think she'll believe you? Will she buy what you're saying?" Before Smith could re-spond, Tierney added, "That would be wonder-ful. If you could convince her that I didn't write those letters and had no romantic involvement with Pauline, it would go a long way toward clear-ing me of her murder and getting them off my back, off my family's back."

Smith stood. "I have to be going, Wendell."

"I'd like to be with you, Mac, when you con-front the police with this evidence."

"I don't think that's a good idea, Wendell. In the first place, it isn't evidence, just a theory of mine based upon having read both sets of documents. I'd like to give Detective Eikenberg Pauline's family history to read so that she, and others in the depart-ment, can make their own comparisons and draw their own conclusions. Is that acceptable to you?"

"You bet it is, Mac. Give them anything you want so they learn the truth."

Tierney walked Smith downstairs and to the back door. "Where's Sun Ben?" Smith asked.

"In his apartment. The attorneys brought him back here last night after the arraignment. I've advised him to stay out of sight, to lay low for a couple of days. That's exactly what he's doing. Would you like to talk to him?"

"No. Just tell him I hope things work out."

"I will."

Smith got in his car, started the engine, and reached under the front seat, where he'd placed the envelope containing the letters and Pauline Juris's family history. He placed them on the passenger seat, turned on the radio, and headed for the city and police headquarters.

28

Detective Darcy Eikenberg had a meeting scheduled that morning with Chip Tierney and had left MPD headquarters minutes before Smith arrived. She'd told Chip on the phone that she also intended to question his fiancée, which prompted him to suggest the three of them meet. Eikenberg vetoed the suggestion. If Chip had been having an affair with Pauline Juris, he wasn't likely to admit it in the presence of his intended.

Once they agreed that the two of them would get together that morning, it became a matter of chosing a place. Chip hadn't gone to work at Tierney Development because of his adopted brother's arrest; Eikenberg had reached him at home. His low voice said that he wasn't anxious for anyone else in the household to know that he was speaking with her. She offered to come to the house, but he was adamant. He suggested the Bistro in the Westin Hotel on Northwest M Street. She knew the place; Nick had taken her there a few times. Trendy, good food and expensive.

Chip was two cups of coffee late, and Eikenberg

didn't attempt to hide her pique. They sat at a table for two by a window. "Sorry, but I got bagged by some business calls," he said. She ignored his apology. "Can I buy you breakfast?" he asked.

"Thank you, no," she said, flipping open a steno pad that rested on the table.

"Mind if I have something?" he said. "It's been such a busy morning, I never got around to breakfast."

"Suit yourself." She uncapped a royal-blue Parker fountain pen. "Being late has set my schedule back, so let's get right to the point."

"All right. Fine. He waved for a waitress who took his order of a mushroom-and-cheese omelet. "Did you get hold of Terri?" he asked.

"Yes. I'm meeting her later today."

"I'm sure she's real shook up about this. I mean, getting a call from a detective and knowing why she's being questioned."

"I've been told you had an affair with Pauline Juris."

The blunt statement had its intended impact. He sat back and placed his hand over his heart; she hoped he wasn't about to raise his right hand and take the Boy Scout oath.

"Did you?" she asked.

She knew the answer by observing him. His hand shook as he returned it to the table; his mouth quavered. He said, "No. Pauline and I were just friends. She worked for my father for a long time and knew me when I was a little kid." He forced a laugh. "An affair with her? No way."

"Why? Because she wasn't attractive?"

"Oh, you mean—no, it wasn't that. Pauline was pretty enough, I guess. In a plain sort of way. She was married once," he said, as though being married were a barometer of physical appeal. "No, I sure didn't have any affair with her. Not because of . . . No, because I'd never mess around with someone that important to my father."

"Did your father have an affair with her? There are the letters."

He averted his eyes and was obviously relieved when the waitress arrived with his tomato juice and coffee. Eikenberg pressed on. "There are a number of people who say you and Pauline were intimate."

"Who would do that?"

"The who isn't important. They're people who knew you and Pauline pretty well."

"They're liars."

"Did Ms. Pete, your fiancée, know about you and Pauline?"

She observed him closely. He was exactly where she wanted him, on edge, not sure of the right thing to say, of what answer would be acceptable and stave off further questions. "I told you—"

"If your fiancée knew about you and Pauline, she would have had a motive to kill her."

"Terri? Come on, Detective. You aren't going to tell her that, are you?"

"Tell her what? About your affair with Pauline?"

"No. Tell her that you think—well, yes, you aren't going to tell her that you think Pauline and I were getting it on?"

"What I tell her is my business."

"That isn't fair," he said. Anger had now joined his mix of facial expressions. "It isn't true. About Pauline and me. You don't really think Terri could have killed Pauline because—"

"Because she was jealous?"

"Of course not. She had nothing to be jealous about." He placed his palms on the table and leaned forward. "Look, I don't know who killed Pauline. It sure wasn't me, and it's absurd to consider Terri a suspect."

"Did she dislike Pauline?" Eikenberg asked.

He sat back again. "She barely knew her."

"What about other people in your family, Chip? Did any of them suspect you and Pauline might have been 'getting it on,' as you put it?"

"I don't know. I mean, they had no reason to suspect anything like that."

"You were discreet?"

"No, I—"

"Your brother is in big trouble, isn't he?"

The younger Tierney seemed relieved that the subject had changed from Pauline's murder to Sun Ben's arrest. "He isn't guilty of what they say he did," he said. "It's a frame-up to cover for Sam Tankloff. Sam is the one they should be looking at, not Sun Ben."

"What makes you say that?"

"Talk to my father."

"What was his relationship with Pauline?"

"Who? Sun Ben? I don't know. He didn't have much to do with her."

"Your sister?"

A small, satisfied smile formed on his lips. "Okay," he said smugly, "now you're talking about somebody who had *real* feelings about Pauline. Suzanne hated her."

"Why?"

"Because Suzanne hates my father, that's why. She's been convinced for a long time that Dad and Pauline were having an affair. She accused him of it many times. When those letters surfaced, she really started attacking him."

"Was he—your father—having an affair with Pauline?"

"No."

"How can you be so sure?"

"Because I know my father. He wouldn't—" He seemed to realize that to issue a blanket denial about a rich, handsome, driving father was sophomoric. He lowered his voice and said, "I just know he wasn't."

Eikenberg glanced at her watch. Time to wrap this up. She felt a certain loathing for the young man seated across from her. She would have preferred him to be brash and arrogant, to refuse to answer her questions without an attorney present, to tell her to get lost. Instead, he was like jelly, spineless, used to getting his way because of money and good looks and family. Darcy had a particular dislike for people like that. She said, "Do you know what I think, Chip?"

"What?"

"I think you and Pauline had something going, at least at one time. I think your father did, too. And if I were at the ballot box, I'd vote for him."

"My father didn't kill her."

"I think he did. I think she was blackmailing him by threatening to tell your mother, which would not only blow him out of the water where she's concerned, it wouldn't be so great for business, either."

For a moment she thought he might be about to admit something painful. She saw the words form on his lips—you could almost see them formulating in his brain—but he held back. He didn't have to say anything else as far as Darcy was concerned. It had been a fruitful forty-five minutes. She hadn't the slightest doubt that he and Pauline had been romantically, or at least sexually, involved. He wasn't kidding anybody. Certainly not her.

She left him sitting at the table and walked out of the restaurant, through the lobby, and onto M Street. The rain continued to fall. She hadn't brought an umbrella that morning and cursed her lack of preparation. She reached her car, which she'd parked on the street a block away, and called in to Homicide. "A Mackensie Smith was here to see you," she was told.

She smiled. "What did he say he wanted?"

"He said it was important that he talk to you about the Juris case. Said he'd be home until one. After that, he can be reached at his office at GW from three till five." The secretary gave Eikenberg both numbers.

She reached him at home. He was brief and to the point. "I have some information I thought you'd be interested in."

"Concerning the Juris case?"

"Yes."

"I can come to your house right now," she said.

"No," he said too quickly. "I'd rather meet with you some other place."

She smiled again. No one that morning seemed

to want her to come to their homes. Maybe his wife was there. Or maybe he was afraid to be alone with her. Darcy liked that scenario.

"Tell you what," Smith said. "I teach this afternoon from one till three and have a meeting after that. Would you consider a drink after work?"

"Of course," she said.

"I'm ending up in Arlington late this afternoon. I'll be free by six. The Rooftop Restaurant at the Key Bridge Marriott?"

This was getting more interesting all the time, she thought. A drink with Mackensie Smith. In a hotel. "I'll be there at six sharp," she said.

29 Annabel's first stop that Friday morning was the National Building Museum where the Great Hall was being transformed into an opulent setting for Saturday night's Scarlet Sin Society black-tie dinner-dance. She bounded up the stairs and joined other members of the finance committee in the pension commissioner's suite. She was the last to arrive. Once everyone was seated, Don Farley closed the door and resumed his place at the table, saying in his usual pleasant way, "I called this meeting for several reasons. One was to have Mr. Factor update us on the schedule for catered parties through the end of the year." Morris Factor headed the museum's catering operation, an important source of revenue. "But circumstances have changed that plan. Morris came down with a nasty cold and wasn't able to come in today. He did tell me on the phone, however, that bookings by private organizations have increased dramatically. Why that is, I don't know, but it certainly is good news."

Annabel looked around the table and noted that Sam Tankloff wasn't present. She returned her attention to Farley, who had other agenda items to cover. Two were disposed of in minutes.

"I thought we might use the remaining time—and I understand how pressed each of you is for time—for Hazel to give us a further report on the missing funds. Hazel."

Hazel Best-Mason appeared ready, even anxious, to speak. Multiple file folders were open on the table in front of her. She said in her usual brisk and efficient manner, "I haven't concluded my audit as yet of the special fund, or where the missing money might have ended up. But I have come to a preliminary conclusion. It's evident that Pauline siphoned off proceeds of the special fund for her personal use." She quickly looked at Annabel. "I realize it's difficult to make such an accusation without being able to confront the accused," Best-Mason said. "But reality dictates that isn't possible. The question was raised at a previous meeting about Pauline's lack of money in her personal bank accounts. That was misleading. Shortly before her death, she'd purchased a sizable tract of land in West Virginia for one-hundred and fifty thousand dollars. The money she used undoubtedly came from stolen museum funds. Hal has verified the land purchase." Hazel's husband, Hal Mason, was D.C.'s planning commissioner, a sensitive and powerful position that brought him into frequent contact—and often conflict—with the area's major builders, including the Tierney Development Corporation.

As far as Annabel was concerned, the conclusion Hazel had reached was still based upon an assumption. But she wasn't about to argue the point. Cases had been made in courts with less tangible evidence.

Comments now flew around the table, most of them expressions of dismay at what they'd heard. Annabel said to Best-Mason, "May I see those vouchers again, the ones Pauline used to withdraw the money?"

"Of course," Best-Mason said, sliding that folder in Annabel's direction. Most of the vouchers had abbreviations scribbled on them in Pauline's dreadful, almost illegible handwriting. Annabel got to the bottom of the stack, then started from the top again.

"Is something bothering you, Annabel?" Best-Mason asked.

Annabel responded without looking up or abandoning her task. "No. Just trying to make sense out of this." She finished, closed the folder, and returned it to the controller.

Don Farley said, "I think Hazel has done a splendid job. And we obviously owe Hal Mason our gratitude for aiding her in getting to the bottom of things. The much larger question now is how we proceed from here."

"That's something for the board to decide," a committee member offered.

"Yes, of course," Farley replied, "but I do think we should be ready to offer our recommendations. Obviously, anything should be done with an eye toward minimizing the public-relations damage to the museum."

"Why do we have to do anything?" Hazel Best-Mason asked. "It happened, unfortunately. But I don't see any reason for it to become public knowledge."

Farley raised his eyes and hands. "If only that could be the case," he said. "But we all know how these things have a habit of finding their way into the press. Frankly, I'm surprised it hasn't happened already."

Annabel offered, "It's been my experience that stonewalling this kind of thing only compounds the problem when it eventually does get out. Remember Mr. Nixon and his tapes."

"Are you suggesting we recommend to the board that they make full disclosure?" Farley asked.

"No. I'm not a PR person. We have a public-relations and advertising subcommittee that should make that decision along with the full board. It just seems to me that those people who've donated money to this institution have a right to know that some of it—and obviously we're talking about a small portion—has been misappropriated by a museum employee." She paused, then added, "*If* that is what happened."

She hadn't expected Hazel Best-Mason to respond so angrily. "Are you doubting the conclusion I've reached?"

Annabel smiled and said, "Of course not, Hazel. I think you've done a good job of drawing a plausible conclusion from circumstantial evidence." She made a show of looking at her watch. "Unless there's something else important on the agenda, I really must go."

She looked to Farley, who shook his head. "I made notes of my conversation with Morris Factor this morning," he said, "and thought I would run down the events that have been booked into the museum between now and the end of the year. But you don't have to stay for that, Annabel. I'll be happy to have them typed up and send them to you."

"Thank you, Don. I appreciate that." Annabel stood, smoothed her skirt, took in the others at the table, and said, "Sorry to run out, but I made the mistake of overbooking my day." One of the committee members laughed and said something about his doing that on a regular basis.

"Best to Mac," Farley said as Annabel headed for the door. She turned and said, "See you all Saturday night."

She stepped into the hallway and closed the door behind her. Standing there was museum director Joe Chester; Annabel had the feeling he'd been waiting just outside the door. "Good morning," she said.

"Good morning, Mrs. Smith. Could I have a word with you?"

"Yes, of course. I am in a rush, though."

"It won't take but a minute."

She followed him into his office. Neither sat; she stood patiently while he paced nervously before stopping at the window and peering through it.

"Mr. Chester," Annabel said.

He turned. "I may be out of place talking to you about this," he said, "but I don't know what else to do."

"Go on. I'm listening."

He spoke rapidly, the words tumbling out as though he'd rehearsed them many times. "I know that your husband is Mr. Tierney's attorney. That's why—"

"My husband is not Mr. Tierney's attorney."

"—that's why I wanted to talk to you."

"You're wrong about my husband."

"I don't want to take the rap for anybody, Tierney included. Those letters he wrote to Pauline say it all. But the police keep looking at me, asking me questions because they were told Pauline and I didn't get along. Maybe we weren't the best of friends, but I had no personal animosity toward her. I know I sure would never think of killing her, or anybody else."

Annabel waited for him to finish. When he had—and she wasn't sure it was because of a need to draw a breath or because the speech was ended—she said, "First of all, my husband is not Wendell Tierney's attorney. You have your information wrong. But even if he were, why talk to me?"

"Who else can I talk to? I've told the police a thousand times that I didn't kill her, but they just look at me with their skeptical expressions and smirks on their faces. A lot of people didn't like Pauline. Some people hated her. Ask Tierney. He was scared to death she'd go to his wife and break up his precious family. Ask his daughter. I heard her attack Pauline twice about the affair she was having with her father. Hell, check out Sy Fletcher. She went to see him the night she was murdered to lay down the law about his spending on Tri-S productions. They all hated her enough to kill her, but not me."

Annabel didn't know what to say, so she said, "I'm sorry you're having these problems, Mr. Chester. But I can't do anything about them. My husband and I and Mr. Tierney are friends. Neither my husband nor I are involved in an official capacity." She thought of the conversation she and Mac had had about the letters to Pauline, and Mac's theory. Why was Chester so certain the letters had come from Tierney? "You don't seem to have any doubt that Mr. Tierney wrote those letters to Pauline. What makes you so certain?"

He snickered. "Everybody knew about their affair. It was the worst-kept secret in the museum."

"You say you didn't hate Pauline. Do you hate Wendell Tierney?"

Her question took him by surprise; a nervous fluttering of hands substituted for a verbal answer. Then, meekly, "Why do you ask that?"

Annabel sighed and said, "It's possible that Wendell Tierney did not write those letters to Pauline. If that's the case, then someone else did, perhaps to make him the prime suspect in her murder."

He turned again to the window, his words coming off the panes. "You aren't suggesting that I wrote them, are you?"

"Mr. Chester, I'm not suggesting anything. I wish I could be more helpful, but I can't. I'm already late for another appointment." She expected him to turn and say something, at least good-bye, but he didn't. He remained standing at the window with his back to her, his shoulders slouched, head lowered.

She went downstairs to where crews continued to ready the hall for Saturday night and used a public phone to check for messages. There were none. She wondered how Mac's meeting with Tierney had gone, how he'd reacted to the news that Mac had the letters and Mac's theory about who wrote them.

She left the museum and stepped into the rain on F Street. Yellow umbrella raised, she crossed the street and wandered through the recently created and moving monument to all the nation's law-enforcement officials killed in the line of duty. She was glad it was raining. The mist against her face, which caused the cement and granite around her to glisten, was cleansing. She would have stayed longer but was scheduled to meet a young college student at the gallery who'd started working part time the previous week. The student, Sally Frasier, was bright and willing but lacked the sense of urgency that Annabel found to be the case in many of her generation. Annabel had promised to spend an hour familiarizing Sally with a recently installed computer system that not only handled inventory and gallery finances but a database as well that had been created to track important pieces of pre-Columbian art in different parts of the country and world. She was tempted to call and cancel the training session but decided to go

through with it. Putting it off would only mean
having to do it another week.

As she walked through the front door of the
Georgetown gallery, she was met with rock 'n' roll
blasting from small, high-tech speakers suspended
in the four corners of the main display room.
Annabel always kept her stereo tuned to WGMS,
which programmed classical music, or played
tapes from a large classical library she maintained
at the gallery. The change in musical format was
not pleasing to her ears.

Sally, a tall, lanky girl with limp, straight blond
hair and a pale face colored pure passive, came
from the rear office at the sound of the front
door's chime. "Sounds like a party in here," Annabel said, having to speak above the music.

The girl stopped in the middle of the room,
looked up at one of the speakers, and said, "Oh,
sorry about that. I just thought with you not here,
it would be all right to change the station."

"Of course it is," Annabel said, "as long as we
don't have customers." She headed for the office
and the tuner, her new assistant close on her heels.

"I guess I'm just not used to that MOR stuff,"
Sally said.

"MOR?" Annabel said over her shoulder.

"You know, middle-of-the-road music. That's
what they call it. Elevator music."

Annabel laughed and pushed the button for

WGMS, catching one of Haydn's six "London" symphonies in midscore. The contrast with the incessant backbeat of the drum machine that had filled the space was heavenly.

"Ready for your lesson?" Annabel asked.

"Yes, I am," Sally said. "But be patient with me. I'm not computer literate."

"Neither am I," Annabel said, removing a dust cover from the CPU and turning it on. "But I'm learning. We'll learn together."

It didn't turn out to be an especially fruitful session because customers came into the gallery, which necessitated either Annabel or Sally leaving the office to serve them. They all turned out to be browsers—no sales; the prices of the art in the gallery precluded impulse buying. At noon Annabel turned off the computer, covered it, and said to Sally, "You're coming in tomorrow, right?"

"Yes, but I won't be able to work again until next Wednesday. Exams."

"No problem. I hate to run, but I have an appointment. I'm taking a tour of Chinatown."

"Where?"

"Where? Here. In Washington."

"I didn't even know we had a Chinatown," Sally said.

"Lots of people don't, but we certainly do. I'm involved with the American Building Museum, which is right on the border of Chinatown. A friend of mine, Sue Yoy, has been conducting tours for a year and has been after me to take one. Today's the day."

"Sounds like fun, Mrs. Smith."

"I'm sure it will be. I'll be back later this afternoon to close up." Before leaving, she called her answering machine again. There was a message from Mac:

My meeting with Wendell went okay. I told him about the letters but didn't show them to him. I'm delivering them this afternoon to MPD after my class and faculty meeting. Sun Ben was there. Wendell says he's laying low for a while, which is a good thing to do, I suppose. Hope your day is going well. I'll check your machine for messages. Love you.

The electronic voice gave Annabel the time and date of the call before a series of beeps indicated it was the final message on the tape. She called her machine and left a message in case Mac called:

Am just leaving the gallery. On my way to meet Sue Yoy for a tour of Chinatown. Should have mentioned it to you earlier. Would love to have you with me. I'll learn everything there is to learn and take you on my own private tour one of these days. By the way, Hazel Best-Mason and the finance committee have come to the conclusion that Pauline stole the funds from the museum and used them to buy that tract of land in West Virginia. And I had a fascinating conversation with Joe Chester, who's uptight that the police keep questioning him. He says Wendell wrote the letters to Pauline. I didn't say anything to disillusion him. Love you, mister. Have a good day, make sure your students know that a tort isn't pastry, and keep in touch. I'll be back at the gallery by five.

30 That Same Day

Tony Buffolino hadn't appreciated being awakened by Wendell Tierney at six that morning. Having agreed to live on the grounds represented sacrifice enough beyond the line of duty. But when Tierney told him the reason for the early wake-up call, his groggy annoyance was replaced by curiosity and excitement.

Tierney hadn't bothered knocking on Tony's door that morning. He had simply walked in, mumbled an apology, and sat in the room's only chair, a cheap wooden one with flaking pea-green paint. Buffolino could see through crusted eyes that Tierney looked like hell, as though he'd been up all night.

"Problem?" Tony asked, getting out of the narrow, lumpy bed and wrapping himself in a flannel robe.

"A big one," Tierney replied. His voice matched his sagging posture. He told Tony about Sun Ben's arrest and the charges brought against him.

"Yeah, I'd say that *is* a big problem," Buffolino replied. "Do you think . . . ?"

"Guilty? I don't know. That's why I'm here."

Buffolino experienced a sudden rush of discomfort. He was about to hear an intimate revelation from Tierney about his adopted son. Buffolino was as curious as the next person about families and their behind-the-closed-door troubles, but he could do without this one. Providing security for the family was one thing. Being taken into its secrets was another. He decided on the spot that Tierney was jinxed. His assistant is murdered, his adopted son gets nailed for laundering dirty money, his marriage is in trouble, his daughter hates him. He'd seen it before, guys like Tierney riding the fast track until the derailment. Once they went off the track, they kept falling, one car after the other until the whole train was upside down. He almost said, Look, Mr. Tierney, none of this is really my business. I'd just as soon not . . .

But of course he didn't. He was doing a job and was being well paid for it. Hear him out.

"I assume you're a discreet man," Tierney said. "A private investigator with a license at stake."

"That's right," Buffolino said, knowing he wasn't always discreet. The letters he'd arranged to bribe out of Joe Chester in MPD Evidence— had Smith talked to Tierney about them, showed them to him? Had he indicated his source, named Anthony Buffolino, private investigator, disgraced former cop?

Buffolino's the name, discretion's my game, he thought, keeping his smile to himself. "I can keep my mouth shut," he said.

Tierney seemed to look right through him. All the muscles of his face had sagged, like silicone injections gone astray. His usually carefully coifed silver hair was tousled. Buffolino waited. Finally, Tierney said, "I believe in Sun Ben's innocence, but that represents the natural feelings of a father. Even an adoptive father. Frankly, I don't know very much about his business dealings with Sam Tankloff except those that directly involve my company. I also don't know the extent of his losses at the gambling table. I'm a businessman, Tony. I try not to let emotions cloud my judgment. I want to know—need to know—how big those gambling losses are. Can you find that out for me?"

Buffolino shrugged. "Depends on where he did most of his gambling. Atlantic City? Vegas? The Bahamas?"

"Mostly Atlantic City. I don't think he's gone to Las Vegas more than once or twice in the past few years."

"Okay, Atlantic City it is. Now, which casino was his favorite, or did he play 'em up and down the Boardwalk?"

Tierney told him.

Buffolino grinned. "Sometimes you get lucky. I

know a guy there who's pretty high up. We go back a long ways. This is a guy that—well, that don't matter. You want to know how much of a high roller—how much money Sun Ben has lost?"

"Yes. I need that information quickly. And, as I said, whatever you find stays between us."

Buffolino stretched and scratched his belly through the robe's folds. "I'll get on it right away. Like today."

Tierney stood. He spoke like a sick man trying to sound strong. "Yes, go today."

"Okay," Buffolino said. "A shower, some breakfast, and I'm outta here."

Tierney went to the door and put his hand on the knob, turned, and said, "You'll need expense money. See me before you leave."

"Gotcha," Buffolino said, wondering whether Smith had raised the issue of the thousand dollars Buffolino had spent obtaining copies of the love letters.

And so here he was on Friday morning, a thousand dollars' cash in his pocket given him by Tierney for expenses, a new shooter at a ten-dollar craps table. He was glad to be there. There was something comforting, at least for him, about a casino. In rare moments of introspective candor, he would question whether enjoying the windowless environment, the stale air, the losers on either side of him, the beady-eyed boxman and stickman and pit boss and the rest, represented his failed side. If so, so what? Could he ever entice Mac Smith to join him on a gambling spree? Fat chance. You had to be a type to enjoy casinos, especially the green felt craps tables where you instantly developed a kinship with other players looking to beat the pants off the casino. You had to be his type. Tony Buffolino, with an *O*.

He'd called his source at the casino, Frankie Brazzo, before leaving Washington. Could they get together? Important. Brazzo had been an undercover vice-squad cop in Washington when Tony was on the MPD, and it was rumored—known by some, including Buffolino—that Brazzo maintained close ties with area mafioso. But no one had ever made a case against him, and he retired on schedule. That he ended up working in Atlantic City surprised no one. The mob took care of its own, the way cops do. Tony and Brazzo had done each other favors during their tour together, favors that would never be forgotten.

Brazzo said sure, but he couldn't see him until one o'clock that afternoon, which was okay with Tony. He hadn't played craps in a long time because Alicia thought gambling was stupid, at best. It was. But.

The table got hot, which attracted more players. There was a lot of whooping and hollering as the dice passed from one hand to another. Tony's turn as a shooter did nothing to cool off the action. He threw sevens on his come-out rolls and didn't seven-out until he'd made money for most people at the table, including himself. The streak ended when an unshaven young man in greasy clothing and smelling of whiskey joined the table and bet "wrong," betting against the players and with the casino. He started to win, which meant all the "right" bettors started losing. Buffolino saw what was happening, left the table, and cashed in his chips. He was eight hundred up over his original thousand. Not bad for a pleasant hour. With eighteen hundred in his pocket he scouted other tables. He played a few losing hands of blackjack and whiled away the rest of the time mindlessly yanking the handle of a dollar slot machine, losing two hundred of his winnings. At a few minutes before one he strolled down the Boardwalk to a hot-dog and pizza stand. Brazzo was waiting. They embraced in the awkward way men do. Tony ordered a dog and beer.

"Well, my man, what can I do for you?" Brazzo asked.

"I need the figures on a high roller. A guy named Sun Ben Cheong. Likes your baccarat tables."

Brazzo, whose face was all chisels and planes, said, "A good customer. I read something about him today. Got nailed in D.C. with dirty money."

"Maybe, maybe not."

"How come you're interested in him?"

"I got a client."

"You working for the feds?"

"Nah," Buffolino said, finishing his hot dog and washing it down with the beer. "Remember me? Strictly a private matter."

"He loses big, Tony. Real big."

"He ever win?"

"Sure. If he never won, he wouldn't come back. But like most, he's into us pretty good."

"To what tune? Fifty? A hundred thou?"

Brazzo shrugged. "Maybe a million. I can find out. Between us, right?"

"Right."

"Give me an hour," Brazzo said.

"Okay. I had a good run with the dice before. I'll play again. Where will I meet you?"

"Back here. And stay away from that table. It won't get hot again until Tuesday—if then."

Tony returned to the fast-food stand an hour later. In his pocket was three hundred dollars. "Took your advice and played another table, Frankie. Shoulda took my wife's. Play none of them. So, what's the score?"

"He's down about two mil."

"You give him that kind of marker?" Buffolino asked, impressed with the amount.

"Yeah. The guy loses big, but he pays—pays off."

"Pays is one thing. Pays off is another. Educate me."

"His big ones always got paid by some rich daddy in Hong Kong."

Buffolino's eyebrow went up. "That so? Who?"

"Don't have a name. Of a person, that is. Usually corporate checks from a company there. MOR Services."

Buffolino screwed up his face. "MOR Services. Rings a bell, only I couldn't tell you why. You sound like you're talking past tense. '*Got* paid.' Who pays now?"

"That's where paying off comes in, Tony. This stays here. Between us. Right?"

"Yeah."

"The Chinaman's got a rabbi."

"Here? The casino?"

"New York."

"That so?"

"The Chinaman's a financial genius, I'm told."

"I'm told that, too, Frankie."

"Good at moving money. Big money."

"He runs a laundry?"

Brazzo nodded.

"For big money."

Nod number two.

"Drugs?"

Shrug.

"Doesn't matter. He barters off his table debts?"

"Uh-huh."

"I see. Anything else?"

"No."

"I owe you. You need anything in D.C., give a call."

"I will. Hey, I heard you got married again. What's that make, two, four?"

"Three. This one's for life."

As Buffolino drove through Atlantic City's slums in search of the highway back to Washington, their sad blight magnified in contrast to the neon and gold-leaf glitter of surrounding casinos, he was dominated by three thoughts.

First, Wendell Tierney was not going to be happy learning that his son, Sun, was a lunatic loser at the baccarat table. Those kinds of losses could push a guy to do almost anything, including breaking and entering, washing money, or taking what didn't belong to him. Tony knew all about that.

Second, Brazzo's clipped comment that Cheong had a New York rabbi chewed at his insides. Brazzo didn't have to elaborate. "New York" meant the mob, at least that faction of it that owned an interest in the casino. Laundering money for the mob? What was with Cheong?

Heading up the Mandarin Mafia? Maybe he lied and claimed he was from Sicily. Tony laughed at that scenario.

His third recurring thought was that he'd broken the cardinal rule of casino money management. Half of his winnings at the first table should have found a safe haven in his wallet, with the other half used to continue playing. Oh, well, it's only money, he told himself. But he wouldn't tell Alicia that. And his expenses as reported to Tierney, if he asked for a written T&E report, would be Tony's first short story.

31 Early That Afternoon

By the time Sam Tankloff arrived at Wendell Tierney's house, Tierney had showered and shaved and "taken a little sun" in his tanning salon. But while he looked better, his disposition had worsened as a result of a phone call. "I'm on my way back from A.C.," Buffolino had said over the sounds of highway traffic. "I was gonna wait until I got back to give you the news, but then I figured you need to know right away, so I pulled off at this rest stop."

"Go on," Tierney had said.

"I hate to be the bearer of bad news, Mr. Tierney. But Sun Ben ranks with the highest rollers at the casino. And he was no winner."

"How bad were his losses?"

"Millions. At least two."

There was a long silence on Tierney's end. "Thank you," he said, and hung up.

Now, in his study with Tankloff, Tierney's voice was an angry growl. "You're telling me you knew nothing about Sun Ben's private accounts in the Caymans?"

"That's exactly what I'm telling you, Wendell.

He and I met with one of my attorneys when we were there. He specializes in setting up offshore bank accounts. I pressed him about the legality of my accounts, and he assured me everything was perfectly legal."

"You said they were investigating you. Who was?"

"Some special unit of Treasury. I didn't pay much attention. What was important to me was that the accounts met the law. My attorney said that any investigations were only routine. Look, Wendell, Sun Ben's problems with the law had nothing to do with the accounts he set up for me and the company. He obviously had his own accounts there. I knew nothing about them."

Tierney's jaw muscles worked as he leaned on his desk. "Where was he getting the money to put in those accounts?" he asked.

Tankloff had draped his suit jacket over the back of a chair and rolled up the sleeves of his white shirt. He didn't like where the conversation was heading and resented his friend's tone. It was as though Tierney was blaming him for Sun Ben's problems.

Simultaneously, he knew the intense pressure Tierney was under and didn't want to exacerbate his troubles. He said in a conciliatory tone, "Wendell, you know I'll do anything to help Sun Ben. He's your adopted son, but he's been like a son to me, too. If he's broken some law regarding his accounts in the Caymans, I'm sure it can be straightened out with the authorities. A deal can be cut, arrangements made for restitution."

"Which is admitting he's guilty."

"If he is, things can be done to lessen penalties he might incur." While Tierney maintained his rigid posture at the desk, Tankloff debated. He decided to say it. "Wendell, are you aware of just how heavy Sun Ben has been gambling over the past few years?"

Tierney turned quickly. Did the whole world know the scope of Sun Ben's addiction except him? Tony's call from the road had shaken him. *Millions?* That could drive almost anyone to break the law. He said to Tankloff, "Sun Ben's love of baccarat is no surprise to me, Sam, no mystery. He's always been open about it."

Tankloff sensed that Tierney was not telling the truth but didn't challenge him. Instead, he asked, "Have you discussed this with Sun Ben in any depth? About the charges filed against him?"

Tierney pushed himself away from the desk and returned to his chair. He shook his head. "No. He's crushed by what happened last night. The embarrassment of it all, being arrested at the airport, having handcuffs slapped on him in front of a thousand people. He'd just been named adjunct professor of economics at GW. His reputation in the financial community is pristine, to say nothing of what this does to *my* reputation."

Tankloff again started to express his support but was interrupted by a sharp knock on the door. Tierney looked up. "Who is it?"

The door opened, and Sun Ben stepped into the room. He wore jeans, sneakers, a gray sweatshirt, and a Washington Redskins windbreaker. Tierney stopped Tankloff's greeting cold. "What do *you* want?" he asked.

"To talk about what happened."

"It can wait." Tierney's voice had its hardest edge. "Sam and I are in a meeting."

"No problem," Tankloff said. "I'd like to discuss this with you, Sun Ben. Maybe I can be of help."

"Do you realize what you've done to this family?" Tierney asked.

"Of course," Cheong replied. "And I'm sorry about it."

"Sorry?" Tierney said. "Somehow that sounds pathetic."

Tankloff forced a smile and extended his arms to embrace the room. "Why don't we all sit down, have some coffee, and hash this out. I'm sure that if the three of us put our minds to it, we'll come up with a way to resolve this so that no one gets hurt."

Cheong ignored Tankloff and took steps toward his father. He stood on the balls of his feet. His body was coiled. "You have a nerve, talking about doing things to this family," he said.

Tierney was physically stung by Cheong's sudden abrasive tone. He sputtered, "How dare you speak to me that way."

"No. How dare you speak to *me* that way," Cheong said, further closing the gap between them. "I came here to apologize for putting you in this position. I came here to see my father. But my father is blind to what goes on around him."

Tierney looked to Tankloff; his expression was profound embarrassment. "Chip wouldn't speak to me this way."

"Chip never speaks the truth to his father. He's afraid because he knows everything that's gone on in this house."

"Including your million-dollar losses in Atlantic City? Your womanizing? Your affair with Pauline?"

For a moment, Tankloff wondered whether Sun Ben was about to attack his father. Tierney had further closed the gap between them; they now stood only a few feet apart, bodies tensed, eyes locked. Tankloff was ready to step in when Cheong muttered an obscenity and stalked from the room.

"That ingrate," Tierney said.

"I don't think he meant what he said, Wendell. He's under a lot of pressure."

"*He's* under pressure? Don't talk to me about pressure."

Cheong was surprised at the level of anger he'd reached. It represented a loss of control that frightened him. He trembled as he raced down the stairs, through the kitchen, and to the courtyard, almost knocking over the security man standing outside the door. He went to his apartment above the garages and exchanged his windbreaker for a blue waterproof jacket with a hood. He rummaged through a dresser drawer until he found the keys to the boat, left the apartment, and went down the long set of wooden stairs two at a time to the dock. It was raining harder now. Visibility had lowered. He put the hood over his head as he stepped into the boat and freed the mooring lines. He looked back at the house. Tankloff, who'd gone to the window of Tierney's study and seen Cheong head for the dock, had come downstairs and through the front door. "Sun Ben," he called. His words were scattered by an increasing wind and reached the dock in fragments. He started down the stairs, heard the Cigarette's powerful engine roar to life, and watched Cheong push away from the dock. As the boat drifted into open water, Cheong advanced the throttles, made a tight arc, and headed downriver, a widening and deepening wake churning behind as he disappeared.

32 As Annabel waited for the Chinatown tour to form at the Building Museum, she wandered into some of its current exhibits. One, "Washington: Symbol and City," was a permanent exhibition whose photographs, architectural drawings, and scale models examined the evolution of the city and its attempt to balance a national capital's splendor with the needs of a thriving city.

She followed a school group into a room in which a series of intricate models instructed, step-by-step, how the Brooklyn Bridge had been built. The children were wide-eyed and giggly. She naturally thought of Great Falls and Mac's recurring nightmare about what he'd witnessed there. Hold their hands tight, Annabel thought, as she entered another exhibit space, this devoted to "Great Places," eight geographically diverse examples of superior planning and architecture. Each had been the recipient of the Urban Land Institute's Award for Excellence—an office building in San Diego, Washington's recently refurbished Union Station, the excellent urban renewal of Norfolk's

Ghent Square, and others that testified to man's ability, if motivated, to meld form and function to create great places for people.

And then she was off to Chinatown in the capable, loving hands of her friend Sue Yoy. Sue not only knew Washington's Chinatown well, she demonstrated immense pride in sharing her knowledge with the dozen men and women on the tour. Of course, there wasn't a great deal of ground to cover. The Chinatown section of D.C. was, in reality, only two blocks square. But there was something of historical significance every few steps.

Naturally, they stopped at the Surratt House, which figured in the plotting to assassinate President Lincoln. "Here is the nest where the egg of treason was hatched," Sue said brightly. "That's how it's usually described. But remember, that was before this was Chinatown. None of my people, at least according to the history books, were involved. Thank goodness!"

They rounded a corner. "Actually, this wasn't the original location of Chinatown," Sue said. "It used to be a few blocks south. But back in 1935 the government started buying up property there, which meant the Chinese community had to look for someplace else to settle. They chose this location and started buying real estate, too." She laughed. "The Chinese spirit of community is very strong. They just picked up and moved here."

"What's on the original site?" a member of the tour asked.

"Federal buildings, a federal courthouse," Sue answered, motioning for them to follow. She continued her running commentary. "Like every other neighborhood," she said, "Chinatown is changing. The Convention Center really put the pressure on the neighborhood and caused it to lose some of its original flavor. But not too much, as you can see." She added, with her tinkling laugh, "No matter what goes on around them, the people of Chinatown never let their daily routine change too much."

They walked through the new Grand Hyatt Hotel, its soaring atrium a chrome-and-steel alien amid the small, dusty shops of Chinatown, and came back around under the arch that spanned H Street. "This arch was built for a million dollars when the neighborhood was moved here," said Sue. "It was a partnership between this city's government and our sister city, Beijing. But there's always been some objection to it. Some groups view it as being too friendly toward mainland China and want to build a second arch as a gesture of friendship with Taiwan. Can't escape politics in Washington. I wonder what the dragons think about it." Everyone looked up at the flame-snorting reptiles on the arch. Some laughed. "Looks like a bunch a' congressmen," a man wearing checkered Bermuda shorts and carrying an umbrella and weighty video camera said.

"Onward," Sue said, and everyone fell in line again. Annabel lingered at the rear of the small group, falling behind on occasion as she stopped to breathe in the culinary cloud of fish cake, bok choy, chicken stock, and Chinese broccoli that drifted from open doorways.

"Sorry about this rain," Sue said, bringing them to a halt in front of the Asia Cultural Society. "We'll go in here and spend a few minutes. There's lots of interesting things to see. Then you're on your own for lunch. As you've seen, this tiny section of Washington probably has more restaurants per square foot than any other part of town. Well, maybe with the exception of Georgetown. But if you eat Georgetown food, you find that ten minutes later you're hungry—for status."

Sue and Annabel had previously agreed to lunch together, and Sue had chosen a restaurant across from the Surratt House on H Street. They entered through an ornate mini-arch, passed huge fish tanks that dominated the lobby walls, and went up a set of stairs to the main dining room, whose windows overlooked the street. Their timing was good; a window table was available.

"Fascinating," Annabel said when they were seated. "I'm so glad I took the tour with you today."

Sue, who'd been a model in New York before marrying a State Department official and moving to Washington, raised her delicate teacup in equally delicate hands and said, "You once gave me a fascinating tour of the pre-Columbian art world. Here's to getting to know Chinatown."

Annabel insisted that Sue order for them, which she did, commenting that while the menu promised Szechuan food, it really was more Taiwanese.

Annabel lost track of time during lunch. She enjoyed being with a friend whom she saw too little of, and basked in the relaxed ambience of the restaurant and its wonderful food. At the conclusion of lunch, they were served complimentary glasses of apricot cordial. Annabel looked at her watch. "Boy, time has flown by," she said.

"We'll go," said Sue. "In a minute. Excuse me." As Sue headed for the ladies' room, Annabel looked down onto the street as she'd done frequently during the meal. The rain had stopped; there was heavy pedestrian traffic flow up and down the sidewalks. Then she leaned closer to the window, narrowed her eyes against her own reflection, and almost said aloud, "Wait a minute." No doubt about it. Sun Ben Cheong was walking up the street at a brisk pace. He paused in front of a small take-out restaurant across the street, looked around, and entered.

Annabel thought of Mac's message, that Cheong was laying low for a few days at home. Obviously, he'd changed his mind. She looked up H Street in the opposite direction. Another man was approaching the take-out place. Sun Ben Cheong? Had she lost a minute of time in which Cheong emerged from the place, went up the street, and was now returning? She shook her head. No time had been lost to her. Sun Ben had a twin. Or almost. The second man was slightly shorter than Cheong and not as stocky, but his face was a mirror image of the young man she knew. He, too, stopped in front of the restaurant, made the same scrutiny of his surroundings, and went inside.

Sue Yoy returned to the table.

"I wonder what they put in this food," Annabel commented.

"Why do you say that?" Sue asked.

"I just saw someone that I know come up the street. And then, a few seconds later, I saw him again—or somebody who is his mirror image."

Sue laughed. "Anyone I know?"

"Maybe. Sun Ben Cheong, Wendell Tierney's adopted son."

"Yes, I know him, but not well. A shame what

happened to him, being arrested like that. I read about it."

"Mac and I were shocked."

"Do you think there's any truth to it?"

Annabel shrugged. "Who knows? I suppose it will all come out through the legal process." She looked out the window again, her face set in thought.

"Is something wrong, Annabel?"

Annabel smiled and shook her head. "No, nothing at all. It was just such a coincidence to see two people look so much alike when I hadn't expected to see one. Well, my friend, I really should be going. This was a delightful experience. The tour was fascinating, the food excellent, and your company is always a pleasure." Annabel insisted upon paying the check. When they were on the street, Sue looked up and said, "Good. The rain has stopped."

"Still looks threatening," Annabel said, observing the gray sky.

They shook hands and promised to be in touch again soon. Annabel walked in the direction of the Convention Center. When she was certain Sue would be out of sight, she retraced her steps and stood in front of the restaurant into which Cheong and his lookalike had disappeared. Next to the restaurant was the entrance to a two-story office building. The front door was open. Out of curiosity, she stepped into the tiny foyer and read from a list of business tenants. Many were in Chinese; a few had English translations below. One that had not been translated caught her eye. She leaned closer to it. Annabel had no knowledge of Chinese symbols, but this one was strangely familiar. Why that was, she had no idea. About to leave, she stopped, opened her purse, and removed the envelope of photographs Mac had given her. She pulled out the shots he'd taken with Tony Buffolino at Tierney's dock. The symbols on the Cigarette racing boat were small, but the photographic print was sharp. Annabel studied it, then looked back at the tenant board. They seemed the same. She looked at the photograph again. MOR. Middle-of-the-Road, she thought, remembering Sally Frasier's comment about music.

She crossed the street, entered the restaurant where she and Sue had lunched, and went to the second floor. "My friend and I just had lunch here, and it was wonderful. I wonder if I might have a pot of tea. I have some time until my next appointment." The host happily agreed and led her to the same table she'd shared with Sue Yoy. Once a waiter had poured a cup from a teapot and placed it in front of her, she settled back to observe the two doorways across the street. She wasn't sure why she was doing this, why she was acting like a cop on a stakeout. If anyone she knew was observing her amateur exercise in observation, she would have been embarrassed. And Mac would tease her. She was spared any such reactions because she didn't know that earlier Sun Ben Cheong had been closing the drapes in his private office when he looked down onto the street as Annabel approached the restaurant and office building. He'd waited, then watched her return to the restaurant across the street, enter it, and take a table at the window. While his brother, John, counted cash from the wall safe, Sun Ben took a final look at the redheaded woman named Annabel Reed-Smith, whose attention was riveted on a place about which people like her were not supposed to know. He quietly closed the drapes fully and sat behind his desk, his broad, otherwise impassive face staring now at nothing. He opened the top right-hand drawer of his desk. In it was a 7.65 by 17 caliber Type 67 pistol manufactured in the People's Republic of China, which he'd purchased last year from an underground Chinatown arms dealer for self-protection—for use in an emergency. Until now, there hadn't been one.

33

"I keep getting his damned machine," an exasperated Suzanne Tierney said, slamming an extension phone down in Arthur Saul's office.

Saul, who wore a lime-green tank top, jeans, and blue rubber thongs, continued tallying checks he'd received that day from his acting students.

"I can't *believe* this is happening," Suzanne said, flinging her hands into the air, then slapping them against her thighs. "Damn it!" She picked up the phone and again dialed Sun Ben Cheong's number at his apartment in the Tierney complex. *"I'm not here at the moment. At the tone . . ."*

"Where the hell can he be? I spoke to Chip this morning. He said Sun Ben was going to be hibernating in his apartment for a few days. Daddy's advice."

Saul looked up and pushed his glasses low on his nose, saying over them, "Call your father. Maybe he's with him."

"I can't call my father. I'll just hear another harangue about why I'm not there in his time of need. What a screwed-up family."

Saul returned to his financial chore as Suzanne paced the room, stopping every few seconds to try the call again. On her previous attempts to reach her adopted brother, she'd left only her name. This time, she pleaded with him to call her at Saul's studio the minute he picked up the message. "Please, Sun Ben, this is extremely important to me."

"Maybe you ought to say you're sorry about his being arrested," Saul said. "Hell, he's got other things on his mind besides giving you money."

"What are you, Arthur, against me, too? He promised me that money. I *earned* that money."

Saul smiled and leaned back in his battered leather chair. "Earned it? How?"

"That's my business," she snapped.

"What the hell did you do, sleep with your brother?"

"You're disgusting," Suzanne said.

She sat on a small chair next to the table that held the extension phone. She was filled with churning emotions, the most pervasive of which was incredulity. She was so close to having the money to mount her one-woman show in New York. And now this. Her source of funds arrested. That didn't mean he couldn't still give her the money. Didn't he know how important this was to her, what anguish she was suffering? But why should she be surprised? He was like the rest of the men in the family, self-centered, egotistical, greedy, thinking only of themselves. The women—her mother and her—were victims of the Tierney men, even Sun Ben, who didn't share their blood. With him it was learned behavior.

Saul wrapped a rubber band around the batch of checks and placed them in a desk drawer. He said to Suzanne, "Look, baby, I have to know whether that money's going to be available or not. I want to do your show, but I have other offers on the table. I can't afford to lose them if your deal falls through."

"What do want from me?" Suzanne asked. "I'm sure I'll get the money. It's just that this thing that happened might delay things a day or two."

"A day or two?" Saul stood and twisted his torso, laced his fingers together, and fully extended his arms in front of him. "Why don't you go back to Washington," he suggested. "I can wait a couple of days. Go down there and talk to your brother. You're not going to accomplish anything here."

Suzanne knew the suggestion was sensible. She'd hoped that being in New York would allow her to placate Saul. But it was obvious the only thing that mattered to him was the money. And that money was in Washington.

She went into a cramped half-bath off the office and fluffed her hair, applied lipstick, then returned to the office and picked up the large duffel bag she'd brought with her. It was empty except for a change of underwear and a T-shirt. "I suppose you're right, Arthur. I'll catch the next shuttle. Call you tonight."

"Won't be here, baby. Call me tomorrow about noon."

"All right," she said. She started for the door when the phone rang. Saul slowly reached for it on his desk, but she was quicker getting to the extension phone. "Hello. Arthur Saul's studio."

"Suzanne?" Cheong's voice asked.

"Sun Ben. Thank God you got my message. Where have you been?"

"You want the money?" he asked coldly.

"Yes. Of course I do." Then, as an afterthought, "I heard what happened to you. I'm sorry."

"Do another pickup. Two hours from now at the usual place. Bring it to me at the office. I'll give you the money then."

"Do you think it's—?"

"Either do it, Suzanne, or forget your precious show."

She glanced at Saul, who observed her with interest from behind his desk. She lowered her voice and said to her brother, "Two hours? All right. But you're sure you'll have the money when I get there?"

"Just do as I say, Suzanne." His hang-up rang in her ear.

FBI Special Agent George Jenkins grinned as the conversation between Sun Ben Cheong and Suzanne Tierney came to an end. He was set up in a small apartment across H Street from the Chinatown office used by Cheong. White take-out containers of cold, half-eaten Chinese food littered a folding table. A small telescope on a tripod was by the curtained window. A ten-inch reel-to-reel tape machine behind Jenkins turned slowly as the wireless tap on Cheong's phone sent the conversation with outstanding clarity to the receiver.

The listening post had been established a month ago once the Bureau, and other federal agencies, had concluded that Cheong was engaged in money laundering. From that point forward, every call made from the office was on tape.

Jenkins turned to the other special agent in the room, Max Johnson, a slender black man who'd heard the conversation through a speaker. "Nice guy, huh, Max? He's got plenty of willing slime-balls to pick up the dirty money, and he recruits his own sister. Class act."

"Family business," Johnson said. "America was built on it."

"Yeah. Well maybe they can get a family group rate at Leavenworth. You hungry? Want me to order up?"

"Sure. If you can find a Chinese soul-food restaurant that delivers. I've eaten my last spring roll."

Off-Broadway drama was not confined to the Arthur Saul School in New York City. In Washington, Seymour Fletcher, director of the Potomac Players, was on the phone pleading with Carl Mayberry, the actor originally scheduled to play the role of Barton Key. Fletcher had received a call from Chip Tierney informing him that due to unfortunate personal circumstances, he would be unable to participate in Tri-S's latest production.

"Carl, I know I was hard on you," Fletcher said. "But I'm a director. It's my job to get the most from my actors and actresses. Frankly, I wouldn't care so much if I didn't think you were the most talented person in the cast."

Mayberry, his brain fuzzy from drinking all night, said, "I know, Sy. But you have to respect my sensibilities. You can't treat me like you treat the others, like some dog. Every actor needs to be handled differently. I don't respond to your anger and yelling."

"I know, I know, and I will be the first to admit that I misjudged how to bring out the best in you.

Mea culpa. Can I do more than admit my inadequacies?"

"I respect that, Sy, but talent isn't something I can turn on and off like a faucet. It needs to be nurtured."

"Of course it does," Fletcher said. "Look, do this thing tomorrow. This show needs you and your insight into the Key character. Don't stick me with this rich, spoiled kid. But let me tell you something else. I may be directing the road company of a big Broadway show when it comes to Washington. I can't say more, but there's a role in that show that was written for you. I mean, like, the playwright knew you in another life when he wrote the part."

"Seriously?"

"I couldn't be more serious. Will you do it?"

"What time?"

34

Detective Eikenberg had left work early and gone to her apartment to shower and to change into something less workaday. She would be working, but maybe more.

It had been important to her from her first day on the force to not succumb to the "uniform" of her work—the drab suits and sensible shoes worn by her female colleagues. Darcy's father had told her to always dress a little better than others at work, no matter what career she pursued. She'd taken his advice. Perhaps she dressed too fancy at times for a detective, she sometimes knew, but that was all right. Better to err on the side of fashion.

She arrived at the rooftop restaurant looking fresh and vivacious, the very words that went through Mac's mind as she came to his window table.

He, on the other hand, did not look fresh and vivacious. He'd been staying up later than usual the past few nights and was tired. The dark beard-line that always appeared at the end of a day was especially pronounced.

"Lovely view," she said. Washington's lights were beginning to be defined against a smudging horizon.

"Drink?" Smith asked.

"Absolutely. Officially I'm off duty." She ordered a vodka-and-tonic. "I must admit, Mac, that I was pleased to receive your call this morning, even happier when you suggested a drink together. Frankly, I'm growing weary of responding to just the official obligations of my life. Nothing but bureaucracy and rules and regulations. Superiors to placate, politicians to appease." She raised her glass, narrowed her eyes, and said, "To a pleasant, *unofficial* evening."

Smith participated listlessly in the ritual; the sentiment of the toast made him uncomfortable. He asked how the investigation was going.

"I thought we were off duty," she said.

"According to the clock? That's union thinking. Civil service."

"You forget I am a civil servant. Salary paid by the taxpayer."

"How's the investigation going?" he repeated, smiling wryly.

"All right. Round one to you. Is that why you suggested we get together? To ask *me* questions? You said you had information *for* me about the Juris case."

"And I do, but I'll get to it in a minute. I

thought you might bring me up to speed. Unofficially, of course."

"Okay. Let's see. Joe Chester."

"The director of the Building Museum."

"Yes. His plaster is cracking. We've kept the pressure on him, knowing it would. No love lost between him and Pauline."

"You think he is a suspect?"

"I think it's an outside possibility. We're going to keep pushing him. I've seen his type, passive but bitter, spill it all when the going gets tough."

Smith thought of Annabel's recent conversation with Chester. Were he the man's attorney, he'd tell the police to either charge him or back off. But he wasn't Chester's attorney, or anyone else's for that matter.

Eikenberg said, "I spent an hour with Chip Tierney this morning."

"And?"

A delicate laugh. "You are amazing, Mackensie Smith. I've been here only a few minutes, and I feel like I'm on the witness stand."

"Which is exactly what I don't want you to feel," he said. "What did Chip have to say?"

"He denies having had an affair with Pauline Juris."

"Does that surprise you?"

"No, but I don't believe him. He's a weak sister. Not much backbone there. Daddy's boy all the way. He also denies that his father had any romantic attachment to Juris. He didn't want to meet me alone. He wanted his fiancée, Terri, to be with us. I vetoed the idea."

"Because he'd be reluctant to discuss in front of her an affair with Pauline."

"Uh-huh. I interviewed her after I left him."

"And, of course, you brought up your suspicion that her fiancé was having an affair with his father's personal assistant."

"You bet I did. I suggested that she might have known about it, which, of course, would give her a motive to kill off her competition."

"Did she? I mean, did she acknowledge that Chip was—"

"No. But I didn't believe her, either."

"That's one of the dangers of being a cop, isn't it? You end up not believing anybody, about anything."

"Not true. I believed you when you said you had information for me." He started to respond, but she shook her head. "I'm in no rush to hear what you have to say, Mac. This is too pleasant to have it ruined by talking business. I like the fact that you and I are not adversaries. I'd like to keep it that way."

"No reason why we should. Become adversaries, that is. Let me get to the reason I called you today."

"Do you have dinner plans?" she asked.

He'd started to reach under the table for the envelopes containing copies of the Pauline Juris letters and family history, and said from that awkward posture, "Yes."

"With Mrs. Smith?" Darcy's grin was mischievous. "What are you doing under there?" she asked.

He returned to an upright position, envelopes in hand. "Yes. My wife and I are having dinner."

"Do you eat out often?"

"Less often than before," Smith responded. "We prefer eating in. I fancy myself a cook, although I suppose my friends are right when they say the secret of my success is keeping it simple and fresh."

"A meat-and-potatoes man. I like that."

"Not so much meat these days. More like tuna or pasta." He placed the envelopes on the table. "I came into possession of—"

"I love a good piece of meat now and then," she said. "I'm partial to filet mignon, although a rare sirloin gets my juices flowing, too."

Smith sat back and fixed her across the table. "I always enjoy talking about food, but the subject is murder."

"I wish you didn't feel that way. I am off duty, Professor. *Very* off duty."

"But I'm not, and really can't stay much longer."

"I'd like another drink. Join me?"

"No, but you go ahead." He ordered her another vodka-and-tonic and continued to nurse his bourbon-and-soda.

"Mac."

"Yes?"

"I don't mean to make you uncomfortable."

"Uncomfortable? I'm not—"

"I think you are, and I can only speculate why."

He came forward again, picked up the top envelope, and opened the clasp.

"I'll be direct with you," she said. "You are—"

He withdrew the sheaf of letters. "These are copies of the letters Wendell Tierney purportedly wrote to Pauline Juris. The infamous love letters."

Her coquettish play was dashed.

"Where did you get them?"

"I refuse to tell you that. You've got a serious leak in your Evidence division. These copies were passed on to an acquaintance of mine, who gave them to me. I'm giving them back to you."

She took the letters and stared at the one on top of the pile. "Damn it!"

Smith opened the second envelope and took out the history. "This is a family history that

Pauline was writing before her death. She'd evidently been working on it for many years."

"What does that have to do with it?"

"A great deal, I think, if you read both the letters and the history with an eye toward comparing them. I believe they were written by the same person."

The expression on Eikenberg's face mirrored her confusion. She started to speak, stopped, looked at the second letter in the pile, then at the cover page of the history. "You say Pauline Juris wrote this history. I accept that. But do I understand that you think she wrote the letters herself. *To* herself?"

"Exactly."

She made another false start, then summed up her feelings with a nervous laugh. "Preposterous."

"That she wrote love letters to herself? Unusual, certainly. But I believe that's what happened."

"She must have been demented."

"Not necessarily. She was madly in love with Wendell Tierney but never enjoyed having her feelings reciprocated. At first, I thought she might have done it in a misguided attempt to create a blackmail scenario. Reveal the letters to Tierney's wife, Marilyn, in the hope it would break up the marriage. But I don't think so. I don't know what the shrinks would call it, but it satisfied a simple need for her. She was providing herself with the very words that she desperately wanted to hear but wasn't about to."

The detective, having regained the composure she'd lost, said, "Who released these letters?"

The staunchly direct Mackensie Smith fudged. "A journalist obtained them and passed them on to the acquaintance I mentioned. Who released them from MPD really isn't my concern—that's your problem. But I do encourage you and your colleagues to read them against the history. I think you'll come to the same conclusion I have. By the way, it looks to me as though the last portion of the history was written on the same typewriter she used to write the letters."

"I must say . . . I didn't expect this when we made a date tonight. Along with all your other attributes, you're capable of delivering big surprises."

He looked at his watch. "Darcy, I really have to go."

Eikenberg returned the material to its envelopes and looked out the window. The ever-darkening city was now studded with the lights of office buildings and the glow of powerful flood-lights that gave the city's famed monuments life after dark. She looked at Smith and said, "Maybe

I do understand a woman writing love letters to herself."

Smith said nothing.

"Will you have dinner with me tonight?"

"I'm afraid I can't, Detective." He scribbled in the air, signaling their waitress to bring the check. "I'm glad to see you," he said. "But maybe having a drink wasn't such a good idea."

"You know, don't you?"

"Know what?"

"How I feel about you. I'm afraid I haven't been very subtle."

The waitress took his American Express card and the check. "Detective Eikenberg, I think there might have been some missed communication between us. If I've done anything to—"

She slowly shook her head, folded her hands on the table, and looked down at them. "No, you haven't done anything—except be Mackensie Smith. I fell in love with you when I was your student. I recently had dinner with Nick, my ex, and he reminded me of how I used to talk about you all the time. Real schoolgirl stuff. Not unusual. Students fall in love with their professors every day. I'm sure I'm not the first to have fallen in love with you. Funny. I sometimes wonder whether that in-your-face crush I had on you contributed to Nick and me breaking up."

"You accused me earlier of being uncomfortable. I am now very uncomfortable. Let's go."

"Can't I at least complete my embarrassing confession?"

"I wouldn't deprive you of that, Darcy." Smith signed his name to the receipt and returned his card to his wallet. "Why don't we forget we ever had this conversation," he said. "Maybe I misled you. I didn't mean to. I don't think I said anything, but maybe my face, my voice, indicated that I find you extremely intelligent, to say nothing of attractive. You were an impressive student, and you're an impressive woman, Detective Eikenberg. But I'm married to another beautiful, bright, and impressive woman. Just that simple."

"Well put, Professor. See? No hearts on my sleeve. Or up them. Shall we go?"

He came around the table and drew out her chair. They walked side by side to the elevators, rode down in silence, and went to the parking lot. She fumbled in her purse for her keys, found them, and he held open the driver's door. They were close. She raised her face and offered him flower-soft lips. The deeply sensuous bouquet of her reached his nostrils. Her large, glistening eyes were, at once, pleading and demanding. "We could be friends," she said softly. "Just talk. I would like that."

As she spoke, she pressed her length against

him and brought her lips to within inches of his. She purred as their mouths met. It began as a tentative kiss, lips lightly touching without breaking shape. Then they pressed harder. No longer tentative.

For Mac, the powerful, compelling sensation of their embrace was tainted by the realization that, like a pilot, he'd reached the point of no return. Cross it and you were committed to continuing on to your destination. No return to home base.

He stepped back. He drew a deep breath.

"Delicious," she said. "We could be good friends."

"I . . . Good night, Darcy."

35 Later That Night

Smith took a detour on the way home, determined to put his mind on other matters. He stopped at the A & B Shellfish Company in Arlington to pick up two live Maine lobsters, cherrystone clams, and a container of red and sweet potatoes with onions. He used a phone booth outside the store to call Annabel and was surprised to reach her machine. He assumed she'd be home by now. A call to the gallery resulted in another recorded message.

He returned to a dark house. No Annabel. No note. No message on his machine from her. He was now worried. This was uncharacteristic of her, of them. They made a ritual of keeping in touch to avoid anxiety. He was about to begin making calls when he heard a key in the front door. "I've been worried about you," he said.

"Sorry, Mac. I know I should have left a message, but time got away from me." She hung up her raincoat and disappeared into the bathroom. They met again in the kitchen. "I bought lobster for dinner," he said.

"Sounds yummy, but I've already eaten. I have to talk to you."

He scowled. "Sounds like something even more serious than lobster."

"It is. Pour me some wine?"

He carried two glasses of a red zinfandel into the study, handed her one, and they sipped. Seated on the love seat, she said, "I've had a provocative day." She recounted her conversation with Joe Chester, told of going to the gallery to train Sally Frasier, getting instead a lesson in and receiving a lesson in radio music programming, and then about her Chinatown tour and lunch with Sue Yoy.

"Sounds busy," he said. "But I have a hunch we haven't come to the good part yet."

"Right." Her face and voice now took on additional animation as she twisted on the couch, placed her hand on his knee, and said, "After Sue and I parted company, I returned to the restaurant. I went back because while I was having lunch with her—she had gone to the ladies' room—I was looking out the window on H Street and saw Sun Ben Cheong come along."

"Sun Ben? Wendell told me he was staying at the compound for a couple of days, depressed."

"He must have changed his plans. Or his mood.

It was him, Mac. No question about that. He appeared, at least to me, to be nervous, kept looking over his shoulder. He stopped in front of a small Chinese take-out place directly across the street from the restaurant I was in, did his swivel-neck routine, and went inside."

Smith sipped his wine.

"Then I saw his twin come up the street and go into the same restaurant."

Smith's eyebrows went up. "Twin?"

"Not a literal twin, but someone who sure looks like him. A little shorter maybe, but the same family. I'd bet my life on that."

"Okay. And then?"

"I went across the street and looked into the restaurant but couldn't see them. Immediately adjacent to the restaurant is the entrance to a small office building. Three floors, I think. The door was open, so I went in and looked at the list of tenants on the wall. Most of the names were in Chinese."

Smith smiled. "Did you learn Chinese before lunch?"

"There was a set of symbols that, for some reason, were familiar."

"From a previous life?"

She slapped his knee. "Stop it. No, I kept staring at it and trying to remember why those symbols looked familiar. Then it dawned on me. I'd taken the photographs with me, the ones you gave me that included the shots of Tony on Wendell's dock. Hold on a minute." She jumped to her feet, went to the kitchen and returned with the package of pictures, went through them, and handed Mac the print. "See? On the racing boat behind Tony."

Smith held up the photograph to better catch the light. "MOR," he said. "I can read that."

She was on her feet again, opened his desk drawer, and returned with a magnifying glass, which he used. "Those Chinese symbols underneath? Is that what you're talking about?"

"Yes."

Smith dropped the photo on his lap and ran an index finger over his upper lip. "Let me see if I follow you so far. Those symbols evidently translate into 'MOR' in English. Your new assistant talked about MOR meaning middle-of-the-road in music programming. And the same Chinese symbols, which evidently mean MOR, were on the tenant board in the lobby of an office building in Chinatown."

"Like I always say, Mac, your mind is a steel trap."

"Don't pick on me, Annabel. Sorry, but I don't see the significance."

"Then allow me to provide it for you," she said pleasantly and not without a certain egoism. "This morning, I went through the vouchers at the museum that Pauline Juris created each time she took money from the special fund. Her handwriting was atrocious, but on more than half of them she'd scribbled *MOR*."

"To indicate where the money had gone?"

"Yes. Who knew? I mean, maybe her jottings on the vouchers indicated companies that had provided services. Contractors. Linen suppliers for the catering operation. No matter. A lot of the missing money, at least according to the vouchers, went to something or someone called MOR."

"To Sun Ben Cheong."

"How else can you read it?"

"No one at the museum ever checked on what this MOR was?"

"No. According to Hazel Best-Mason and Don Farley, the only people who had access to the account were Pauline and Wendell. It started small, petty cash really, but then grew. Farley told me that because Tierney was such a strong force at the museum and raised so much money, nobody was about to challenge him."

"I see," Smith said.

Annabel refilled their glasses. "Well, that's almost all my report. I gave Tony Buffolino a run for his money today, became a real snoop. Even staked out—that is the expression, isn't it?—staked out the building."

Smith couldn't help but smile. "How did you do that? Where did you do that?"

"From the restaurant across the street. I ordered a pot of tea and watched."

"Sure nobody saw you?"

She shook her head. "No, no one saw me."

"And what was the result of your stakeout?"

"Ready for this?"

"I'm not sure, but try me."

"I was tempted to leave but decided to gut it out. After a few hours I stayed for dinner and continued my surveillance. The baby bok choy was excellent. So was the asparagus."

"Skip the vegetables, Annabel."

"I'd paid the tab and was getting ready to leave—I realized how late it had gotten and felt terrible having you come home and not knowing where I was—and I took one last look out the window. Suzanne Tierney."

"She went into the restaurant?"

"No. Into the office building. The restaurant is in the same building. The doors are next to each other. She was carrying a very large duffel bag. It looked heavy."

"What do you think was in it?"

She shrugged. "Beats me. But isn't the connection interesting?"

"Yes, it is. We'll have to give it some additional

thought. You say you've eaten. What am I going to do with two live lobsters?"

"You eat them. I'll just nosh a little. That Chinese food didn't . . . well, you know."

Annabel, whose appetite was voracious but who also possessed an internal engine that burned up food as fast as it was ingested, ate one of the lobsters and a hearty portion of potatoes and onions. They cleaned up and returned to the study. "I had a drink this evening with Darcy Eikenberg," Smith said.

"You did. Why?"

"I called to make an appointment with her to discuss the letters and decided not to do it at headquarters. I ended up in Arlington late this afternoon to touch base with Jerry Malone—he thinks I ought to shift some of my Keogh assets into some livelier investments—and met her at the Key Bridge Marriott."

Annabel's smile was knowing. "Riskier investments, you mean. She must have been thrilled."

"I'm not sure I'd characterize it that way."

"I just mean that she's obviously infatuated with you."

"Oh, maybe once—student-and-professor sort of thing, way back."

"Go on. How did she take the news that you had copies of the letters?"

"Stunned her. Naturally, she wanted to know how I got them. I gave them to her along with the history Pauline had written and suggested she compare them. I told her I was certain Wendell had not written them, and that I was convinced Pauline had."

"And what was the ravishing detective's reaction to that theory?"

"Skepticism at first, a little more open-minded after that. She commented that she could understand a woman frustrated with unrequited love falling into such fantasies."

"Meaning you."

"Yes. It was awkward at best."

"Do you find her attractive? No, strike that. Of course you do. I find her attractive. Were you tempted to follow through?"

"No."

"Not even a little?"

"A little. Not to follow through, as you put it. I did have a fleeting visceral reaction."

"I love it when you talk euphemisms."

"I straightened her out."

"Gently, I hope."

"Gentle but firm."

"Good."

"I kissed her."

"You did?"

"It just happened. Actually, she kissed me. No. We kissed each other. That was it. I thought you'd want to know. She wants to be my friend."

"A kissin' cousin?"

"No more kisses. I have a feeling you understand her."

"Why?"

"Because you're both beautiful women. You know how it is. I remember talking with you about it not long after we met. How beautiful women—and men who are too handsome—aren't always taken seriously. Takes a while for people to get past their looks and recognize they have brains. In your case, a big one."

"In Darcy's case?"

"Also a big brain."

"I love you, Mac."

"And obviously I love you, Annabel."

"You won't kiss her again? Even as friends?"

"No, I won't."

Mac awoke with a start in the middle of the night.

"What's wrong?" Annabel asked.

"A nightmare. I saw that child go over the edge at Great Falls. Only it was me. Falling, spinning, screaming."

She cradled him until his trembling stopped

and his breathing was normal. "Sorry to wake you," he said.

She started to say, "Go back to sleep. It was only a dream." But it hadn't been. He'd seen the child in the water, and she wished there were something she could do to erase that dreadful, haunting vision from his mind. She'd never loved him more than at that moment.

36 The Next Morning—Saturday

The Scarlet Sin Society evidently had a friend in high places. Saturday morning dawned sunny and cool, a perfect day in Lafayette Park for a murder.

The weather had coaxed people to the park far in advance of the noon production. The few permanent, perpetual protestors who called the park their home were joined by hundreds, soon over a thousand, theatergoers, curiosity-seekers, and tourists of all ages. Many carried folding chairs or blankets and staked out the best plots. Individual pieces of turf assured, they strolled the park's seven acres, pausing at the five large statues that dominated the square, some to read the plaques, others to have their pictures taken while striking their own heroic poses.

National Park Service ranger Lloyd Mayes stood proudly next to the statue honoring the Frenchman for whom the park was now named, Marie-Joseph-Paul-Yves-Roch-Gilbert du Motier, marquis de Lafayette, the adopted American son who'd become a Revolutionary War hero, and whose friends and military colleagues called him Gilbert. At Gilbert's feet was a nubile, partially naked young woman who, Mayes had learned in his training sessions, symbolized the fledgling nation of America. One of her delicate arms held aloft a sword. Supposedly, Mayes was taught, she was pleading for Marquis de Lafayette's help. But depending upon the individual tourist group—especially those comprised primarily of young adults whose sensitivities would not be offended—Park Service rangers often remarked on what the young woman was actually saying to Lafayette: "Look, I'll make a deal. You give me back my clothes, and I'll give you back your sword."

Mayes would have preferred to be at his old post on Roosevelt Island, but he'd been transferred to duty in Lafayette Square following the discovery of Pauline Juris's body. Although he hadn't been the one that night to leave open the gate across the pedestrian causeway, a particularly nasty superior had decided that he, too, was culpable. His change in assignment was a form of punishment.

Mayes knew the transfer to be blatantly unfair, but everything and everyone seemed to be unfair to him these days. Marge had packed up and gone home to her mother in Cincinnati. While her departure created a certain peace in his life—at least there was no one to fight with—he was lonely.

The only thing that made him smile occasionally was that she'd gone to Cincinnati instead of Los Angeles, Detroit, or Miami. Cincinnati was a funny word, he thought, almost a funny city, and he would smile. Other than those infrequent moments, these were dark days and long nights for Lloyd Mayes.

By the time Mac and Annabel arrived, the crowd had swelled to justify calling it a throng, perhaps even multitude. A Dixieland band had set up in the center of the park at the foot of the statue of Andrew Jackson, "Old Hickory," for whom the park had originally been named until the dashing marquis de Lafayette upstaged him. Still, his was the most dominant of the statues that defined the center and corners of the park. And his was the only statue of an American hero in the park, the first president ever to be elected by the Democratic party, which, in gratitude, had raised funds in 1853 to create their winner's metal-and-marble tribute.

The Smiths had approached the park from Sixteenth Street, pausing in front of St. John's Episcopal Church at the corner of H, the "Church of the Presidents," where Washington's *Social Register* was synonymous with its list of parishioners. They managed to make their way to a knot of people gathered at the side of a makeshift stage that had been erected for the performance. Behind it a long rented house trailer served the cast.

"Mother Nature's been kind to you," Mac said to Monty Jamison, who stood with Chip Tierney, director Seymour Fletcher, and some diehard Tri-S members.

"Yes, I would say so," Jamison said, shaking Smith's hand and kissing Annabel on the cheek. "Splendid day for a murder." They looked up into a cloudless cobalt sky.

"Excuse me," Jamison said, walking to the trailer. Smith asked Chip, "How are things going?"

The young man slowly shook his head. "Terrible. You know about Sun Ben, of course."

"Of course," Smith said. "Me and the rest of Washington. Is your dad here?"

"No, and you know how upset he must be to miss this. He's secluded himself in his study."

"What about Sun?"

"The same, I guess. I really haven't seen him. I tried to talk to him about it the night he was arrested, but he didn't want to. I guess I can't blame him. This family has been rocked by one scandal after another. I just wish it would end."

Smith remembered that Chip was to play a role in the production and asked if he was ready to go on.

"God, no," Chip replied. "I told Sy Fletcher there was no way I could go through with this, considering what's happened at home. He got the original actor to come back."

Sam and Marie Tankloff joined them. "Amazing, the number of people who show up for these productions," Sam said. "Like the garage sales Marie loves to run. They come out of the woodwork, descend in hordes, and usually hours before it's supposed to start." Marie laughed and playfully punched her husband's arm. She punched his arm often in appreciation of things he said, or did.

Annabel and Marie had their own chat as Tankloff took Mac aside. "Have you spoken to Wendell?" Sam asked.

"Not since yesterday morning."

"I'm concerned about him, Mac. You know Wendell. Depression isn't in his vocabulary. But I swung by there this morning. At first, he wouldn't see me. When he decided he would, I was faced with an utterly dejected and demoralized man. This thing with Sun Ben has really shaken him. I was there yesterday afternoon when they had quite a confrontation. Frankly, if I didn't know how strong Wendell was, I'd worry about him taking his own life."

"Frightening," Smith said. "Do you think he's capable of it?"

Tankloff shrugged. "Who ever knows about those things? Someone on Marie's side of the family took her life a few years ago. No one thought she knew how to spell suicide, but she did it."

"Any suggestions?" Smith asked.

"No. I wish Wendell had come today. I think it would have done him some good, taken his mind off his troubles. You know how important Tri-S has always been to him."

"Do you think he'll attend the dinner tonight?"

"I hope so. I asked him this morning, but he was noncommittal. Maybe a call from you would push him in that direction."

"I'll call as soon as I get home."

The trailer was a frenzy of activity. Sy Fletcher, Monty Jamison, and the cast and crew were making last-minute preparations before taking the stage. Suzanne Tierney, who would play the role of Congressman Dan Sickles's indiscreet, adulterous wife, Teresa Bagioli Sickles, had arrived late, which wasn't unusual for her. It was a chronic bad habit that upset most people but had not seemed to bother Fletcher. Until this day. To the surprise of others in the trailer, he lambasted her, saying, "Your lack of responsibility matches your lack of talent."

Equally surprising was Suzanne's calm acceptance. She smiled and said pleasantly, "Coming from you, Sy, I take that as a compliment." And she walked away, humming.

"Is the president here?" someone asked.

"No, but I heard the secretary of agriculture is in the audience." Groans.

"Could I please have your attention," Fletcher asked. "We go on in a few minutes." Everyone in the trailer continued to talk. "Damn it!" Fletcher shouted. The chatter trailed off. Before addressing the cast, Fletcher turned to Monty Jamison. "Are you ready?" he asked.

The roly-poly professor went through his throat-clearing routine. "Yes, Sy. Ready, willing, and able." Usually, Wendell Tierney was the master of ceremonies at these events, but in his absence, Jamison had been pressed into service. Little pressing was needed. He left the trailer to address the crowd.

Fletcher stood on his tiptoes and held his hands in the air. "Ladies and gentlemen, may I please have your attention."

The trailer door opened, and Chip Tierney entered, followed by Sam Tankloff. "I wish you were still playing the part," a young female cast member whispered to Chip as he stood next to her. Her infatuation with him hadn't been a secret during rehearsals.

"Wardrobe, wardrobe," an actor shouted. "This damn button just popped on my cutaway coat."

Fletcher clapped his hands. "Listen up now," he said. "Is everyone's energy level high? Your energy must be at its peak and transmitted to every individual in the audience if we're—"

Tankloff threaded his way through the group and went to a small bedroom at the far end of the trailer that housed costumes and some props. The woman in charge of wardrobe had responded to the actor's cry for last-minute button surgery, leaving the prop girl alone in the room. "Everything ready?" Tankloff asked pleasantly.

"I think so," the girl said. "Excuse me." She left to deliver the handkerchief to Carl Mayberry he would use to signal Teresa Sickles that they were due to rendezvous. When she returned a few minutes later, the prop room was empty. Tankloff had gone back outside to join his wife, Mac and Annabel, and a dozen others.

Monty Jamison stepped up onto the outdoor stage, went to the microphone, coughed, and said, "Good day, ladies and gentlemen. Welcome to murder most foul from yesteryear."

"Sorry to hear about your brother," the young actress said to Chip.

"What? Oh, yes, thank you. All a mistake, I think."

"I hope so. I tried to talk to him before, but he didn't seem in the mood for conversation. I suppose I can't blame him."

"Sun? He was here?"

"Yes. I was one of the first ones to arrive. Ran

into him here. But he didn't want to, like, talk, you know?"

"He'll be fine. Everything will be fine."

Jamison explained to the crowd the circumstances that had led to the February 1859 murder. He introduced the major characters, each coming onstage as a thumbnail sketch of their background and role in the drama was presented. The opening scene, Jamison explained, was set in a boardinghouse run by a gentleman named Lorenzo Da Ponte, a ninety-year-old Catholic priest who'd been a librettist for Mozart and close personal friend of the legendary Casanova and, besides running Washington's most eclectic boardinghouse, managed a grocery store. The occasion was a party to celebrate the engagement of New York Tammany Hall congressman Dan Sickles to fifteen-year-old Teresa Bagioli. At the party was an assortment of friends and well-wishers, including James "Old Buck" Buchanan, future president of the United States, who at the time was ambassador to the Court of St. James. In a few days he would designate his close friend Dan Sickles to be his secretary of legation. Although Philip Barton Key, district attorney of the District of Columbia and son of Francis Scott Key, author of "The Star-Spangled Banner," had not yet become a friend of the couple, scriptwriter Madelon St. Cere had taken the liberty of hastening their friendship in the interest of introducing the character early on and had placed him at the party.

Jamison ended his introduction by announcing that Tri-S membership information and applications were available at selected locations throughout the park. "Next month's meeting has been especially planned for newcomers. We shall present an overview of murder in fiction, honoring, of course, the great Edgar Allan Poe and his analytical approach to discovering why that poor young girl was stuffed up a chimney in 'The Murders in the Rue Morgue.' But we'll also be going back in time much farther than that, to the Apocrypha and its murderous tales solved by none other than the prophet Daniel himself. In one—"

"Psssst!" Seymour Fletcher hissed from the side of the stage. He pointed to his watch.

"Yes, yes," Jamison said. "We must forge ahead. Without further adieu—let the play begin!"

A dozen scenes leading up to the shooting of Barton Key by Congressman Dan Sickles were acted out. Sickles's seduction of the young Teresa was tastefully presented, avoiding its more sordid aspects and stressing the role played by Lorenzo Da Ponte, who was actually Teresa's adoptive grandfather and who, according to the script, had nurtured the premarital affair. And there was a pivotal scene in London between Sickles and Buchanan that preceded Buchanan's election to the White House.

Once Buchanan became president, Sickles's place in Washington political and social circles was assured. While he kept himself busy, including making frequent visits to area brothels, his close friend Barton Key became Teresa's "official" escort to charity events and other social gatherings. They soon became lovers, frequently having their clandestine grapplings in the Congressional Cemetery on the tranquil, rolling banks of the Anacostia River.

But, as so often happens with such affairs, things began to unravel for the unfaithful Teresa and the lecherous Key, who once bragged that given thirty-six hours with any woman, he would have her doing his bidding. A young man named Beekman, who worked for Congressman Sickles and who'd become a close family friend, fell in love with Teresa. He got wind of the affair she was having with Key and took it upon himself to follow them to their graveside assignations. He reported his findings to another friend in government, who passed it on to yet another individual, who, predictably, made sure that Sickles knew. Confronted by Sickles, Key vehemently denied everything, which seemed to satisfy his suspicious friend.

Eventually, Key and Teresa decided to move their affair indoors. With shocking audacity and mind-boggling stupidity, Key rented a small brick house on Fifteenth Street, close to Vermont Avenue, but two blocks from Sickles's home. There, the lovers met with increasing frequency, much to the amusement of their working-class neighbors, who quickly understood the purpose to which the house was being put and the identity of the participants.

One day, Sickles received an anonymous note informing him of his wife's infidelity. The note went into considerable detail, including the fact that Key would signal to Teresa in her bedroom window that he was heading for their love nest by standing in Lafayette Square and waving a white handkerchief at her. Teresa would then follow.

Sickles hired people to confirm the rumor and soon knew the truth about his wife. She confessed to him—in writing. Sickles convened a meeting of his closest friends to discuss the situation. Should he challenge Key to a duel to maintain his honor? That was a serious possibility until, during the meeting, Sickles went to his window. Below, on the street, in broad daylight, was his friend Barton Key, waving a handkerchief at the upstairs windows.

Simultaneously, Sickles's greyhound, Dandy, ran across the street and licked Key's hand.

"Scoundrel," Sickles snarled. Even his dog was betraying him. He told one of his friends, Sam Butterworth, to go outside and detain Key while he fetched his pistol.

The actor playing Butterworth, Clarence, a tall, slender young man with a neatly trimmed black mustache, approached the Philip Barton Key character on stage. " 'Morning, Philip," he said. "Beautiful day for February."

Key, who was about to head for the rented house, replaced the handkerchief in his breast pocket and exchanged banalities with Butterworth as a dozen extras sauntered by. Some carried parasols; two female cast members dressed in period costumes held the hands of small children. But Key noticed that while Butterworth was friendly, he seemed nervous, kept looking over his shoulder. He was about to comment on his behavior when Dan Sickles, played by Stuart Gelb, approached, a pistol in his right hand. Butterworth backed away.

"You bastard!" Sickles said to Key, his voice matching the threat in his hand.

Key raised his hands in feeble defense. "Don't, Dan," he said. "Don't shoot me!" He slipped his hand beneath his vest.

The revolver's report violated the day's tranquillity. Key grasped at his shoulder. "Murder," he said, lunging at his attacker.

The strolling extras stopped, stared, and gasped. They braced like mannequins, mouths and eyes opened wide. Key pulled a small pair of opera glasses from a vest pocket and threw them at Sickles. They bounced off his chest.

Key slowly backed away, his hands again raised as though shields against another bullet. "Don't murder me," he said. "Please don't murder me."

Another shot. Key's hand went to his groin. When the real murder had taken place in 1859, the second bullet had struck Key just below his groin, passed through his thigh, and exited where his right buttock joined his leg.

The look on Carl Mayberry's face was more bewilderment than pain. "I'm shot," he gasped. In an attempt to stay erect, he wrapped his arms around a tree that was nailed to the stage floor. But as his thigh and groin melted into a wet red stain, thanks to vials of raspberry juice concealed there, his body melted, too.

Sickles stood over him. Key propped himself up on an elbow. "Murder, murder," he repeated.

Sickles held the gun inches from Key's head and pulled the trigger. The weapon misfired with a dull, metallic *thunk*. Sickles recocked the gun, put it this time to Key's ribs, and fired. Key twisted into his death spiral. Sickles again held the revolver to Key's head. Another misfire. No matter. You can only die once.

"Is he dead yet? Is the bastard dead?" Sickles asked, now facing the large audience in the park. He smiled, calmly placed the hot revolver in his pocket, and walked offstage to thunderous applause.

37 That Same Afternoon

"It should have ended with the murder," Mac Smith said gruffly as he and Annabel walked to their home in Foggy Bottom following the performance.

"I know," Annabel said. She started to giggle. "That trial scene was torture. And the reverend playing Buck Buchanan—I thought he was going to burst into a sermon any minute."

"Well, as you say, it's all for a good cause. Shame Wendell wasn't there. He might have enjoyed it, although murder is not an entertaining subject in his life these days. It went off quite well, and the crowd certainly was large enough."

Rufus greeted them as they came through the door, his powerful tail beating a staccato rhythm against the foyer wall. "I'll walk him," Smith said.

"Aren't you going to call Wendell? You told Sam you would."

"A matter of priorities," Smith said, fetching the leash from the kitchen. "Rufus has to be walked to go to the bathroom. Wendell doesn't."

Annabel busied herself in the kitchen while Mac was gone. She realized they hadn't checked their answering machines and went to the study where they sat side by side. She pressed Play on hers. There was only one message: *"Be careful!"* She played it again, and a third time.

"I'm back," Mac shouted from the hallway.

"Mac, please come here." She played the message for him. "Recognize that voice?" she asked.

"No, but it's hard to identify a voice based upon two words. Play it again."

Back in the kitchen, Annabel said, "I have to admit a certain preconceived notion, if not outright prejudice."

"What do you mean?"

"I keep trying to detect a hint of Asiatic in that voice. Maybe Sun Ben did see me playing Sam Spade and isn't happy I know about his MOR company, whatever that might be. I keep thinking about his lookalike and Suzanne joining them. What do you make of it?"

"I don't, but let's see what we have here. Based upon your observations: It appears that Pauline Juris was skimming money from the museum's special fund and passing it on to Sun Ben, perhaps through some company like this MOR entity. Maybe he has a relative from Hong Kong who's come here to visit him. Then there are the charges of financial crime. He obviously had some sort of secret account in the Caymans, which doesn't necessarily mean the money in it was illegally obtained." Smith frowned. "But, as we all know, offshore accounts are often used to launder dirty money from the sale of drugs, the Mafia, whatever. It's all interesting speculation, but that's all it is. Speculation.

"The bigger question is how this might relate to Pauline's murder. We know she purchased land just before buying the parcel from her ex-husband. The strategic combination of the two tracts is evidently valuable because Wendell is planning to go in there with a major development."

"Fair to assume, isn't it, that she knew how valuable the land would be before grabbing it up?"

"Sure. My question is, if she managed to steal enough from the museum—what did you say it amounted to, a hundred and eighty thousand?— to buy the land, why involve Sun Ben? She didn't need him."

"Or maybe she did. Maybe the land cost a lot more than was available through the museum fund."

"If she bought the land cheap from her former husband knowing its true worth, he'd be pretty upset," Mac said.

"Mad enough to kill."

"Could be. But he wasn't the only person who might have been upset with Pauline. If I'm wrong about the letters and Wendell did write them,

Pauline could well have threatened blackmail.
There's Chip Tierney, too. Was *he* having an affair with her? And how about Suzanne? Tony says
she's totally alienated from her father and accused
him of a relationship with Pauline. As I said
before, all speculation. The list could include all
sorts of people with whom she came into contact,
businesspeople unhappy with her, a secret lover,
and Sun Ben. If she was funneling stolen museum
money to him, there might have been a web of
financial dealings that went sour. As many potential suspects as there are motives. As far as that
message on your machine goes, I'm going to dub
a copy and file it away. There's probably nothing
to worry about, but let's stay on our toes. I'll call
Wendell and see if he's planning to attend tonight.
I told Sam I'd try to persuade him, but I'm not
sure I want to do that. He's probably better off
avoiding the social scene for a while."

Annabel asked, "Is he coming?" when Mac returned to the kitchen.

"No. I suggested it might do him good to get
out. Frankly, I'd like to skip it, too."

"I know." She finished polishing the second of
two silver candleholders. "We don't have to stay
late," she said, drying her hands. "Unless, of
course, you take a notion to dance after dinner."

"Which I just might do," he said, wrapping his
arms around her from behind. "I'm ready for a

. . . what do they call it these days, a meaningful relationship? And a vacation."

She turned and kissed him. "Let's do it. A real vacation. We'd talked about going to Bermuda, but maybe you should come with me to San Francisco. The actual conference is only two days. We can extend the stay and hang out, drive up to redwood country, watch the fog roll in over the Golden Gate from the Top of the Mark, maybe even spend a few days in Carmel, or the Napa."

"Sounds good to me. Call your travel agent and tell her to make it *two* tickets."

38 That Night

Until the Scarlet Sin Society launched itself into the mainstream of Washington's social whirl, the city supported three major fund-raising annual balls. One was to benefit the Opera Society, another to raise funds for the Corcoran Museum, and, perhaps the most lavish of all, the yearly gala to benefit the National Symphony Orchestra. The problem with adding a fourth high-powered event was finding enough ladies committed to such an undertaking (and with enough money to indulge that commitment). There were always those highly visible women whose lives revolved around fund-raising and who could be counted on to lend their names, zeal, and organizational talent to worthy events. But mounting a successful fund-raiser demanded dozens of such dedicated women. There simply wasn't an abundance of them anymore, not with so many having returned to the workplace, whether for money or to be politically correct by having forged a career away from the home.

When Wendell Tierney had suggested mounting another major yearly fund-raising extravaganza, his close friends counseled him to scale down his aspirations. But big had always been beautiful for Tierney, and he set out to enlist the services of the city's leading "ladies of the balls," as they are known in Washington, D.C. "The reason they'll work hard for Tri-S is that it's different," he often said. "Arias, art, and overtures are fine, but murder is so much more fun."

He proved himself right. Not only did Washington's movers and shakers find Tri-S to be "delightfully different," the charities that benefited from its yearly production and dinner-dance jogged the civic conscience of those involved. Opera societies, orchestras, and museums certainly needed money. But no one in them was likely to miss a meal. Inner-city meal programs, drug-rehab centers, ghetto youth centers, and senior-citizen outreach projects benefited directly from Tri-S's extravaganzas. Those whose lives were Mozart, Puccini, and Picasso could now say they had touched the city's underbelly and fed it. It made them feel good, which, as Ayn Rand espoused, made the lives of others a little better. Productive self-interest. A good deal for all.

The annual production and dinner-dance had been a success from the outset. This year's event saw an increasing number of the rich or mighty or both seeking tickets. More than six hundred Washington couples, along with well-heeled fun-seekers from other cities, paid seven hundred dollars to attend a night of cocktails, exotic food, and plenty of dancing to Washington's premier society orchestra led by Gene Donati. Hundreds of others had taken expensive ads in the ball's journal and had donated an impressive array of door prizes, including an all-expense-paid week at the Ritz in Paris, the use of a Rolls-Royce convertible for a year, and a number of other, less glamorous but not necessarily less expensive favors.

The British embassy had been persuaded to co-sponsor the affair to the tune of eight thousand and provided a boxed set of six Agatha Christie murder mysteries as a favor for each guest. In addition, the embassy would host two intimate parties over the weekend for individuals who donated fifteen thousand dollars in return for VIP treatment. These favored few, by virtue of their generosity, joined what Tierney called the Cozy Club, in honor of that brand of genteel murder mystery.

An eight-piece contingent from the larger Donati orchestra played during cocktails as the guests poured out of their limousines in front of the National Building Museum and made their entrances.

Monty Jamison, resplendent in a tuxedo that was as natty as his office was tatty, held court next to one of the eight soaring Corinthian columns that dominated the Great Hall. A dozen couples surrounded him. He was in a particularly jovial mood, as was usually the case when he'd captured the attention, and ears, of people interested in the historical tidbits he dispensed. He raised his voice above the increasing noise of cocktail blather-skate coming from every corner of the huge room to announce, "We may be standing next to proof that the assassination of Honest Abe Lincoln in-volved considerably more than historians would have us believe. President Lincoln's son Robert was secretary of war when his father was slain in Ford's Theater. That was the same period when this magnificent building was being erected under the watchful, albeit irrational, supervision of Quartermaster Montgomery Meigs.

"One of young Lincoln's many responsibilities as secretary of war was to approve Meigs's plans for this, the Pension Building. It has never been proved, but there is considerable—and I might add credible—speculation that Robert Lincoln came into possession of many documents sup-porting the wider conspiracy theory. Rather than release them to a worried, jittery nation, he chose to give them to Meigs to hide in one of these columns for posterity."

Jamison smugly surveyed the faces around him.

"Any proof of that?" a literal-minded Wash-ington attorney asked.

Jamison laughed, concealing his annoyance at the question. "No, not any more than proof that men on transparent horses canter these halls at night, or that the footless ghost whose eyes are empty sockets stalks the corridors. But that particular ghost sent one of the building's night watchmen to an asylum after a midnight confrontation in this very room."

There was laughter as husbands and wives gently nudged their spouses in pursuit of other conversation.

Mac and Annabel were late arrivals, having had trouble commandeering a cab in front of the Kennedy Center. Annabel always enjoyed attending functions for which Mac had to don black tie. He looked especially handsome in it, she thought, and was quick to tell him so.

As for the ravishing redheaded creature who was his wife, he was always proud to have her on his arm, but she was especially stunning in a Cerruti *terre-verte* evening gown purchased especially for the evening from Saks-Jandel in Chevy Chase.

They'd no sooner presented their tickets to the women at the desk and had stepped into the Great Hall when Joline Lazzaras, wife of the area's preeminent plastic surgeon, and a leading lady of Washington society, took Mac by the arm. She said to Annabel, "You won't mind if I take your husband for a spin, will you, Annabel? If I don't do it now, the line will be too long later in the evening." Annabel smiled at the mixed emotions written on her husband's face—I mustn't be rude, but do something to save me.

Annabel was quickly surrounded. Because she was tall, she was able to see over most heads and watched her husband valiantly keep pace to the band's spirited version of "Just in Time." She spotted Tony and his wife, Alicia. Tierney always invited an assortment of people outside the society's social realm; it amused him to mix but not match. The Buffolinos were camped in front of one of many long tables which bloomed with hors d'oeuvres. One table featured massive ice sculptures of Sherlock Holmes and Dr. Watson, each with their arms bowed in front to cradle sizable silver bowls heaped with cooked shrimp. Although dozens of waiters and waitresses passed finger food among the guests, Tony obviously preferred a do-it-yourself approach.

Annabel plucked a profiterole of duck-liver mousse from a waiter's tray. A waitress carrying glasses of champagne passed by, and Annabel relieved her of a glass. (Ever since the Great Hall had been carpeted, red wine was prohibited in the building.) She looked for Mac again and saw him chatting with Joline and her husband, whose tummy tucks were considered the best in town. He disengaged from them and headed for the closest bar. Annabel smiled.

When he returned, he said, "I just talked to Tony. He looks lost. I should have thought to ask Wendell to put them at our table."

Annabel laughed. "Tony always manages."

"I wouldn't mind getting lost myself."

As he said it, Chip Tierney approached from behind and tapped his shoulder. Mac turned. "Good evening, Chip."

"Hello, Mrs. Smith," Chip said. He leaned closer to Mac's ear and said, "Would you mind coming with me for a few minutes? Dad would like to speak with you."

"He's here?" To Annabel: "You don't mind, do you?"

"As long as he isn't stealing you for a dance," she said. "No. You got your wish." She answered his quizzical expression: "To get lost."

"Annabel, how wonderful to see you," the wife of the British ambassador said. Annabel was happy to see her. She'd been the one who'd introduced Annabel to Mac at an embassy party. "Enjoying yourself?"

"Yes. Very much." She caught a fleeting glimpse of the back of her husband's head before he disappeared behind a Corinthian column.

"Dance?" a regular customer of the gallery asked.

"Love to," Annabel said, suddenly remembering he was fond of dipping. "Where or When" came from the bandstand at the same tempo at which every other song seemed to be played. Annabel was spun around and weathered her first dip of the evening.

Smith assumed Chip was going to lead him to another area of the Great Hall. Instead, the young Tierney started up the stairs at the building's west end. Smith was about to follow when he heard someone call his name. He turned. "Darcy," he said.

"Professor Smith," she replied. "Surprised to see me?"

"Yes."

"Mr. Tierney is a generous man. He invited the commissioner and some of the detectives who've addressed his Scarlet Sin Society over the years. I imagine my invitation represents a more pragmatic decision." She smiled.

Smith glanced at the stairs where Chip Tierney waited. "With you in a minute," he said. He turned to Eikenberg and said, "Well, enjoy yourself. Wendell always throws a good party."

"Is your dance card full?" she asked.

"Afraid so. I've danced once. That exceeds my limit."

"I haven't seen Mr. Tierney. He's here, isn't he?"

"If so, I haven't seen him, either."

"Nice to see you again, Mac. I came with my former husband, Nick."

"That sounds encouraging."

"Not at all. But he's the best dancer I know. Never goes over his limit."

Smith and Chip reached the first balcony. Chip started up to the second. "Where's your father?" Smith asked.

"Fourth level."

"As far away from the festivities as possible?"

"Something like that. He could have used any of the museum offices, but he preferred the one Tierney Development rents up there. Kind of a private place for Dad to get away and think. You're less likely to be interrupted." What could such interruptions be? Smith wondered.

He'd been on the fourth level only once before, visiting a government attorney whose office was there. Because the building was maintained as a partnership between the General Accounting Office and the museum board (the government maintained it and allowed the museum to function rent-free; all other expenses were covered through fund-raising activities), federal agencies had first dibs on office space on the third and fourth levels. Obviously, with Tierney's clout at the museum, he hadn't had any problem becoming one of the few private tenants. The fourth balcony, unlike the lower three, was nothing more than a five-feet-wide wrought-iron platform with an ornate wrought-iron railing that had been installed as a safety precaution and painted gold.

As they continued to climb, the bouncy music, happy voices, and clinking glassware faded into a surrealistic single sound. When they reached that fourth level, Smith followed Chip to a large office located in the northeast corner. Smith paused and looked down on twelve hundred reveling guests. The band was playing a mambo.

He saw through the glass door that Tierney was seated at a desk, a lamp with a green shade casting a small lagoon of pale yellow light on the desk. Chip opened the door, and Smith entered, expecting the young man to follow. Instead, Chip closed the door and was gone.

"Good party going on downstairs, Wendell," Smith said. "You ought to be there."

Tierney was costumed for a party, in his tux and tan. But his actions were uncharacteristically subdued, even somber. His customary exuberance had abandoned him. He said quietly, "Sorry to pull you away from the good times."

"Not a problem. Chip said you wanted to see me."

"Yes. Please." He gestured to a mellow brown

leather chair with chrome arms. "What's happened over the past month has had a profound effect on me, Mac. They say that young people don't have a sense of mortality, that they forge ahead assuming they'll be alive and healthy for eternity. I guess I've always been a kid, because I've felt that way right up until Pauline's murder. And now Sun Ben's troubles have really kicked the skids out from under me."

"That's to be expected," Smith said.

"We are betrayed by what is false within."

"Shakespeare?"

"I don't know. Somebody. I just remember that phrase from someplace. I'm not a well-read man. No time. I set my sights on making a million when I was very young and never took my eye off that prize . . . and more. You know what that can mean."

"Everyone needs a goal in life, Wendell."

"True. But some goals are harder to attain than others. I suppose your goal was to become the best damn lawyer in Washington."

"No. I decided to become a lawyer. My *goal* was to have a happy life."

Tierney maintained his position at the desk, hands folded in front of him, arms resting on the surface. He swiveled in his chair so that he now faced Smith, the lamp's light illuminating only one side of his face and leaving the other masked in gloom. "You make my point," he said. "I don't suppose you've had to hurt a lot of people to achieve your goal."

"I hope not, but maybe I have. If so, it was never intentional."

"I wish I could say the same. But you don't build what I've built without stepping on people. Bodies buried along the way. Lives broken. Too much sadness and sorrow left in your wake."

Smith said nothing.

Tierney continued. "It's easy to rationalize, isn't it? Especially with a family. As long as I provided all the creature comforts, all the things money could buy, I considered myself a good husband and father."

Smith shifted in his chair. Was this why Tierney had asked to see him, to use him as a sounding board to clear his conscience? As always, he was willing to listen but hoped it would end soon. He was never comfortable playing priest without benefit of collar. He thought of Annabel in her green gown.

"I was always confident that I could handle anything, Mac. I could always fix any problem my family and business had. The hassles Marilyn and I have been having aren't indicative of our entire marriage. It was good in the beginning, good until a couple of years ago. I don't know what went wrong. She changed, I guess." He expelled a half-hearted chuckle. "Lord knows I didn't change. Maybe I should have. But I couldn't. You don't ride the fast track all your life and then blithely and suddenly decide to get off."

Smith thought of his own decision to leave his pressure-cooker law practice for the sedate life of a professor. He considered mentioning it, but this was Tierney's speech.

"I hope you don't mind my venting like this, Mac. You're the only person in this world I've opened up to. I'm not what you'd call an intro-spective man. I've never been to a shrink and don't spill my guts to clergy. The last time I went to church was when I bid on a big renovation. Once I got the job, I gave a healthy donation and never set foot inside again, at least not on Sun-days.

"No, I don't talk to anyone about what's going on inside me, which, I'm told, is unhealthy. Let it all hang out, they say. Good for the soul. Maybe they're right, but I haven't noticed any change in my soul over the last few minutes."

Smith wanted to bring the conversation—the monologue—to a conclusion. "Wendell, you've been under tremendous pressure since Pauline's murder. I don't know much about the charge against Sun Ben, but that has to weigh heavily, too. I'd like to be of help, but I really don't see where—"

"I know, I know. You want to get back to that lovely wife of yours, do a little jig on the floor, enjoy the food you paid through the nose for. But give me another minute, please. Just another minute.

"All the talk about Pauline and me having an affair was garbage. Yes, she was in love with me and let me know it. We got close to climbing into the sack a few times, but I always backed away." He waved his hand in the air. "Yeah, I was the one who backed off. Don't get me wrong. I'm no moralist, no angel when it comes to other women. But I didn't follow through with Pauline because I knew what it was she really wanted."

"Which was?"

"Power. And money. She had power by virtue of being my right hand, and she carried it off well. She was an incredibly efficient person. I don't think I would have achieved what I have without her. As far as money was concerned, I run a tight ship. Now and then I'd pass on some insider information on a stock. She'd buy a few shares and make a buck. When I decided to go into West Virginia with a major mall project, I learned that she and her ex-husband owned property smack-dab in the middle of the tract. I suggested she buy him out—hell, the property couldn't have meant anything to him in its present state, just pine trees and scrub oak. And I tipped her to an adjacent parcel that would be part of the complex. I told her that if she grabbed the piece she owned with Lucas and bought that other parcel, we'd buy the whole thing back from her at ten times what she'd paid."

"And she took your advice."

"Sure. Only she didn't live long enough to enjoy it."

Smith thought of Dr. Lucas Wharton. Was Tierney pointing the finger at him?

Instead, he shifted to talk about Sun Ben and his legal problems. "He's a million-dollar loser at the tables, Mac. More. Did you know that? I assume that's why he did what he did."

He was admitting Cheong's guilt.

Tierney leaned forward and moved the chair closer to Smith. Their knees almost touched. He said, the oblique light distorting his handsome features, "You've been straight with me, Mac. You've been there whenever I called. I know you haven't asked for this, but I'm afraid you're going to have to accept it."

Smith's brow furrowed. "Accept what?" he asked.

"Knowing who killed Pauline Juris."

Had Suzanne Tierney not been a member of the cast, she would have avoided the Saturday-night extravaganza. But she was there, director Seymour Fletcher her escort. Since rebellion did not take the form of staying away, she accomplished it with dress—a pink sweatshirt she'd studded with rhinestones using a kit she'd ordered after watching television, long blue denim skirt, and hoop earrings. She'd sprinkled metallic confetti in her hair, which picked up the light and turned her head into a walking Fourth of July. Fletcher wore a tux shirt and black bow tie beneath a short purple waiter's jacket, black trousers, and black sneakers. They gravitated to the table where Tony and Alicia Buffolino stood. The pile of shrimp in Sherlock Holmes's icy arms was almost gone, but it would not take a Holmes to solve the mystery of where it had disappeared.

"Hello, Suzanne," Buffolino said.

"Oh, hello, Mr. Buffolino." She said to Fletcher, "This is Tony. He's my father's bodyguard."

Buffolino shook Fletcher's hand. "I'm not his bodyguard. Bodyguards guard the person. I provide all-over security."

Fletcher was not much interested in what Buffolino had to say and showed it. He looked past him to where Hazel Best-Mason and her husband, Hal, Washington's planning commissioner, were coming off the dance floor. "Mr. and Mrs. Shakedown," Fletcher said.

Buffolino, whose immediate dislike of Fletcher

was as strong as his love for shrimp, looked at the couple to whom Fletcher referred. "Huh?"

Fletcher said to Suzanne, "A couple of typical D.C. whores. I applied for a license to operate a theater in vacant space off Dupont Circle. The application went to Mason, but it was his wife who called me. She said the request would be considered provided I donated a portion of the proceeds to what she called a general Dupont Circle development fund." He sneered. "General development fund. Translation, kickback. Pay-off."

Suzanne and Seymour's presence was enough to drive Tony and Alicia from the shrimp in search of more palatable company. The problem was that they knew so few people. "Dance?" Tony asked.

"Love to," said Alicia, taking his hand. The band played a slow fox-trot version of "Our Love Is Here to Stay," which was just Tony's speed. He pulled Alicia close, extended his left and her right arm high into the air, and shuffled to the beat, spinning her in an occasional embellishing circle.

Annabel and a new dancing partner, a George-town antique dealer who specialized in Carolean furniture and who was one of her favorite friends, maneuvered close to the investigator and his wife. The two couples stopped dancing. "Annabel,

great to see you," Buffolino said. "You look terrific."

"And I might say the same about you both.
That's a lovely dress, Alicia."

"Thank you, Annabel."

"Where's Mac?" Tony asked.

"That's exactly what I'm wondering. Have you
seen him? He went off to see Wendell Tierney."

"Tierney's here?" Buffolino said. "Last I heard,
which was this afternoon, he wasn't going to
make it."

"I haven't seen him," said Annabel, "but Chip
told Mac that his father wanted to speak with
him."

The orchestra shifted from the safe fox-trot
medley to rock 'n' roll. "That leaves me out,"
Buffolino said. Annabel started to agree, but her
partner began gyrating. "Down and dirty," he
said to Annabel. She laughed and began to match
his movements. "If you see Mac, tell him I'm the
captive of a dancing fool," she said. Buffolino
laughed and led Alicia from the floor.

"Enough," Annabel said minutes later after the
band had segued into another rock tune. Her
partner returned her to the friends with whom
she'd been talking before being hijacked as a
dancing partner. Others had joined the group by
this time, including, to Annabel's surprise, Detec-

tive Darcy Eikenberg, who stood next to D.C.'s police chief.

"Good evening, Mrs. Smith," Eikenberg said. She introduced the commissioner, whom Annabel had met before. "Has anyone seen my husband?" Annabel asked.

A sly smile crossed Eikenberg's lips. "I have," she said.

"Good," said Annabel. "Where is he?"

"I don't know, but last time I saw him, he was heading up the stairs over there. He was with Wendell Tierney's son."

"Upstairs? Is there a party going on up there, too?"

"Not that I'm aware of," said Eikenberg.

"Excuse me," Annabel said. She headed toward the staircase at the western end of the museum.

"Please find your tables," the chairwoman of the event announced from the microphone. "Dinner is about to be served, and we are in for a scrumptious treat."

Annabel's progress was impeded by the crowd. But she eventually reached the perimeter of the Great Hall and stood at the foot of the broad brick staircase. Behind was a festival of lights, music, and cheerful chatter. In front of her and above were silence and furtive darkness. She debated going farther. Mac would not have stayed this long unless there was a pressing need, and she didn't want to barge in on the middle of an important conversation. On the other hand, she decided he might need rescuing. Once Tierney had your attention, he was a master at keeping it, especially with someone like Mac, who was, among other things, a patient listener.

She was about to turn, rejoin the party, and find her table. Surely, Mac would have heard the announcement that dinner was being served and would break away from Tierney. But her feet took a contrary position, and she started up the stairs.

When she reached the first balcony, she wasn't sure what to do. It ringed the Great Hall, as did the balconies above it. She went to the railing, held a hand over her eyes to shield them from the party lights downstairs, and scanned the three upper balconies. As far as she could tell, there were no lights on in any of the exhibit rooms and offices. All was dark. But from the northeast corner of the fourth level, she saw a faint light. Is that where Mac had gone? she wondered. Why all the way up there?

Should she make the climb? It was either that or forget about her husband, go downstairs, and join their table alone. No, that wouldn't do.

She completed her ascent to the fourth level, somewhat out of breath, and slowly walked in the direction of the light from the corner office. It looked to be miles away. She stepped carefully, one foot slowly placed in front of the other, tentative, one shoe secure on the floor before the other was moved. It occurred to her that she probably appeared to be drunk. Alcoholics often walked that way, reaching with uncertainty for the ground.

She paused and looked over the railing. The milling partygoers almost one hundred feet below were smaller now. Like going up in an airplane, she thought. She tried to blot out party sounds and to focus on her immediate surroundings. It was hard to see in the somber light. A fleeting vision of a small child toppling into Great Falls came and went. She drew a breath and continued toward the light from the office. A sound stopped her. It had come from her left and in front. She looked in that direction, squinting against the blackness. Nothing. She cocked her head. No such sound now. What had it been? It sounded like a dull thud. Someone's hand coming in contact with a wall? A foot inadvertently hitting a desk or chair? Maybe it hadn't emanated from the balcony. Maybe it was a sound that had drifted up from the party.

She looked up. Above her head was a metal document track that circled the Great Hall. When the building had housed the Pension Bureau, trolleys traveled the track, each loaded with documents. A dumbwaiter in the northwest corner, now covered by a wall, had moved papers vertically.

Annabel moved closer to her destination, passing a number of doorways, each leading to an office, workshop, or display room. She turned the corner and began her trek on the long leg of the balcony. When she reached the halfway point, she stopped.

"Mac?" she said in a quiet voice.

Silly, she realized. He—no one would hear her. She gripped the gold railing with her right hand and waited. She'd come this far and intended to find her husband and return with him to the festivities.

A thin, amplified voice from downstairs drifted up to her ears. *"Before the first course is served, there are so many people to thank for making this wonderful evening possible. Goodness, I hope I don't forget any."*

Annabel glanced down. She was not afflicted with a fear of heights but suddenly felt dizzy. She pushed away from the railing toward the security of the wall. But instead of coming in contact with a hard surface, she was in someone's arms. Her scream was primal and loud.

"Quiet," a male voice whispered.

"Who is it? Let me go!"

The man maintained his grip on her as someone

else stepped into view. It was Sun Ben Cheong's lookalike. "What are you doing?" she asked. "Let me go! My husband is—"

"Shut up, Mrs. Smith," Sun Ben said, his arms still wrapped tightly around her.

She screamed again. "Mac! Mac!" But her words coincided with a drum roll and fanfare from the orchestra and an accompanying burst of cheers and applause. The microphone voice said that someone had won a Saint Laurent Rive Gauche gift certificate.

As Annabel struggled to free herself—she thought of the young woman who'd been pushed to her death from a balcony in the National Building Museum by a disgruntled lover—her husband was about to leave Tierney. "Naturally, Wendell, I'm shocked and dismayed by what you've told me. You're certain?"

"Unfortunately, yes. I feel betrayed, of course, but not shocked. I made it too easy for him, gave too much. Strange, isn't it, how his actions parallel Ziang Sun Wan. He was the Chinese student who murdered officials of the Chinese Educational Mission back in 1918. We've studied that case at Tri-S a number of times but never produced a re-creation of it. Too sensitive. Too easy to be accused of prejudice against Orientals. I know one thing, Mac. No matter what I feel, I won't abandon him."

"Of course you won't," Smith said. "As difficult as it may be, the only course of action for him is to come forward to the police and cooperate fully. The attorneys I've recommended are the best. They're not only superb criminal attorneys and litigators, they're decent, sensitive people who'll do everything they can to minimize the impact upon the family."

Tierney stretched his arms above his head, twisted his torso, and yawned. "Money does corrupt. At least it has in this instance. It makes me think that—"

Smith snapped his head in the direction of the door. "That's Annabel," he said.

"What?"

"That scream. It's Annabel." He was on his feet, moving toward the door.

"I didn't hear anything," Tierney said to Smith's back; he'd run out to the narrow balcony. Smith wasn't certain he'd heard Annabel scream. It was more like a mother sensing a child's dilemma when no one else would, or could. A sixth sense.

"Annabel!"

"Mac—"

He started toward her voice and the vague shapes in the shadows but stopped when John Cheong's revolver flashed reflected light in his direction.

"Let her go," Smith shouted.

"What's going on?" Tierney said from behind Smith. At the sight of his adoptive father, Sun Ben reflexively released his grip on Annabel. She'd been trying to pull away, and the momentum carried her toward the railing. At that instant, Chip Tierney stepped from a doorway and grabbed her. He'd been sitting silently in a small, dark room since delivering Smith to his father.

". . . and the winner of the luxurious trip to gay ol' Paree is—"

"Chip . . ." Annabel said, her voice mirroring her relief.

Tierney walked past Smith and extended his hand to John Cheong. "Give me the gun, John. You and your brother have done enough hurt."

"The winner is—Mackensie Smith!" The band began to play "April in Paris."

Tony Buffolino had left Alicia with the wife of a detective friend and was on his way to the men's room when Smith's name was announced. "Son of a gun," he said as he scanned the vast hall for Mac and Annabel. *"Let's not be shy, Mac Smith,"* the chairwoman said into the microphone.

Buffolino fixed his attention on the dais. When neither Mac nor Annabel stepped forward to accept their prize, Buffolino's antennae went up. Something's wrong, he thought. He looked up into the soaring recesses of the building, to the domed roof and the balconies. Smith had gone to meet with Tierney and obviously wasn't back yet. Dinner was well under way. Where was Annabel?

His eyes went to the upper reaches of the northeast corner. There seemed to be people up there. He went directly to the stairs and bounded up three at a time.

"Seems Mac and Annabel Smith are hiding on us," said the chairwoman. *"We'll move on to one more prize, and then the main course will be served."*

"The gun," Tierney said.

John Cheong handed the weapon to his brother, who pointed it at Tierney.

Tierney halted his advance, raised his hands, and forced a smile. "We'll work things out, Son," he said. "I've told Mac everything. He'll help. We'll go to the police together. We'll hire the best lawyers and—"

"No!"

Everyone now looked to Chip.

"Get away from him, Annabel," Smith said. She looked quizzically at her husband, then into Chip's eyes. Tears came from them. His grasp of her had been comforting. But his moist eyes gave sudden credence to her husband's warning. Smith repeated it. "Annabel, come here. *Let her go, Chip.*"

"What the hell are you doing, Chip?" Tierney asked. "Shut up."

"I won't shut up, Dad. I can't shut up any-more."

"Damn it. Everything is worked out."

"Meaning having me take the fall," Sun Ben said. "That's what he wants," he said to Smith.

"I know," Smith replied. He said to Tierney, "I didn't buy what you told me, Wendell. Too neat. Sun Ben's problems with the law create a perfect setup to pin Pauline's murder on him."

"I didn't kill her," Cheong said.

"Get the police," Tierney instructed Chip. "Get them up here."

"To arrest me?" Chip said.

"To arrest *him,*" Tierney said, pointing at Sun Ben.

Sun Ben slowly lowered the revolver to his side. He turned to Chip. "I know why you killed her, Chip, to help me, to keep her quiet about the money. It doesn't matter now. It's over. Let's stand together and take whatever they dish out. We're brothers. We can—"

"I won't go to prison," Chip said. His voice, soft, frightened, now had a harder edge. He grabbed the weapon from Cheong's relaxed hand and held it to Annabel's head. "I tried to do the right thing for you, Dad. Pauline knew everything about the family, about Sun Ben laundering money through his diamond business, the land deals, the payoffs, all of it. She would have ruined us all."

Smith took a step in his direction. "Hurting another person won't help anything, Chip. Give me the gun." He saw over the young man's shoulder the crouched figure quietly creeping up behind Annabel.

"And now, let's see who the lucky person is to drive that magnificent, sleek Rolls for a year. The winner is—"

Buffolino's movement was sure and quick. His right hand struck Chip's hand, sending the revolver into the air and down into the Great Hall. Simultaneously, the investigator drove his shoulder up into Chip's back, which bent him over the railing.

Chip Tierney didn't have to go over the railing. Everyone could see that.

Buffolino reached for the collar of Chip's tux jacket in order to straighten him up, yank him back to safety. But the young Tierney moved quicker. He pushed up and out, his feet leaving the ground and following him over the rail.

"No," Tierney said, lunging for his son.

But he was gone, arms and legs akimbo, falling, twisting, spinning, until he landed facedown in front of the dais.

The band was playing "A Foggy Day."

39 Two Weeks Later

Mac and Annabel finished lunch in Les Princes, the stylish restaurant in the George V, the opulent hotel included in their Paris "package." Mac had enjoyed his *entrecôte* cooked perfectly *à point;* Annabel opted for a regional stew, *blanquette de veau.* Their bottle of Beaujolais was empty.

They'd attended Annabel's conference in San Francisco, then taken the polar route to Paris. The glorious week was almost up. One more day and they'd be heading back to their normal lives in the nation's capital.

"I suppose the Tierneys are what they mean by a dysfunctional family," Annabel said.

"I suppose so. Functioning in many ways—but in the end . . . Tony made a comment the day we took a ride on the river. He said that when men like Wendell fall, they fall far and they fall fast. That was certainly the case, wasn't it?"

Annabel tasted a petit-four. She said, "Imagine Suzanne a bagman for Sun Ben."

"Bagwoman," Smith corrected.

"Sounds wrong," said Annabel. "How hard will they be on her?"

"Hard enough. She claims she never knew what she picked up for him, but that'll be tough to establish."

"I'm still not clear on how Sun Ben's laundering operation worked," she said.

"A complicated setup, Annabel, but not original with him. John Sims did a good job of explaining it to me." Sims, a Treasury agent, and Mac had been friends for years. "It only works if the bankers involved are greedy enough, which too many are."

"About eight years ago, according to John, some South American gold merchant set up a laundering system for the Medellín cocaine cartel. He established an office in California where drug money was delivered in large quantities. That's what Suzanne did for Sun Ben. She was one of dozens picking up the cash and delivering it to the laundry, in this case his diamond business.

"The guy in California who worked for the Medellín cartel used the cash delivered to him to buy gold. The trick was to buy the gold at a premium price, way over market—which rewarded those dealers selling to him for moving the money through their bank accounts—and then selling the gold quickly to pay off the drug dealers in Colombia. Problem was that consistently buying high and selling low was sure to attract attention. As I understand it, he solved that by claiming the gold had been bought out of the country, rather than from within the United States. Something to do with foreign gold being lower-quality. Anyway, it was a big operation. His slice off the top was worth millions to this guy."

"And Sun Ben did the same thing?"

"Yes. Only he used diamonds bought through his brother in Hong Kong."

"The profits must be enormous to entice otherwise honest people to get involved."

"Potentially. Of course, Sun Ben had an additional motivation to set up his laundering operation. He lost so much playing baccarat, he couldn't keep up with what he owed the casinos. His reputation as a financial guru caught the attention of the mob, which had all this drug money to launder. They cut a deal. Sun's been very upfront about how it happened. The mob had its hooks in him pretty deep. Deep enough to get him to throw over a sterling career in finance to launder drug money in a diamond bath. Tragic."

"Do you believe Sam? That he knew nothing about what Sun Ben was doing on the side?"

"Yes, I do. Tankloff's a straight arrow, Annabel. He trusted Sun like a son. The accounts Sun set up in the Caymans for Sam were legit. Sun's other, private accounts obviously weren't. John tells me there's to be no further investigation of Sam. They took a look at him because of his close connection with Sun Ben. Evidently, he's clean. And broken up about Sun. He took it hard."

"Harder than Wendell, I gather."

Smith nodded and ate a petit four. "Boy, that's good."

"We keep this up and we'll both be ungodly fat."

Mac had one more.

"Merci," Annabel said to the waiter, who poured café filtre.

"Wendell seems to be taking a perverse comfort in the police not being able to *prove* that Chip murdered Pauline. At least not in court. Our statements about Chip's confession just before his death close the case, as far as the police are concerned. But the family won't have to go through a murder trial."

"Small comfort," Annabel muttered. "A son is dead."

"Wendell's biggest problem, it seems, is Sun Ben's testimony against him. He's cooperating with the police in the case against Wendell."

"I wonder if he would if Wendell hadn't tried to set him up to take the fall for Chip in Pauline's murder," said Annabel.

"Probably not. Sun Ben really loves the family. Or did. A father attempting to sell his son down the river—adopted son or not—isn't calculated to foster love, or loyalty. Wendell ran his own funny-money operation, including all the bribes to Hal Mason and others. Insider stock trading. Fraudulent land deals. Father and son both gone astray."

"But different motivations," Annabel said. "Sun Ben had his terrible weakness for gambling, which led to a gun being held to his head."

"And with Wendell, it was pure greed. One thing's for certain. There're lots of chips still waiting to fall in our beloved D.C."

"*Chips* waiting to fall?" she said.

Mac said, "Unintentional. I don't go in much for tragic puns. Forgive me."

They spent the misty afternoon walking the narrow streets of the Left Bank. They stopped to admire a young artist's efforts. Annabel's enthusiasm was greater than her husband's. "There's a Monet quality to this," she said, picking up a small watercolor and holding it up to the sky's diffused light.

"If you insist. It doesn't do much for me. Like Ben Jonson said about the 'adulteries of art,' it strikes my eyes but not my heart."

"It scores a bull's-eye on my heart," she said gaily.

They bought the painting from the grateful artist and continued their stroll. The sun broke through at five, and they whiled away an hour in an outdoor café along the Seine.

"Not unlike the Potomac," Smith said. A young couple embraced on the riverbank.

"A lot more peaceful."

"We'll find that peace again back home," he said.

"Were you truly concerned that a real gun might be used during the Key-Sickles reenactment?" Mac had casually mentioned that to her during their long polar flight.

"It crossed my mind as we stood there and watched. Make a good plot, if nothing else."

"Shame the Scarlet Sin Society is no longer. You could have brought it up at a meeting."

"Another missed opportunity in the life of Mackensie Smith," he said.

Annabel broke a silence of short duration. "Pauline knew too much."

"What?"

"She knew too much. That was her only crime, and it got her killed."

"It's been known to happen. According to Sun Ben, Pauline threatened to blow the whistle on both his and Wendell's illegal activities. He'd confided in his brother about the hold the Mafia had on him and what he was doing in servitude. Pauline already knew everything about Wendell's shady financial dealings. When she and Chip were having their affair, he told her about Sun Ben. Now she knew enough about two members of the family to go after what Wendell claims she always wanted more than anything else—money and power."

"And Chip killed her to keep her quiet. To protect his family."

"Sounds noble, doesn't it? It isn't."

"No, it isn't."

"One thing we'll never know," said Mac.

"Which is?"

"How Chip got Pauline's body to Roosevelt Island. Took her out in a boat? Dumped her in the river and didn't worry where she'd end up? Carried her across the pedestrian walkway and tossed her over it?"

"I suppose it doesn't matter."

"It does to Tony. He says he won't enjoy a good night's sleep again until he figures it out."

"Poor Alicia."

They fell silent again. Mac held a glass of house wine in both hands in front of his lips, his brow knitted.

"A frame for your thoughts," Annabel said.

"I was thinking about Darcy Eikenberg."

"You were?"

"Yeah. Not a bad person. And a good detective, I think."

"She was taught by a pretty good professor."

"Nothing to do with it. It's all instincts. Tony has good instincts. So do you, as a matter of fact."

"About solving crime, or when another woman has set her sights on my man?"

"A little of both. There's something inherently sad about the Darcy Eikenbergs of this world."

"Because of what you said the other night? Too attractive to be taken seriously?"

"That coupled with being a cop. A female cop. An alien intruder into a male domain, no matter how far you've come, 'baby.' Who does she talk to? Other cops? She's brighter than most. Needs a higher level of discourse."

"A college professor, for instance."

"Hmmmm. Know what I want to do the first weekend after we get home?"

"Tell me."

"Go up to Great Falls."

It was her turn for a creased forehead. "Why?"

"Because I don't want to be a victim of what happened there. Like falling off a horse and getting back on, I suppose. It's so beautiful up there. I want to be able to enjoy that beauty again. Maybe if I go, it'll put a rest to my vision of the child going over."

"If it will, I'm all for it. We were all headed for a fall, in your dreams. Speaking of the river, you promised me a day of fishing."

"And you shall have it, Mrs. Smith. Maybe Tony will drive us to a peaceful spot on the river in his Rolls. His for a year. Ready for a nap? We should pack for our getaway tomorrow."

"Nap? Yes. Pack? That wasn't exactly what I had in mind."

"And what was on that pretty mind?"

"A nap, during which we celebrate our last night in Paris, the painting we bought—that you will learn to love—and maybe find the fireworks."

Look for these at your local bookstore

American Heart Association, *American Heart Association Cookbook, 5th Edition* (Abridged)
Dave Barry, *Dave Barry Is Not Making This Up* (paper)
Peter Benchley, *White Shark* (paper)
Barbara Taylor Bradford, *Angel* (paper)
Barbara Taylor Bradford, *Remember*
William F. Buckley, Jr., *Tucker's Last Stand*
Leo Buscaglia, Ph.D., *Born for Love*
Michael Crichton, *Disclosure* (paper)
Michael Crichton, *Rising Sun*
E. L. Doctorow, *The Waterworks* (paper)
Dominick Dunne, *A Season in Purgatory*
Fannie Flagg, *Daisy Fay and the Miracle Man* (paper)
Fannie Flagg, *Fried Green Tomatoes at the Whistle Stop Cafe* (paper)
Robert Fulghum, *It Was on Fire When I Lay Down on It* (hardcover and paper)
Robert Fulghum, *Maybe (Maybe Not): Second Thoughts from a Secret Life*
Robert Fulghum, *Uh-Oh*
Peter Gethers, *The Cat Who Went to Paris*
Martha Grimes, *The End of the Pier*
Martha Grimes, *The Horse You Came In On* (paper)
Lewis Grizzard, *If I Ever Get Back to Georgia, I'm Gonna Nail My Feet to the Ground*
David Halberstam, *The Fifties* (2 volumes, paper)
Kathryn Harvey, *Stars*
Katharine Hepburn, *Me* (hardcover and paper)
P. D. James, *The Children of Men*
Naomi Judd, *Love Can Build a Bridge* (paper)

(continued)

Judith Krantz, *Dazzle*
Judith Krantz, *Lovers* (paper)
Judith Krantz, *Scruples Two*
John le Carré, *The Night Manager* (paper)
John le Carré, *The Secret Pilgrim*
Robert Ludlum, *The Bourne Ultimatum*
Robert Ludlum, *The Road to Omaha*
Cormac McCarthy, *The Crossing* (paper)
James A. Michener, *Mexico* (paper)
James A. Michener, *The Novel*
James A. Michener, *The World is My Home* (paper)
Richard North Patterson, *Degree of Guilt*
Louis Phillips, editor, *The Random House Large Print Treasury of Best-Loved Poems*
Maria Riva, *Marlene Dietrich* (2 volumes, paper)
Mickey Rooney, *Life Is Too Short*
William Styron, *Darkness Visible*
Margaret Truman, *Murder at the National Cathedral*
Margaret Truman, *Murder at the Pentagon*
Margaret Truman, *Murder on the Potomac* (paper)
Donald Trump with Charles Leerhsen, *Trump: Surviving at the Top*
Anne Tyler, *Saint Maybe*
John Updike, *Rabbit at Rest*
Phyllis A. Whitney, *Star Flight* (paper)
Lois Wyse, *Grandchildren Are So Much Fun I Should Have Had Them First*

The New York Times Large Print Crossword Puzzles (paper)

Will Weng, editor, Volumes 1–3
Eugene T. Maleska, editor, Volumes 4–7
Eugene T. Maleska, editor, Omnibus Volume 1